PRAISE FOR *THE REBEL NUN*

"Vividly imagines one of the most fascinating events to occur in sixth-century Gaul…Marj Charlier's *The Rebel Nun* brings the sights, sounds, and smells of this event and its aftermath to life in a richly imagined story that is firmly rooted in equal parts rigorous historical research and inspired, creative imagination."

—DORSEY ARMSTRONG, PHD,
professor of English/medieval studies at Purdue University, and lecturer for *The Great Courses* ("The Medieval World," "The Black Death," and others)

"*The Rebel Nun* is a boldly imagined story of one early medieval woman's struggle against the societal forces that constrained her…The result is an engaging and thought-provoking tale."

—SAMANTHA KAHN HERRICK,
Associate Professor of History, Syracuse University

"*The Rebel Nun* is a wildly original, suspenseful account of a group of nuns in medieval France who must endure hardships and treachery from both outside and within their walls. It feels both historically authentic and startlingly contemporary, and I loved every word of it."

—ELIZABETH STUCKEY—FRENCH,
author of *The Revenge of the Radioactive Lady*

"A gripping tale of heroism and audacity in the least likely of guises…With meticulous research and in exacting detail, Marj Charlier brings to light the remarkable exploits of Clotild, who leads her fellow sisters on a daring escape that culminates in bloody revolt, and a place in history."

—DENISE HEINZE,
author of *The Brief and True Report of Temperance Flowerdew*

"A startling look into a world I never imagined visiting—a sixth-century nunnery, where one bride of Christ…makes it her mission to battle the corruption of bishops oppressing the sisters of the Holy Cross. A well-wrought yarn reflective of historical fact."

—DARRYL PONICSÁN,
author of *Eternal Sojourners*

THE

✝

REBEL

✝

NUN

OTHER BOOKS BY MARJ CHARLIER

Putt for Show (2013)

Drive for Dough (2014)

Hacienda: A South American Romance (2014)

Professional Lies (2015)

Thwack! (2015)

Gracie's Revolution: A Johnson Station Novel (2016)

Jackie's Campaign: A Johnson Station Novel (2017)

Marcia's Revenge: A Johnson Station Novel (2018)

ROMANCES BY MARJORIE PINKERTON MILLER

One Way to Succeed (2016)

No Way to Win (2017)

THE ✝ REBEL ✝ NUN

MARJ CHARLIER

**BLACK
STONE**
PUBLISHING

Copyright © 2021 by Marj Charlier
Published in 2021 by Blackstone Publishing
Cover, illustrations, map, and Rebel Nun Sans font by Kathryn Galloway English
Book design by Amy Craig

Printed in the United States of America

First edition: 2021
ISBN 978-1-09-409275-1
Fiction / Historical / Medieval

1 3 5 7 9 10 8 6 4 2

CIP data for this book is available
from the Library of Congress

Blackstone Publishing
31 Mistletoe Rd.
Ashland, OR 97520

www.BlackstonePublishing.com

To Ben

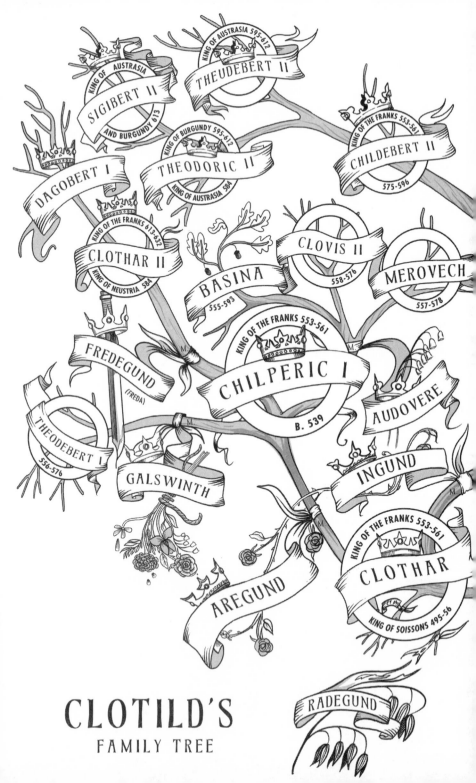

CLOTILD'S
FAMILY TREE

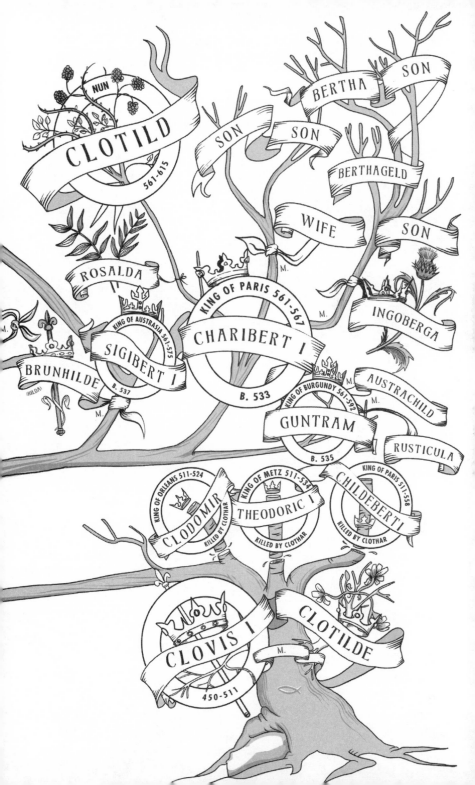

AUSTRASIA

SOISSONS

PARIS

NEUSTRIA

TOURS

POITIERS

CHALONS-SUR-SAONE

BURGUNDY

LYON

AQUITAINE

ATLANTIC OCEAN

KINGDOM
OF THE
FRANKS

MEDITERRANEAN SEA

PROLOGUE

ANNO DOMINI 613

The hour I learned of Hilda's death, the cool autumn mist had crept into my garden, telling me it was time to call a truce with the weeds and bugs for the night. From stiff knees, the effort of rising forced a low moan from my lungs. I brushed the dirt from my hands and picked up a sack to gather the herbs I had harvested that afternoon.

It was the time of day when, usually, I would look forward to a comforting fire and a quiet evening meal of fresh cheese, bread, and watered wine in the villa's garden shack that I had made my home. Then I would crawl under an old blanket and bid the world goodbye for the night—or perhaps forever, for all I knew.

But that night, I would not sleep. Under the full moon, my friends and I would celebrate the moon goddess Máni with the pagan rituals we revived when I returned to this village twenty-two years ago and found the women eager to reclaim our ancestral rites. They joined me in the daytime for lessons in the healing power of herbs, wild roots, and allium—secrets I had learned from my mother and grandmother decades ago in this very garden. And twice every cycle of the moon—at its fullest and its darkest—we gathered to remember the goddesses who rule the celestial realm and to affirm our ancient beliefs.

Careful to keep my balance, I bent to collect bundles of borage for stomach ailments, betony to relieve headaches, sage to treat the village children's persistent colds, and rosemary to ward off nightmares. Hens scuttled out of my way, flapping their wings, irritated at me for interrupting their feast of cabbage worms. At first, their flurry and cackling kept me from noticing the lone rider coming through the chestnut trees between my garden and the main house.

"Sister," he called out, startling me. I looked up and froze. Only one kind of visitor would address me as a nun: a messenger from the posse loyal to my Aunt Hilda, known as Queen Brunhilde to most of the world. She had been the one to rescue me from the church's suffocating grasp but had never stopped referring to me as a penitent.

My heart clenched painfully. Only one thing would bring this envoy to my door after so many years. "When?" I asked, tears already swelling under my eyelids.

"A week ago." The large man slipped off his mount and walked toward me with the horse's reins in one hand, his fur cap clenched against his chest in the other. "I am sorry for my delay. The queen's enemies swarm like wasps, even now. I had to avoid the roads, and many times I had to stop and hide for hours."

I studied him. He looked like so many of Hilda's men—tall, exceptionally strong, with long blond hair and sky-blue eyes. Not so different from the man who had held my heart for so many years, now traversing the heavens with the Valkyries, as only the worthiest are chosen to do.

"Come inside." I motioned toward the door of my hut. "You must be weary, and the autumn chill is creeping into my bones. I need to know everything."

The news was worse than I could have imagined. Nearly eighty years old—the oldest person I had ever known—my aunt—queen to the late King Sigibert—had been dragged by the hair and torn limb from limb by horses, surrounded by a drunken, cheering horde of her political and religious enemies.

Few women in our time have acted so bravely or had so much influence over our kingdom as she did. But, in the end, Hilda had fewer friends than powerful foes. A gang of Catholic bishops and counts allied themselves with Clothar, my evil great-nephew, and ordered Hilda's execution. Clothar and his bishops now reigned over Austrasia and the territory known as Neustria, which my own father once ruled.

The women who gathered for the full-moon ceremony later that night were as distraught as I was over the news. Through clouds of incense, we chanted praises to the moon goddess until our voices were hoarse from song and smoke. We passed communal goblets of wine and cider and tossed bundles of herbs and fragrant branches into the bonfire.

These were the same rituals as ever, but hanging over us was a raw fear, a new awareness of how vulnerable we were. If Hilda, with all her cunning and wiles, could face such a brutal end, we knew that the king who ordered her execution could, at any time, command men to storm our gatherings, lay axes to our altar and swords to our flesh.

As could any man of the church.

✛

Days later, Hilda's death haunts me still as I sit with Gregory's *Ten Books of History*, rereading his account of our rebellion at the female Monastery of the Holy Cross, which Hilda abetted and from which she rescued me. In his book *Decem Libri Historiarum*, Gregory, the late Bishop of Tours, has distorted the truth for his own polemics, painting me as a prideful and brash perpetrator of a reckless rebellion and my sisters as feckless pawns. As one of the few who was there and is still living, I have long been tempted to refute his fabrications with my own story. They have stoked the hatred that precipitated Hilda's murder. By penning this, I will honor her heroism to preserve, for posterity, the truth, both on her behalf and in the memory of the other brave women who joined our rebellion: Covina, my closest friend and our staunchest rebel; Basina, my sometimes rebellious, sometimes fragile cousin; Bertie, brave despite her tiny stature; and Veranda, whose stoicism in the face of danger and death was far greater than I could ever muster.

As I write this account, I will not attempt to dodge my share of blame for the death of those women whose bodies bled dry onto the cold stone floors of the monastery just outside the city walls of Poitiers. But the story does not begin or end with the bloody clash at the Holy Cross.

It began when Christianity first swept across Gaul, and the church demanded the obliteration of the pagan rituals, shrines, and deities that had guided our tribes for centuries. It continued as the church declared women unclean, threw us out of the clergy, and denied us the right to sleep with the priests to whom some of us were married. Our monastery's founder, Radegund, who had the powerful status of a queen, was able to retain her status as a deaconess, and bequeath her boldness and independence to Agnes, who became our abbess. But when Agnes died, the church moved quickly and cruelly to assert its control over our monastery.

The story of our struggle will end only when our kingdom is no longer at the mercy of the patriarchy and the church, the matriarchy flourishes anew, and pagan traditions are again celebrated across the land with impunity.

ONE

ANNO DOMINI 588

The abbess's body was still warm when Maroveus, Bishop of Poitiers, blew through the door of the Monastery of the Holy Cross and commenced his campaign to destroy us.

I had just risen from my vigil at her deathbed, and with my head bowed, I trudged back toward the dormitory through the reception room. The wide front door stood ajar, and the dim light of the rainy afternoon exposed the decades of dirt ground into the rough stone floor. Distracted, I nearly collided with the bishop in the narrow entryway. His robe flapped around his arms and legs as he swept past Bertie, the old nun who had held the door open for him. His sleeve wrapped around her thin arm, threatening to pull her down, but I caught her as she toppled sideways.

Maroveus strode directly ahead toward the oratory, his bulky frame sucking the room's air along in his wake. I feared the draft would pull Bertie over again.

"Clotild!" he commanded. "Call the sisters. I will address you as soon as they have gathered."

I steadied Bertie. With an arm around her shoulders, I helped her to her bench by the door, retrieved the handbell from a shelf over her head, and laid it on her lap. "Ring if you need help. I will go get our sisters."

I watched the bishop stride down the center aisle of the chapel and step up to the altar. He stopped with his face tilted up toward the modest crucifix that alone adorned the wall, hands folded at his chest, the robe settling around his knees. I lifted my stiff linen dress above my ankles and hurried off to gather the nuns.

Slowly, sixty hooded residents and novices filed into the nave behind the bishop, weeping and sniffling, their eyes lowered. I fell in behind the slowest and oldest and stood at the rear of the chapel as they slunk into the nave. Heavy clouds dripping a cold March rain darkened the sky outside the tiny windows high along the outer wall. The gloom suited a convent in mourning.

Maroveus stood with his back toward us until the shuffle of feet and rustle of linen quieted. He turned around to face us and traced the sign of the cross in the air. His countenance, dominated by a bulbous nose and flabby chin, was coarse, his scowl permanently affixed by years of habit.

He grimaced conspicuously as one of my sisters lost control over her grief and let out a staccato sob. He waited as the sound echoed through the chamber before starting his address with a whisper. I strained to hear him.

"I have first a message for you from Bishop Gregory of Tours," he said. Gregory, we all knew, had been a steadfast supporter of both our abbess, Agnes, and our founder, Radegund, so I was not surprised at this.

"My fellow bishop says," Maroveus began to read. "Blessed are those gathered here in mourning for Sister Agnes, whose soul surely begs our prayers as she aspires to join her espoused, Jesus Christ, for eternity. As a pious yet sinful soul, she serves as an example for all manner of trespassers striving to overcome the vexations and degradations of our tortured kingdom."

Maroveus looked up and frowned at us as if we were all pitiless sinners. "The passage to heaven is assured to none of us," he said. "Not to Agnes, nor you, nor I." He rolled up the papyrus containing Gregory's message and continued with his own. "There has been much extravagant behavior here at the Holy Cross that your abbess accepted and that was condoned by your founder, Radegund. This cannot continue. I trust that you will spend the next few days of your vigil in penitent prayer, and that you will seek your own rectitude as you beg for the passage of Agnes's soul." His oratory ran on, casting doubt on Agnes's passage from purgatory to heaven and vaguely recalling her time on Earth, about which he showed himself to be mostly ignorant. I watched the backs of the veils crowded between me and the bishop, but the sisters' heads moved neither in affirmation nor disagreement. No one lifted her face to him. The bishop had few admirers among us.

"Do not be misled by your sorrows or your pain." As he continued, his voice swelled to a roar, a tone I had always thought signaled his anxiety about his authority. "The devil seeks these opportunities to encourage betrayal and perfidy. Your grief is no pretext for laxity. Indeed, sorrow is the seedbed of sin and damnation, and home to wicked, venomous snakes that swarm the countryside with their deceitful pulchritude." As always, the bishop did not veer from his focus on sin. I wondered, where was the love in his theology—the love that Radegund had extolled? Where was the joy in the creation? In the resurrection?

Fumbling for a pocket in his outer robe, he extracted a slim manuscript and thumbed to a page marked with a thin black ribbon. From the back of the room, I could see it was Caesarius' *Regula virginum*—the rule book Radegund had copied and brought to the monastery from Arles a decade ago. Our founder had adopted it to deflect the hostile and mercurial directives of Maroveus, whom she despised. The hatred had been mutual. His opinion had deteriorated further when the Council of Bishops of Tours officially recognized the *Regula*'s binding force over us.

"These things first befit your holy souls," Maroveus bellowed, reading from the page. "If a woman, leaving her parents, desires to renounce the world and enter the holy fold to escape the jaws of the spiritual wolves by the help of God, she must never, up to the time of her death, go out of the monastery."

His message was unambiguous: We would not be permitted to leave the monastery to accompany Agnes's body to the church of St. Mary, where it would lie in the mausoleum with Radegund's body, whose soul had departed for heaven two years earlier. I recoiled. How dare the bishop now use Radegund's shield against us, when he had protested its enforcement in the first place?

Muffled sobs filled the room. The women who loved Agnes and Radegund best—those who had come to the monastery to escape the tortures of marriage and childbearing more than any "spiritual wolves"—would not be allowed to visit the crypt that would cradle the women's corporeal remains for eternity. Not until we, too, were without breath and heartbeat, bound for our union with Christ in heaven.

The bishop snapped the thin volume closed and slipped it back into his pocket. He paused only a moment before sticking his chin in the air and, with hands clasped under his outer vestment, he marched back down the center aisle toward me, the floor under our feet vibrating with his steps. There would be no gracious benediction from him that day; he would waste no more breath on us.

"I will pay my respects now." It took me a moment to realize Maroveus was speaking to me, and then another moment to realize what he was demanding. He wanted to visit Agnes's deathbed. Perhaps he wanted to assure himself she was, in fact, departed. "Clotild! Did you hear me?"

"But the *Regula* forbids it." My words tumbled out before I stopped to think. No man was allowed beyond the sanctuary, the dining room, and the reception room of the monastery. Even the doctors called to tend to the sick in the Holy Cross—truly a rare event—had to minister from afar. What the bishop intended to do violated Caesarius's *Regula* immediately after he had invoked it to exclude us from Agnes's funeral procession.

"Sister," Maroveus's glare matched his growl, "I am not asking. You will escort me."

I lowered my eyes below my hood to veil my anger and turned down the hall toward the infirmary with the bishop at my heels.

✝

Maroveus had arrived at our door much sooner than I had expected. Less than a day had passed since Agnes had slipped free of her pain and suffering. When Radegund founded the monastery, in her humility she chose her handmaid, Agnes, to be its first abbess. Mercifully, Agnes's death had come quickly, but it left the business of naming our new abbess unfinished. I was considered the likely successor, as Radegund had been married to my grandfather, Clothar. Although a *bastardis* and not her grandchild—she had no children—I was her favorite among the nuns. Continuing in the tradition of our monastery, I expected to be named abbess by the others as soon as Agnes was laid to rest.

News of her death had somehow traveled five hundred furlongs to Limoges where Maroveus was visiting another bishop, and once it reached him, Maroveus traveled the same distance back—a full day's trip, possibly more now that the spring rains had started.

It might have seemed odd to some that he would find Agnes's funeral such an urgent matter, when he had made himself unavailable for Radegund's interment two years before, leaving it to be attended by another bishop in his absence. The enmity between our founder and Maroveus had myriad roots. Namely, Maroveus coveted our relic of the Holy Cross—a splinter of the cross on which Christ died—and craved authority over our small community of penitents. He had tried to bully his way into our monastery when Radegund died, but Agnes and our loyalty to her stymied him. His renewed effort to conquer us this time did not surprise me.

Maroveus's rush was understandable. Unable to get us under his thumb previously, he saw this as his chance to do so, as well as steal our precious relic. Across Italy and France, Maroveus's fellow bishops had seized control over female monasteries that had once operated independently, unmolested by clerical interference.

As the monastery's next abbess, it would fall on my shoulders to stave off the bishop's aggression and retain our independence. It was a challenge I found daunting, but I would accept.

I led the bishop back to the infirmary and vowed to myself this was the last time he would get past the door of the Monastery of the Holy Cross. It was the last time I would bow my head before him.

How naive I was! I had seen enough of the church's actions by then that I should not have been fooled about its tenacity. Since the first Council at Nicaea one hundred fifty years before, bishops had denied women ordination, even going so far as to suggest women had no souls. Women were declared unclean, and we were prohibited from touching the sacramental objects. Priests could no longer sleep with their wives, and the Council of Macon advised married clergy to avoid their spouses completely. It seemed only a matter of time before priests would not be allowed to marry at all.

Somehow, I had let myself believe that our monastery could resist that hateful onslaught. Somehow, we would retain our independence. Somehow, our story would be different.

I had no idea then just how different it would be.

TWO

Two days after the bishop's acolytes, accompanied by townsfolk and clergy, carted Agnes's body to her crypt, Maroveus returned. In a morning meeting between the sunrise Hour of Lauds and midmorning Hour of Prime, we gathered in the chapel to elect our new abbess under his watch. Or at least, that's what we thought.

Maroveus began his address with a prayer. "Lord God, your servants Radegund and Agnes were faithful to Christ's habits of poverty and humility. May their cenobitic example help us to perform faithfully His calling and instill in us the perfection you showed us in your Son, who lives and reigns with you and the Holy Spirit, one God, forever."

My heart pounding, I waited for him to get through his preliminaries. This was going to be my day, my inauguration, the day I accepted the reins of the monastery and could thenceforth turn this arrogant bishop away at the door.

Besides being our founder, Radegund was my heroine and my teacher. As a child, she had been captured as war booty, dragged from her homeland of Thuringia, and married to Clothar. But when he murdered the last members of her family, she escaped from his court, shook off the king—one who was powerful enough to unite the warring and fratricidal Franks—and then turned around and wrangled from him enough money to build our monastery. Clothar was my grandfather. His son, Charibert, was my father.

After Charibert's death, I was delivered to Radegund and the Holy Cross for protection and a life of prayer and abnegation. Only a month into my cloister, I had become Radegund's most fervent disciple.

I was shaken back to the present moment when Maroveus's tone took a sudden turn.

"Agnes now awaits entry to heaven, but her passage will be blocked without your extreme devotion and humility." His expression of admiration for the founders, already weak, had shifted to condemnation. "Agnes's sins must be extinguished with your prayers."

As he denounced our first abbess for decadence and immodest independence, I surveyed the startled faces around me. The others had not expected this hateful blast any more than I had.

"I know of your licentious and extravagant celebrations, your meals of flesh and fowl," he continued. "You undress before each other in your dormitory. You greet poets and princes in your dining room. You play games and, lacking devotion, you gossip through your prayers."

Where had he heard these things? The cloister's guests were few. True, one was the revered poet Venantius Fortunatus, who had escorted me to the Holy Cross when my father died and had befriended Radegund for the rest of her life. But the only other regular visitor was Gregory of Tours, a friend of the monastery, and another devotee of Radegund. Otherwise, only a few relatives were allowed to visit, and even then, only under the supervision of other nuns.

"It is time for this wickedness to end." His tirade drew from a seemingly bottomless store of synonyms for sin. "Your new leadership must denounce the satanic temptations of the past. You must beg forgiveness for your vanity and profligacy. The Lord knows your transgressions and He is condemning you. Only through renewed sacrifice and penance will you save your souls from eternal damnation. This monastery will be shuttered, and its walls demolished. Your treasured relic of the Holy Cross will belong to the basilica of St. Hilary's where it will no longer suffer the disgrace of your proximity."

He had never wanted Radegund to acquire that relic—that precious sliver of the cross on which Christ was crucified. She had appealed to Hilda's husband, King Sigibert, to request it from the Byzantine Emperor without asking for Maroveus's permission. Although it was Maroveus's duty as bishop of our territory to accompany the holy fragment to the monastery, he refused. In his absence, Sigibert ordered the bishop of Tours to install the relic. Fortunatus wrote a beautiful hymn, *Vexilla Regis*, for the large procession that accompanied the relic through Poitiers to the monastery:

> *Vexilla regis prodeunt:*
> *Fulget crucis mysterium*
> *Quo carne carnis conditor,*
> *Suspensus est patibulo.*
> *O Crux ave, spes unica,*

Hoc passionis tempore
Auge piis justitiam,
Reisque dona veniam.
Te, summa Deus Trinitas,
Collaudet omnis spiritus:
Quos per crucis mysterium
Salvas, rege per saecula. Amen.

The Royal Banner forward goes,
The mystic Cross refulgent glows:
Where He, in flesh, flesh who made,
Upon the tree of pain is laid.
O Cross! all hail! sole hope, abide
With us now in this passion-tide:
New grace in pious hearts implant,
And pardon to the guilty grant.
Thee, mighty trinity! One God!
Let every living creature laud;
Whom by the cross thou dost deliver,
O guide and govern now and ever! Amen.

It was not long after that Radegund asked Caesarius of Arles for his *Regula virginum*.

Maroveus's reprimand at the altar was losing steam. I returned my focus to his words. The time had come for my election. Instead, Maroveus surprised me and my sisters yet again.

"There will be no vote in this house today." He lowered his voice to a growl. "Through your sinfulness, you have lost your privilege to select your own spiritual guide. You will accept my judgment as I name your new abbess." He paused as we pulled in a collective, audible breath. Maroveus's tiny smile qualified more as a sneer. He enjoyed polluting the room with his malice. "Your new abbess is the devoted and humble Sister Lebover."

We drew in our breath again. I glanced around as everyone quickly looked toward and then away from each other. No one met my eyes. I turned and searched the veiled faces behind me for Lebover. A few feet away, the "devoted and humble" nun looked pleased and unsurprised. The muscles in her face jerked up and down as she smiled and then forced the smile to drop. She was trying to appear humble.

"Anyone who objects to this election will be thrust through the doors of this cloister into the streets and condemned with excommunication!" Maroveus shouted. His authority to decree this was questionable, but the threat of excommunication was horrible, and it would serve his purpose.

Dizzy from surprise, I slipped to my knees. Sister Covina's strong hands slipped under my arms and lifted me back up onto my feet. Silently, she shook her head: I could not dare to show my dissent. But did Maroveus have the power to take away our right to elect our own abbess? I did not know. However, given the attitude toward women the church had taken lately, I feared that his fellow bishops would back his decision.

I struggled to my feet as Maroveus motioned for the nuns to rise and then spat out a crude blessing on Lebover's ascension to leadership. He mumbled a brief prayer for forgiveness to spare us from hell's imminent flames, and strode, head high, back toward the monastery entrance.

"So much for the love of God," whispered Covina.

"So much for the future of this blessed house," I answered.

THREE

I knew why Maroveus had chosen Lebover. As one of the few nuns at the Holy Cross who was not from some branch of the Merovingian royal family, she had no loyalty to us. Maroveus could bribe and sway her in a way that he never could me.

And I knew why she was willing to go along.

When Lebover first arrived at the monastery more than a decade before, I had pitied her. I understood her discomfort, as my first few months at the monastery were equally as miserable. When I arrived in Poitiers, barely a teenager, I was physically homesick for our garden hut and my mother. I vomited daily. As a result of the meager meals and heavy labor on my body, I shrunk rapidly to little more than a skeleton, and my skin aged to a dusty gray. I was confused by the chatter of multiple foreign dialects and depressed by the ceaseless prayer, interrupted sleep, and freezing rooms of monastery life. I cried in my cot at night, muffling my sobs with the rough blanket and blowing my nose into my under-garment. By day, I kept my head down, my face covered by my hood, and tried to hide my raw nostrils and swollen eyes from the stoic, hardened women who surrounded me.

My home in the garden hut of my father's villa had not been luxurious but it was much more comfortable than my new home. The monastery was a safe place, solidly built, thanks to my grand-father's money, but it was drafty and stark. The cold stone floors lay bare or were occasionally littered with straw to collect the mud and melting snow from our shoes. The small windows at the top of the bare limestone walls were open to the outside air rather than inset with stained glass, as was common in less austere Italian monaster-ies. The crucifix above the altar was the only object to draw our eyes upward in the chapel. Even the altar cloth was simply embroidered with matching linen threads, as required by the *Regula*.

Radegund saw my anguish, and soon after I arrived, she rescued me from the laundry room and my gloom by assign-ing me to fulfill the *Regula*'s requirement for a sister to sit with her when she and Gregory met at the monastery. Frequently, she asked me to make a written record of their meetings. Because we came from the same part of the kingdom and were related by her marriage to my grandfather, we spoke the same language. And I knew how to write, having been taught alongside my father's legitimate children at the insistence of my mother.

Sitting and listening to their conversations, I was enthralled with Gregory's knowledge of our kingdoms' histories. He was eager to try out the theories behind his analysis of the past and tradi-tions of the Franks with Radegund, whose intellect was outshone by no man's. At times, caught up in their banter, I would forget to take notes, and Radegund would reach over and tap on the parch-ment, a friendly reprimand that refocused my attention.

I had been lucky to enter the cloister when I had and to be

favored by the founder of the most famous female monastery in Gaul. By the time Lebover came to the Holy Cross, however, Radegund was old and infirm, and her days were spent largely with her bible and Agnes. She was too ill to expend her energies easing an initiate's distress.

Lebover was a Breton, an outsider amongst Franks. Many of my sisters had come together from different regions and kingdoms, and our dialects made it difficult at first to communicate with one another. But our ways of life were similar, and our adjustments swift. Lebover's Celtic traditions, however, were as foreign to us as ours were to her. She could not speak a Germanic language; hers was Celtic. And her Latin was crude and limited to the words of the scriptures and liturgy.

At first, she smiled nervously whenever her eyes met ours, but over time, she dropped even that pretense of solidarity. More and more, she had kept to herself, in part because the cultural differences and language barrier never seemed to abate, but also because of her growing physical limitations. She suffered from pernicious gout, a swelling of the feet and legs that progressed over the years to making her nearly immobile. Now, she shuffled about with the aid of two canes on good days; on bad days, she never left the dormitory for prayer hours or meals. One of the other nuns was assigned to bring food to her bedside, a task that most of us resented, as it pulled us away from the quiet gossip of the dining room.

I imagined she resented us too, as she had never been able to participate in the idle chatter that Radegund allowed at meals or in the sewing room. Now, she could get even: she could keep us from talking amongst ourselves as well. Given a little power and Maroveus's backing, she could attain a status she never would have gained on her own.

☩

The first month after Lebover's ascension, I submerged myself in prayer and meditation to drown my disappointment and try to see the justice in Maroveus's choice. I knew she had suffered from her isolation within our walls. And it was a sin to covet someone else's fortune. If I was going to spend eternity in hell, I wanted to go there for something that made me happy, not something that had made me miserable.

It would be a fierce mental battle though. I turned to the certainty of the Hours that filled much of our days for comfort. The ritual and the humble intent one brought to prayer mattered more to the pagan in me than the expectation that a deity would listen and grant me health and prosperity. Unlike the others—as far as I knew—I had never abandoned the gods of my mother and grandmother, and I still said as many prayers and hymns to the goddesses of Thuringia as I did to the Virgin Mary and Christ, but I did so in secret.

The afternoon of Lebover's naming, I waited until she had taken her few possessions from the dormitory and moved them to her new private quarters before I slipped away from the study where I was transcribing a manuscript. I sat on my cot with my knees pulled to my chest, my rough linen shift tucked around them. I closed my eyes and fashioned a prayer to Maroveus's God, moving my lips but giving no voice to my words. "Father, I know you make things right, and you are just. Help me understand and accept this decision. Help me find peace under Lebover's rule and find my own manner by which to serve you."

It was not one of the hundreds of official prayers that we recited at the Hours. I had memorized those but I had also developed a habit of talking with the Christian God as if he were my earthly father, not just the heavenly one. Keeping him earthbound in my mind allowed me to set him alongside the gods and goddesses of my youth and consider him as an optional, rather than the only, deity.

Tears stung my eyes, and with nothing more to say to the Lord, who either did not exist or had betrayed me, I let them gather, fall, and soak into my dress, and I murmured a pagan chant from my youth. The other sisters were in the sewing room, the kitchen, or the study, as I should have been. I had the long, narrow room to myself.

Once during the next week, Lebover sent for me, but I ignored her summons. I did not want to hear what I assumed would be her supplications; nothing she could say would make me feel less cheated, less tortured.

For years, I had been preparing for the day that Agnes's reign would supposedly pass to me. For the strength of my mind, I had been chosen by Radegund as her personal scribe despite my illegitimacy as a king's daughter. Before coming to the Holy Cross, I had been a studious and quiet child, content to stay in the garden hut behind my father's villa that I shared with my maternal grandmother and mother as much as possible. My mother, Rosalda, was a beauty, a slave whom King Charibert could never convince to marry him, despite my birth. A gangly child with a Merovingian head of unruly hair, I had amused my father with my audacity, curiosity, and temerity in his presence. Unlike his legitimate children, I acted as if I had nothing to lose by asking bold questions or disobeying his rules. Recognizing my inquisitiveness, he made an exception for me as a girl: I was assigned a tutor and allowed to study alongside his sons, my half brothers. Under a scholar's guidance, I prepared for life as the devoted wife of whatever low-ranking royal relative my father would eventually choose for me. I grew into my long limbs and my sculpted face; I was considered handsome, not pretty. I learned Latin and spoke both the Thuringian tongue of my mother and the Frankish German of my grandfather, my father, and his brothers.

My favorite classroom, however, was the garden where my mother raised herbs and vegetables for the villa's kitchen.

I remember sitting patiently in the deep grass of summer when I was very young, watching my mother and grandmother gently pull weeds and bugs from the tender stems of herbs while they talked about the remedies they promised: hyssop-chicken stew to ward off sadness, poultices of comfrey for cuts and scrapes, sprays of angelica to ward off evil spirits. I was a curious child, but I feared my questions would interrupt their inadvertent lessons, which I absorbed with precocious concentration.

My silence prompted my mother to look up occasionally, searching for me on the perimeter. "Are you listening, child?" she asked. She sat up straight and arched her back, stretching her arms high over her head. "You must remember all this because Grootmoeder and I will not always be here."

"I know." I nodded and pulled a bright yellow flower—a weed—from the grass and held the stem to my nose. It smelled bitter. "What is this?"

"Lion's tooth," she said.

"Can we eat it?"

"Yes."

"Then why do you not plant it in the garden?" I squinted my eyes and waved the bright flower back and forth, focusing on the yellow streak I was sketching against the green backdrop of the garden.

"We do not have to." Mother leaned back down on her hands and crawled ahead to start weeding another section of her row. "It grows on its own. And I do not like it much."

I bit into the flower, which tasted as bitter as the stem smelled. "I do not like it either."

Grootmoeder was a stout woman, stronger and healthier than my mother. She attacked the rot of stems and roots in the spring, hunching over the spade with her entire body, shoving the blade deep, turning over a clod of dirt and plant detritus, and never pausing before initiating her next plunge. The violence with which she churned the garden was her way of shedding her winter lethargy and warming the body for the hard summer's work of laying by food for winter.

Once she had tamed the tangle of weeds and last year's litter, my mother and I joined her with pointed sticks, breaking up the clods and smoothing out the surface for sowing. Then came the planting, weeding, pruning, and harvesting that brought us our rewards. As I grew old enough to discern the difference between nutsedge and the tender young leaves of a carrot top, they assigned me my own rows to weed, and I thought myself no longer a child, but a young woman helping to feed the villa. I still listened to my mother and grandmother talk, but by then I had stored most of their herbal knowledge in a place where it still remains years later, long after the memory of those golden afternoons started to fade.

As much as she knew about the natural world, my mother knew little of Christianity in any of its forms—Catholic or Arian or Pelagian or Manichean—and she had no use for any of it. Christianity had spread across Gaul faster than the plague, and my father had instructed his priest to school me in its creed. Under the priest's tutelage, I memorized enough Psalms, prayers, and liturgy to lead a parish—had the church not banned women from the clergy before my birth. But in the dark of night, my grandmother and my mother performed the rituals of the ancient Thuringian cults with which they had been raised and which had been outlawed by the Romans and the Franks before my father's time. Fortunately, the ban was not enforced against Germanic slaves, whose souls mattered little to the local clergy or kings. Our celebrations of Kalends and the turn of the seasons continued unabated. I joined them in each one. Occasionally, Charibert sent servants out to stop us from banging on pots and pans, which was how we brought the new moon back from the dark, but he never forbade our celebrations. As a result, even as a youngster, my religious beliefs were polytheistic.

After entering the monastery, I added the ritualistic prayers of the Hours to my invocations while keeping my pagan observances a secret. Now in my anguish over Lebover's ascension, I exploited that full portfolio of prayers and chants to keep my frustration at bay and seek acceptance.

The other nuns dealt with the surprise of Lebover's appointment with a kind of quiet revolt. Rather than turn to contemplation, prayer, and penance, they huddled, gossiped, and grumbled. They prayed less, not more, Maroveus be damned.

Their grumbling did no good. Lebover moved quickly to cement her authority under Maroveus. She named the tiny niece of Gregory of Tours, Justina, as her prioress, a strategic move intended to bolster Gregory's hitherto unenthusiastic support of Lebover and Maroveus. And, after ordering her personal effects moved into Agnes's old chambers, she and Maroveus met daily to discuss the changes he thought necessary to render our cloister a haven for abstinence and asceticism.

I had no doubts that the bishop's intent was not to save our souls, but to confiscate our relic.

✝

Radegund and Agnes had both participated in our menial daily chores, not holding themselves above the other sisters. With them in the room, the mood lifted. We sang hymns as we sewed and teased each other about our poor voices and our uneven stitches. Lebover, on the other hand, removed herself from such quotidian tasks—either begging illness or asserting privilege. And while Radegund had enjoyed an intellectual life of contemplation, writing, and reading, Lebover chose to live hers as a prison guard.

Gout swelling her feet and ankles, she limped through the cloister on a cane throughout the day to monitor our behavior. She prohibited conversation, and only when we were separated from her in the middle of the night, could my sisters gossip and commiserate. The dark dormitory hissed with angry whispers, often right up to the call to Matins—our 2 a.m. prayers. We slept in one room on narrow cots lined up against the cold stone walls. Caesarius's *Regula* said our tongues were supposed to be reserved for prayers, readings of the *Regula* at dinner, and recitation of Psalms at the eight prayer sessions, called Hours, in each day.

One night, the whispers woke me a few minutes before the crier announced the Hour of Matins. Shaking off the vestiges of a sour dream, I listened to Covina, who lay on the cot next to me.

"Are you certain?" she asked her neighbor on the other side.

"Yes, he was there again," answered the nun. "I saw them go together into her chambers."

"Alone?"

"Yes."

"Are you sure it is a man?"

"Well, he dresses like a woman, but he has the chest of a man. His face was covered by the hood, but I saw hairy arms peeking out from under the sleeves of his robe."

"Were they not covered by the linen?"

Whomever the nun had seen, it was not one of us. We wore shapeless, long-sleeved shifts under our outer clothing, even when bathing, to keep from seeing our own skin or the skin of others. The temptations of the flesh were considered too intense to risk nakedness.

That this man was regularly coming to meet with Lebover in the reception area, even without another nun present, also violated the *Regula*. But this new rumor surprised me. If he was now staying in Lebover's chambers, that was worse than breaking the *Regula*. It was a sin.

As we rose minutes later for Matins, I slid in next to my cousin, Basina. "Have you heard about a man in Lebover's chambers?" I whispered.

"Oh, the eunuch? Yes. And so have others." Basina sounded annoyed and she turned her head away from me. I knew about the man who visited Lebover's room, although I did not know what his purpose was, or if he was, indeed, a eunuch. Maroveus had either given his approval for his visits or pretended not to notice them, but it was news to me that he was living there. I wondered if Maroveus knew that.

"Are you angry with me?"

"Yes! We all are!" Covina interjected. I had not realized how closely she was following us.

Of course, I had noticed the scowls thrown my way,

increasingly over the past few days. The longer I said nothing and did nothing about Lebover, the more obvious their disappointment in me had become. I had lost any official authority when I was denied election as abbess, but wallowing in self-pity, I had neglected to realize the others still expected my leadership.

"But, what can I do?"

"Help us!" Basina whispered harshly.

I usually let Basina's anger roll off my back. My young cousin was unreliable, mercurial, and generally more afraid than courageous. She had good reason: Her stepmother Fredegund had murdered her mother and her brothers to secure a place for her own son as heir to the throne of Austrasia, the westernmost kingdom of Gaul. Attacked and raped by her father's soldiers on Fredegund's orders, Basina had fled to the monastery for protection.

Basina's story was a common one. Our monastery was more a community of women with shared motivations than a punishingly strict cloister. We fulfilled our obligations to pray for the sick, the wounded, and those awaiting passage from purgatory, but we shared so much beyond our Christian faith. This home, populated largely by Frankish women of royal and noble birth—Lebover being the exception—was our refuge from marriage, childbirth, and murder at the hands of jealous relatives.

We reached the chapel where the morning prayers were held. I was glad that I would have some time to think before I had to respond to Basina and Covina. Could I fix things? How?

Clearly, my sisters were expecting more from me, and by keeping my head down and thinking only of myself, I had let them down.

FOUR

For three decades, my sisters had endured the cold, hard, and plain surfaces without complaint because of the warmth and camaraderie Radegund infused into our monastery. Despite Lebover, we tried to retain some of that. As we sat in the atrium sewing room in the afternoon between the Hours of midday Sext and midafternoon None, Basina and a couple of sisters talked softly about letters they had received from home. Our conversations were usually in Latin, the only language we all had in common, or in the most shared of our German dialects.

"My brother's wife is with child again." Vivian said.

Basina chuckled. "How many is that now?"

"I have lost count! She does not know where they come from." Vivian's giggle, which sounded more like the tinkling of bells mixed with the gurgle of cider poured from a jug than a human laugh, never failed to amuse me. It was contagious and without much reason, we all burst into laughter.

Suddenly, Basina dropped her embroidery needle on the floor

and clapped her hand over her mouth. I followed her eyes to the doorway, where Justina stood, surveying our gathering with a scowl.

"Did someone announce the second arrival of Jesus Christ?" the prioress asked. I wondered if she was serious at first; it seemed like such an odd question. But she held her frown. "Otherwise, I see no excuse for this levity. I will see if Lebover has something more appropriate for you to discuss while you work. Or perhaps you can help each other practice your prayers for Advent. She has not been impressed with your recitations so far."

"We were only—" Basina started, but Justina had stomped away, making a beeline to report our misbehavior to Lebover, I suspected.

Sneaking around and dropping in unexpectedly, Justina and Lebover succeeded in eroding whatever joy we had regained after Agnes's death with anxiety and melancholy. Even when they were out of the room, we worried about spies among us. It would be easy for Lebover to coax secrets out of anyone with a bribe of a little extra food, a private visit with relatives, or some treasured personal possession.

Still, our nighttime conversations continued. One night, Greta, the sacrist who stored the goods we brought to the monastery and maintained the sacred objects used in the sacraments, told us the abbess had demanded a silk altar cloth from the treasury and had used the fabric to make a robe for her niece's wedding trousseau.

Most of the nuns—those of royal lineage—had bought their way into the monastery with fine household items, clothing, and jewels. The goods went into the monastery's treasury and were sold or traded as needed for food, cloth, or wine that we could not raise or make ourselves, and for the parchment and ink we needed to copy the manuscripts sent to us by parishes in the diocese. The gold, jewels, fine linens, and animal skins were no longer ours to wear or enjoy.

Greta's cot was on the other side of mine from Basina's, and she started her story in a whisper. A cold draft whistled through the dormitory, preventing the others from hearing her.

"Speak up, Sister," hissed a nun far down at the end of the row of cots. "Have no worry. Lebover will not hear you over this howling wind."

"I questioned her about it, and she threatened me," Greta said, louder. Her voice trembled as if she were still shaken by what had happened. "She told me to be quiet about it, or she would take away my position. I would scrub pots day and night."

"She cannot do that," another said.

"Oh, yes, she can," I countered. "With Maroveus behind her, she can do anything she wants."

"And she took some of the silver and gold jewelry from storage," Greta said, gaining composure as we encouraged her. "I do not know what she did with them, but I suppose they will be wedding presents as well."

"How do you know she took them?" Basina asked.

"Only she and I have keys to the treasury," Greta said. "And I have not loaned mine to anyone."

While I knew some of the nuns were prone to concocting stories and gossip to get attention, I did not suspect that of Greta. Like so many, she had come to the Holy Cross to sidestep a treacherous royal marriage—in her case, to a royal cousin known for his whoring and violence. Her very life depended on her cloister in the monastery where neither the rejected cousin nor her father, a prince, could reach her. As a result, she had always been a careful and humble penitent.

"That is nothing compared with those men in the bath today," Basina snorted.

That afternoon, as we made our way to None, our afternoon

Hour of prayer and recitation, we had to avert our eyes from the men in the bathing tank that had been built for us. The money for its construction had come from a royal prince, the father of one of the sisters who had only recently arrived at the monastery. Lebover had said the bath was not safe for us to use yet; the mortar between the flat stones of its walls had not yet cured sufficiently. But the men laughed and splashed in it as we passed through the courtyard to the chapel.

"Who were they?" Greta asked.

"Her brothers and cousins," I answered. I had seen them before, gathering just inside our garden walls, laughing and talking with Lebover and her male companion who was dressed as a woman. When I had questioned her about letting men inside the convent walls, she had retorted that they were her relatives, and as such, she could meet with them as long as another sister accompanied her. That was true, but I doubted that the *Regula* identified "sister" as an ersatz woman from the outside. I had kept that opinion to myself.

As the fall wore on, we faced new deprivation. Despite the bitterly cold autumn, the bishop cut our wood rations and food. We had no idea why—we had plenty of treasure to sell or trade for fuel. Lebover gave us no chance to ask. She was now eating alone in her chamber, instead of sharing our meals. She sneaked into the chapel for the Hours at the last moment and left before the rest of us turned around.

Soon the nighttime conversations in the dormitory were peppered with plans for escape, but I knew they were just wild fantasies generated by empty stomachs. Hardly a one of us had a safe place to go; we would have ended up back in the precarious situations that had sent us to the cloister in the first place.

FIVE

Despite the joy and freedom the founder had allowed us in our cloister, Radegund had been pious and generous without fault, leading by example, not exhortation, and allowing us to express our devotion to Christ in whatever way we chose. That included paths to martyrdom, if that was what our souls required.

A year after I arrived as a thirteen-year-old at the monastery, one of the older nuns—suffering from disease, her eyes and ears failing, her breath weak—wanted to spend her final days in solitude and prayer without interruption. With Radegund's permission, her family provided the materials to build a small stone cell, just large enough for the old woman to lie down, and after tearful goodbyes, her sisters sealed the cell, leaving only a small hole by which to hand her a minimum of water and food, so she could live out her days with only the Lord's voice guiding her to her reunion with Him.

I respected such piety—was even frightened by it. I strove to develop the love for Jesus that the old woman pronounced as she entered her cell. But that kind of devotion evaded me, and seven years later, I still turned my eyes away as I hurried past the old woman's cell-turned-crypt on the path to the garden. This radical Christianity, this asceticism was so different from the joyous pagan rituals I had shared with my mother and grandmother in our garden. I wondered how immurement could be reconciled with Christian doctrine—the fine line between walling oneself up and suicide seemed slim indeed.

Even though the routine of prayer and work satisfied me in the way it absorbed the hours and left no time for idle dreams, Lebover's rule had poisoned my attitude, and I began to think about how the cloister left me bereft of purpose. I obeyed the rules and learned the liturgy, but other than to save my own soul, I was not sure what good it was doing. Jesus had preached care for the poor, but we were only caring for ourselves. To add to my confusion, I was intimidated by the perfection of the Virgin Mary—virtuous in her devoutness, obedience, acquiescence, and self-sacrifice—and I ached for the more accessible and flawed goddesses of my Germanic ancestors. Only the levity of the unscripted times with my fellow inmates had stilled my nostalgia, and Lebover—under Maroveus's orders—had taken that away.

Radegund, whose practice of Christianity I chose to emulate, was cut from a different cloth. She was pious but generous, strict but reasonable, God-fearing but hopeful. But it was her intellectual curiosity, intimacy with the classics, and philosophical deliberations with Gregory and Fortunatus that constituted what I considered a life worth living. As one of Radegund's favored nieces, I had spent my first few months at her side, listening, reading, and learning.

It was her intelligence, not her devotion to Christ, that led me to my work in the scriptorium as a transcriber and copier of texts. I apprenticed with Ethel, a former deaconess and transcriber who had been forced from her parish. As a woman, Ethel's hands—like all women's hands—were impure, a church council had declared, and she was no longer allowed to touch the sacred documents in her diocese. She came to the Holy Cross where she reclaimed her pen and resumed her worship with ink and parchment.

Her fingers were ink stained, but Ethel's face was wise, and her patience great, and she taught me the tedious tasks of scraping old parchments clean and mixing inks for new texts. I had no artistic talent to illustrate the manuscripts, but I was literate, and my fingers were nimble, and when the old deaconess died, I was the only one left in the convent who could read and copy old manuscripts. I worked alongside the monastery's illustrator, Desmona, whose eye for color and shapes humbled me, and we prepared copies for churches and other monasteries around Gaul. The money we were paid for the work helped support our cloister.

Up until Lebover's ascension, Desmona had been a bright spark in the monastery. Her high, lilting voice brightened our Psalms and rose above the droning hymns the poorer singers among us uttered. She was younger than most of us, and her light, skipping steps cheered me. Her blond hair was frequently falling out from under her veil, hanging in long, wavy strands in her face. She brushed them aside with impatience, eager to get on with whatever task beckoned her.

One day as we worked late, taking advantage of the long summer daylight, I heard her start to hum a sweet folk song I had heard as a child. I looked up to see her smiling and tilting her head from side to side to the rhythm of her tune, even as her brush continued its confident strokes.

"Desmona," I asked her, "what fills you with such joy? What do you hear that fills your heart with song?"

She pushed a stray lock away from her face and looked up at me. "What you are asking?" The flickering light from the candle that illuminated her desk sparkled in her bright blue eyes.

"Why are you so cheerful?" I asked. "I was once like you, back when I was a free and silly child, running around my mother's gardens. How do you retain that here inside these cold monastery walls?"

Desmona diverted her eyes. Her eyebrows furled, and she frowned—the first I had ever seen cross her face.

"No, I am not censuring you!" I tried to assure her. "I think you help us all remember to let light into our hearts and find joy in this life, not waiting for our reward in heaven. But I know no one who is as good at it as you."

Desmona put down her paintbrush and wiped her hands on the ink-spattered rag she hooked through the belt of her cloak. Her frown dissolved, and she looked at me with eyes full of thought. "There are so many things I love about this place," she said quietly. "Radegund was the mother I never had. You are the closest I have ever known to a sister. I have a bed and work and music and the Psalms. I could not imagine a happier place to be. Even heaven will have to be pretty special to impress me after the Holy Cross."

I nodded and looked back down at my work, giving her permission to return to hers. I had no answer for her but I realized she made a good point. I, too, had enjoyed a surrogate mother in Radegund, even though I had always missed my birth mother. Here, I had sisters I never had before. I had a bed, food, shelter, a garden, and useful work. I had the certainty of a life with Christ after death, a future my mother's rituals and beliefs had never predicted. Why not be happy?

When Radegund ascended to heaven two years before,

Desmona suffered as profoundly as any of us. Her own mother had died at her birth, and Radegund literally had been the only mother she had ever known. Although she never regained quite the same childish demeanor after Radegund, she did eventually pull out of her deepest sorrow, and her soprano once again lifted our hymns.

That bright summer ended with Agnes's death. Desmona's downward spiral under Lebover's reign was like the sudden silencing of birds right before a storm. The atmosphere had become so toxic, even her song was silenced. At the same time, more parishes in the kingdom were renouncing the service of women, and fewer sent us manuscripts to copy and decorate. Desmona and I had less of the work we loved—and that kept us busy.

Besides my share of the sewing, which was assigned to each of us with enough eyesight left to do it, I took on more responsibility in the monastery kitchen, kneading and forming sticky dough into loaves of bread every morning, and tending and gathering the herbs in the garden for the cooks. When there were no manuscripts to copy, I spent the entire day cooking, using the knowledge of herbs I had learned from my mother. A benefit of working in the kitchen was a measure of wine each day, which sometimes improved my mood, but often worked in the opposite way.

On our idle days, Lebover reassigned Desmona to the laundry. It seemed an odd choice for such a wisp of a girl. The woolen outer dresses and the abundance of sheets and tablecloths were a heavy load for the strongest nuns. Desmona's demeanor had begun to sink even further under the burden, and I worried about her.

Lebover's austerity weighed heavily on the kitchen and my sisters. My loaves of bread got smaller as the daily rations of wheat and barley were cut, and the porridges were thinner. We were already denied meat or fowl most days by Caesarius's harsh dietary rules, and now the eight daily Hours of prayer and Psalm readings were accompanied by the gurgling growls of our stomachs.

On Mondays, Wednesdays, and Fridays, from the first of September to the first of November, the *Regula* required us to fast, eating only one meal a day. Except for that portion allowed the cooks, wine was served only on feast days, of which fewer were now observed at the Holy Cross. As Advent approached, our fasting increased to every day. We all grew thinner, but Lebover seemed to be accumulating our lost pounds around her already substantial circumference under her robes. Her gout worsened.

I had expected the new abbess would speak to me privately, soon after her appointment, to express counterfeit surprise and humility for her selection, maybe even apologize for my disappointment. But instead, Lebover walked steps out of my way to avoid me for weeks. Perhaps it was for the best.

Just before Christmas, as we were finishing our single afternoon meal, and the brief sunlight that filtered into the cloister had grown dim, Justina, the prioress, approached me. My sisters' eyes widened with expectation.

"The abbess, Sister Lebover, wishes to meet with you in the chapel," tiny Justina whispered.

"When?" My stomach clamped tight. I knew it had to happen—a meeting to clear the air and forge some path forward through our mutual animosity, but I dreaded it.

"This evening. After Vespers."

It would be over soon, I told myself. I closed my eyes and imagined myself two hours into the future, well past the confrontation, breathing easier again.

SIX

Two hours later I carried a candle through the dark corridor, shielding its wavering flame with one hand, and stepped into the chapel. Lebover knelt in the front of the nave with her back toward me—a lump of dark humanity surrounded by a halo of altar candles. A cold draft blew down from the windows near the ceiling and extinguished my flame. I picked my way in the dark over the uneven stone, knelt, and crossed myself before sliding into the bench a few feet from the abbess.

I waited several minutes for Lebover to speak. I had begun to wonder if she had fallen asleep, when the front door of the monastery behind us slammed closed against the winter wind. I turned to see Maroveus push past Bertie and, without kneeling or acknowledging his proximity to the relic he craved, he shuffled into the bench in front of us, lifted his knee onto the seat, and turned to me with a frown.

"Have you started?" he asked Lebover.

"No, I was waiting so you could hear her excuses yourself,"

Lebover said. With difficulty, she rose from her knees and sat heavily next to me.

She turned toward me. It was the closest I had been to the abbess in months, and I was startled at the puffiness in her cheeks. She was certainly eating well, but the deep, dark circles under her eyes told of profound sorrow. What price was she paying for her privileges? How much pain was she enduring working under the thumb of Maroveus?

"I am not here to make any excuses," I whispered. I looked back at the bishop's large nose.

"Good. Then we should be able to get to the bottom of your transgressions quickly," Maroveus said.

"I am a sinner, which I have confessed to our priest and to our Lord, but I have done nothing unusual. I have no unconfessed transgressions." It was true that I had done and said nothing to improve morale. If I had anything to feel sorry for, it was that: I had been keeping my head down and waiting. Waiting for what, I now wondered. How did I think this miserable atmosphere would end?

"But it is you who spreads rumors about me!" Lebover's voice shot out, causing me to flinch. Anger flashed in her eyes, replacing what I had interpreted as hurt, and I quickly dropped the sympathy I had just started to feel for her. Now I understood what was coming: she would blame me for the dark mood in the monastery and the restlessness among the sisters.

"What rumors?" I asked. In a way, my professed innocence was not an exaggeration; I barely listened to the whispered gossip and complaints in the night.

"Let us not belabor this," Maroveus cut in. "We know the hatred you harbor in your heart. I need not tell you, as John has,

'Anyone who hates a brother or sister is a murderer, and you know that no murderer has eternal life residing in him.'"

He was right; I already knew that. It was in the *Regula*. The *Regula* also said that if a nun sinned and had repeated the sin after a reprimand, she should be disciplined to the greatest severity. Was this a warning? Would they order me to side with Lebover or be punished?

"I do not hate her." My voice barely carried over the howl of the wind rushing through the high open windows. But was I being truthful? Did I hate the woman for stealing my position as abbess? Or for denying my sisters decent rations? Did I hate Maroveus? I was distracted by the question. It was a sin to hate, but that was not the one I usually confessed. Usually, I acknowledged wanting more than I deserved—more food, more wine, more freedom to walk about, read, and study. I was vain and covetous. But hateful?

I shook my head to clear my thoughts. I had to pay attention. Whatever trap they were setting for me; I would need to concentrate to steer clear of it.

"Your lies are the devil's stories," Lebover said. "You will destroy yourself and others with them. You and your cousin Basina will not be spoiled by me as you were by Agnes before. You are not special. Your privilege has ended."

Why bring Basina into this? I did not want my cousin to be tainted with my mistakes, imagined or not. I waited for Lebover to continue. Would she volunteer what gossip it was that had wended its way to her ears?

"You have nothing to say?" Lebover shifted her wide girth to turn toward me, shaking the bench under us.

"No. I have spread no gossip. I know nothing of whatever gossip you have heard."

Lebover emitted a staccato huff. "I expected you would feign innocence." She and the bishop nodded at each other. "Then you will move your cot to the corridor outside the bedchamber. You will sleep there until you have asked for forgiveness and I have granted it."

"It is not for you to forgive my sins or condemn me. My sins are for the priest to hear and the Lord to forgive," I shot back. "And the *Regula* says all nuns shall sleep in one quarters—"

"You will not tell us what the *Regula* says!" Maroveus interrupted, his voice suddenly booming in the hollow heights of the chamber. "You claim to be a student of the *Regula*, so you know there should be no quarreling. 'Abstain from strife and thou shalt diminish thy sin.'"

"Yes, Ecclesiastics 28:8," I said. I had transcribed the Bible so many times, it was etched, nearly verse for verse, in my memory.

The bishop's arm shot out from under his robe, and I jerked back, certain he was about to strike me in the face. But he stopped, a finger pointing at my nose.

"I will not stand for your insolence, Sister." His finger shook violently just inches from my eyes. "It is my station, my responsibility, to watch over every Christian in this diocese, and as much as it pains me, that includes you and your noxious, venomous allies." Seemingly exhausted by his short outburst, the bishop kept his trembling finger in my face, but ended his screed as abruptly as he had started it, breathing heavily.

"I wonder if you can tell me what sins I have committed?" I asked "What hatred do you think I harbor? What lies have I concocted?" If I was to be punished for rumors I had only heard, not started, then at least I should know which ones they were.

"That I am cruel to the sisters. That I am hoarding food.

That I ration food needlessly. That I am starving you." Lebover answered for him.

I had heard the nuns whisper a lot of things, but not those. I imagined they were products of Lebover's own guilty conscience.

"Have you not said those things?" Lebover asked. Her arms encircled all my misdeeds as if they were wrapping them up in a succinct package.

I shook my head. "No, I have not said them. Perhaps you know more about those things than I do."

"What have you heard? Tell me now, or I will have you punished further."

I thought about the question for a moment. Would it be wise to mention the sins the abbess was committing in front of the bishop? Did he already know about them? Maybe if he knew nothing of it, the news would make him reconsider who should head the monastery. Even as scurrilous a man as he would not approve of Lebover's recent activities.

"You are entertaining a man in your chambers," I said to Lebover's face. "He is there almost daily."

"No. No. No!" Lebover labored to her feet. She stood, leaning over me, her heavy breasts crowding my shoulder. I suspected that her belligerence had more to do with Maroveus's presence than her own cold heart.

"But others have seen him with their own eyes." I forced myself to sit still in her shadow, faking calm even as my heart pounded in my throat.

"They have not! They imagine things with the devil's eyes."

"How about the men who have been seen bathing in the tank that was built for the nuns?" I asked, catching the bishop's eye.

Maroveus lowered his finger from my face and looked at

Lebover. Was this the first he knew of that? He opened his mouth as if to talk but paused for a moment. He had lost control of the inquisition, and if there was one thing I knew about him, it was that he needed to be in control. Could that possibly be his Achilles heel as well? He snapped his mouth shut and waved at Lebover to sit down. "This conversation has gone on long enough," he said. "I have heard enough. You will sleep in the corridor until you receive the abbess's forgiveness."

That will be a cold day in hell. I stifled a smirk.

"And, you will fast for the next seven days," the bishop continued, his voice much louder than necessary, even given the cold wind howling outside. "You will not join the others in the dining room, and you will be brought bread and water. You will not attend Matins, Lauds, Terce, Sext, None, or Compline. You will attend only Vespers but you will lower your eyes, acknowledge no one, and ask for no acknowledgment. You will recite the prayers and Psalms without opening your mouth and follow the readings for Advent and Christmas with only your eyes. You will spend the remainder of the Hours in solitude and prayer, asking the gracious Lord for forgiveness you do not deserve. You will not speak with anyone other than your Savior, and then only in prayer."

"Is this clear?" Lebover bellowed at my side.

I looked at her and felt tears burning in my eyes. Two things were crystal clear: One, I was going to miss the Christmas feast, the thought of which had sustained me and my sisters through the past weeks of hunger. And two, I was never going to win a battle over these two hulking humans from within the monastery. They held all the power.

The Holy Cross I had come to love and trust was lost. My sisters and I were doomed, and some of us might be ejected from the cloister to a life of deprivation, or worse, to our deaths. None of us who had known what a beautiful place our monastery had been before Lebover could survive this new, degrading existence.

"You make yourselves clear, yes," I finally answered. "But it is not right that you have made us miserable where we were once full of joy."

"Obedience!" the bishop shouted. "Do not argue with us. You are risking excommunication and eternal damnation with your attitude and your perfidious behavior. One more word from you, and you will spend the rest of your days in silence and solitude."

I had heard of nuns in other monasteries who had been sentenced to live out their lives in solitary cells, sealed away from the rest of the world with only a small window at the ground through which to receive food and water. I could not imagine a worse fate. The nun I had known who had committed herself to her entombment at the Holy Cross at least had done it voluntarily.

So, of course, I said nothing.

Once again, Maroveus offered no benediction or prayer for my soul. He dismissed me rudely with a wave of his arm, and I walked out into the dark corridor without relighting my candle.

The other nuns were sitting up in their cots whispering when I walked into the dormitory, but they immediately fell silent. I could feel their eyes on my back as I rolled up the clothing under my mattress, put it on top of my thin blanket, and pulled the cot through the door and into the breezy corridor.

I let the door clang closed behind me, and settled into my first of many cold dark nights in the solitude of my own regrets.

SEVEN

What I regretted most was not listening to my mother.

Rosalda was her name, and like Radegund, she was a war-booty child whom King Clothar had brought to Paris from Thuringia as a slave and given to his daughter-in-law upon her marriage to Charibert. But with her red hair, bright blue eyes, and freckles, my mother looked like an adolescent, and Charibert's wife, Ingoberga, was threatened by her unique, foreign beauty. Immediately, my mother was exiled to the king's villa outside Paris. With youthful energy, Rosalda tended the villa's gardens, and when Ingoberga sent her children to the villa to get them out of her hair, Rosalda watched over them. Charibert first noticed my mother as she was kneeling, weeding a low patch of herbs in the villa garden as he passed through one day. That evening, she was summoned to his side.

Ingoberga was in Paris while Charibert entertained Rosalda in his bed for the next fourteen nights. My mother had learned Latin alongside their children, and she impressed him with her fine mastery of its complex inflections. When Charibert's wife returned, Rosalda went back to the small house at the periphery of the villa grounds and gave birth to me nine months later. Summoned by my mother, my grandmother crossed the Rhine to live with us.

Even as he married more wives and had more children, Charibert looked for me when he returned to the villa from Paris, from whence he ruled his quarter of Gaul. He frequently called my mother to join him at night. Although Rosalda gladly warmed his sheets when his other wives were pregnant, nursing, or away, she refused to marry him.

"I will not be the fourth on the list," she told me when I was old enough to understand the difference between marriage and concubinage. "I would rather be who I am—a Thuringian slave and a whore—than stand on the lowest rung of a tall ladder of wives."

I remember that vow, if not its precise words. Like most of the memories of my preconvent years, I fear losing it to time. Months go by between flashes of the time I spent with her and my grandmother in the garden and in the kitchen. Only when I returned to the convent garden each spring and began its annual renewal did I dwell on those memories long enough to recover more than mere glimpses. Now these scenes seem to hover just out of reach.

My life in that garden with my mother and grandmother, however, was cut short. A year after the poet Fortunatus arrived at the villa, where he found a haven from political enemies in Rome, my father fell ill and died. Immediately, his wives began jockeying for position, seeking the best political appointments for their sons, and Fortunatus feared for my life. No one wanted me around to produce a possible contending heir.

"Clotild cannot stay here." Fortunatus had come to our hut to talk to my mother. He called me in from the garden to hear his warning. "She will be murdered within a fortnight if she does. Charibert's widows will see to it."

"As long as she does not claim any inheritance, what danger does she pose to them?" Rosalda argued. "We have asked for nothing but this modest hovel and work in the gardens." We had only two three-legged stools in our one-room hut, and I stood behind my mother as they talked.

"It is too risky." Fortunatus continued to press. "Charibert's wife Ingoberga is treacherous and not above murder. Clotild will be far safer at the Holy Cross. Her grandfather's wife Radegund will watch over her. And if Clotild chooses not to stay after her novitiate, she can leave."

My mother said nothing. Her eyes swelled with tears. Other than my grandmother, I was the only family she had. Finally, she let out a long sigh. "She will decide for herself," she said. She turned to me and pulled me into her arms. "You will never know the warmth of a man's arms around you at night, the beauty of a babe at your breast, the joy of your child's laughter. The cloister is death, the end of your dreams. Think of that before you decide."

I hated to sadden her, but for me, it was an easy choice. As much as I loved my mother and grandmother, as much as I knew I would miss our garden and our warm, tight but snug cottage, my heart leapt at the thought of getting far away from my male cousins and half brothers, who constantly taunted me with such words as, "*Bastardis! Bastardis!* Your mother is a whore. Her mother is a whore. You shall be a whore," while my half sisters, Bertha and Berthageld, stood by and tittered.

This abuse was the dark secret of my childhood, which I hid

from my mother as I did not want her to see me as weak. She always held her head high and her eyes level when surrounded by my father's wives, even as they sneered at her to her face.

As I got older, the boys became more aggressive, groping at my budding breasts and grabbing at my crotch. Bertha and Berthageld's mothers had drawn them into the villa's parlors to learn to sew, to mewl, and to modestly tilt their heads and drop their eyes in the presence of their male cousins, to whom they would soon be betrothed.

As a *bastardis*, I was not allowed in the salons and parlors; I was not expected to secure a marriage that would bring wealth or honor to the family, only one that would get me safely out of the way. But neither did I belong among the children of the farmers and tenants of my father's kingdom. I had no assurances that I could stay at the villa once my mother died, and I was of no use to the Merovingians, except as a slave, the daughter of a slave.

✝

On the night before I was to leave with Fortunatus, I joined my mother and grandmother in a ceremony under the full moon, calling down the moon goddess, Máni. Sweet incense filled the small space between our hut and the garden, and our candles flickered in the night breeze. We chanted the rhymes I had known by heart from infancy, my child's voice adding but a whisper to my mother's hearty song and my grandmother's scratchy one. My mother poured three cups of wine and handed me one without diluting it.

"Where is the water?" I asked.

"Tonight, you will have trouble sleeping," she said. She was wise and could see into my heart. "You will need the wine, not the water."

We sat in the moon's glow, and I sipped my sour wine while my mother and grandmother filled their glasses several times. I studied the spidery shadows the willows threw on the ground. Already homesick for the garden, I worried that someday I would forget the place. I listened to the murmur of their Germanic chatter—not the words, just the sound of it—and tried to memorize its cadence.

I drifted off to sleep on the ground, and the last sound I heard was of my mother weeping.

The next morning, Mother sobbed and threw her arms around Fortunatus as he loaded my small trunk onto the wagon. "Please, do not take her from me. She is all I have left of Charibert. She is all I have in this world."

I remember feeling little that morning except for nausea from the wine, an eagerness to start our adventure, and joy at escaping the torture of my cousins. I rebuffed my grandmother's hugs and kisses and gently pushed my mother away. As the wagon rolled up the lane toward the old Roman highway to Tours and Poitiers, I did not look back.

My heart softened toward my mother over the next few years, as I took up gardening for the convent, which brought back memories of our life together at the villa. The warmth of my new sisters compensated for my loss of her. Under Radegund's special tutelage, I learned diplomacy and patience, which burnished my reputation inside the cloister's walls as a fair and thoughtful sister, worthy of being a future abbess. And before I had even completed my novitiate, I had set my sights on that future.

Now, sleeping alone in the cold, drafty corridor, away from my whispering sisters, I regretted having left my mother so eagerly. I longed, painfully, for the garden of my youth. I pulled myself into a ball on my side to conserve my body heat, and for the first time in ten years, I wished I had not left with Fortunatus. I saw my mother only one more time, when she made the trip to see me in the monastery, and I knew the worms had entered her brain. I think she was aware of it too, and she had come to visit me before it was too late. Now, I was forgetting her face. I remembered the moon's sharp shadows in the garden but I failed to conjure up her image.

Seven days into my nighttime solitude, the Christmas vigil began directly on the heels of Vespers. Starting at three hours past sunset, we gathered in the chapel for six readings from the Prophet Isaiah before midnight's Nocturnes, and six readings from the Gospels after Nocturnes. At the Hour of Terce, our liturgy included twelve readings of Psalms. And then the glorious feast could begin.

I had spent the entire day before helping to prepare the Christmas meal, including venison and boar donated by hunters from the noble family of one of the sisters, none of which I would be allowed to eat. At the smell of the roasting meat, saliva gushed in my mouth and swamped my throat, puddling with nausea in my empty stomach. Perhaps to make my misery sharper, Lebover sent Justina to tell me I could attend the feast, but I could not eat. Nearly dizzy with hunger, I decided that smelling the repast was better than nothing, and I joined my sisters as they filed into the dining room at midday.

Surrounded by my favorites—Desmona, Greta, Covina, and my cousin Basina—I joined in the blessing of the food and the prayers of thanks for its abundance. Looking up after the amen, I fought dizziness. The huge plates of food weighed down the far end of the table, fragrant and steaming in the cold dining room. A large goose was surrounded by bright globes of beets and glowing onions. Chunks of moist pork lay on a bed of sliced cabbages, sprinkled with shavings of carrot.

I wondered if I could experience hunger as a good sensation if I put my mind to it. Perhaps I would feel the rapture of the presence of Christ on this day of his birth if I could turn that suffering into pleasure.

But the smell of browned goose skin and salty pork was torture and it defeated me. I was not strong. I bowed my head and prayed. I diverted my eyes as the abbess and prioress began passing the heaping plates around the tables. As I accepted the first platter from Desmona and passed it along, I noticed she had not taken any of the luscious goose. Still under orders not to speak, I could only raise my eyebrows to ask the question.

"I am not eating until you are," Desmona said quietly, not meeting my eyes.

I shook my head. It was wrong for me to be punished for misdeeds I had not committed. It was even worse if Desmona was punished for them as well. Desmona nodded her head toward the rest of the table. I looked around and realized that none of the other nuns were taking food either. Plate after plate passed us by, and no one took a morsel.

The heaping dishes circled unmolested and returned to the head of the table. Justina watched, her face turning red with anger. By resisting temptation to feast on that rare and succulent meat, the nuns not only showed how strong they were, they showed how willing they were to stand by me.

Justina looked ready to kill, but Lebover simply lowered her eyes. Sadness, not anger, was written on her face. Had she realized her attack on me had failed? Had she understood how it jeopardized any chance she still may have had to make friends or win love and support from my sisters? Again, I had a fleeting feeling of pity for her.

I glanced around the table and saw no other face soften with Lebover's obvious regret. As the abbess rose from the table and slowly, laboriously clawed her way out of the room, leaning heavily on her canes, a murmur rose, and soon, nearly a cheer. Furious, Justina stood and ran after Lebover.

My sisters wasted no time. They eagerly passed the plates around again, starting each one at my place.

It was the beginning of our rebellion.

EIGHT

My sisters' show of solidarity with me at the Christmas feast weakened Lebover's resolve and strengthened mine. As we gathered in the nave for Vespers on Christmas night, the abbess limped up to me and said, "In the spirit of the love of the season and the gift of Jesus Christ, I have decided you can move your cot back into the dormitory and resume eating our meals." Her tone was cold, stiff, and labored.

I did not answer but stared straight ahead with exaggerated piety. Out of the corner of my eye, I could see her staring at my face, but I refused to acknowledge her.

Lebover's change of heart was too little too late. By then, the consensus in the monastery was that she was a monster—perhaps even worse than Maroveus. Adding to the abbess's vulnerability, the bishop had either tired of his role overseeing the quotidian details of the monastery or was sufficiently distracted by serious matters elsewhere. Or, perhaps he simply abhorred the cold streets of Poitiers in the dead of winter. Whatever the cause, he came less often after Christmas, and the first two months of the year went by without a single sighting of his pudgy face. The parish priest, a diffident and unassuming man of God, came with little fanfare to officiate over the services for the Epiphany and the Presentation of the Lord to the Temple.

The particularly cold winter did not improve Lebover's status amongst us. The dearth of wood she requisitioned for the monastery barely kept the water from freezing in the pitchers on the dining tables, and we shoved our cots closer together, hanging sheets from the ceilings to block the icy draft in the cavernous dormitory.

Meanwhile, Lebover continued to add layers of fat, even as her gout worsened. She shuffled through the convent, stabbing her cane into the ground ahead of her feet and leaning her heavy frame against it. A complete pass through the sacristy, the kitchen, the infirmary, the cellar, and the dormitory absorbed a couple of hours, and her daily rounds declined to one and then none. By the time Lent arrived, we saw her only at the Hours, and other than the cellarer, the sacrist, the infirmarian, and Justina, no one had reported a word from her for more than a month.

Colder, but free of the dispiriting presence of Lebover and Maroveus, our convent regained some of its earlier cheer and camaraderie. Regular gifts of grain begged from royal relatives boosted the supply of bread at meals, and until the fasting before Easter began, many of the other nuns had regained the weight they had lost in the days leading up to Christmas. After my long fast, however, I was still the thinnest I had been since I reached puberty.

One afternoon, as we sat silently over our embroidery, the elderly portress Bertie walked into the sewing room and motioned for me to follow her. The great poet Fortunatus had arrived at the door of the monastery and asked for me. My heart leapt in my chest, and I jumped up, dropping the scarf I was mending, and ran ahead of her to the reception room. Fortunately, he had shown up at a time when Lebover had secluded herself in her chamber with her decidedly male-looking guest. I was not inclined to interrupt her, but careful to follow the *Regula*, I asked Bertie to sit in with us.

"What a blessed pleasure to see you, old friend!" I greeted the poet with more emotion than I had expected to show. "What news do you bring us from the world of our fathers?"

Fortunatus had come to show me the progress he was making on Radegund's hagiography, the long paean to her life that he had been writing since her death. He looked on as I read his latest installment, which described a monastery unlike the one we now suffered. I had started to wonder if my memory of Radegund's reign had been clouded with nostalgia, but in Fortunatus's words, I saw that it was not.

The poem made me shake with anger and self-pity. I had not planned to complain to Fortunatus, but once I read his verse, my grievances poured out. "Oh, dear friend of Radegund! Our beloved cloister is draped in such sorrows now, you would not recognize it. We are starved, frozen, and belittled by Lebover and the bishop, Maroveus. This is no longer Radegund's blessed monastery. It has decayed into darkness and despair." I told him about the items taken from the sacristy. I told him about the food rations and the cold.

When I finished, he studied my face for a long minute. "Is it possible that you are simply jealous of her position?"

I wondered if he found my stories outrageous, perhaps even

incredible. I had thought, as a friend, he would listen and sympathize rather than doubt me. "I admit that I wanted to follow Agnes as abbess," I said. "And, yes, I perhaps am a little jealous, but—"

"Do you want to live with such envy?" he interrupted.

The question stung. I stood and paced across the room to shed the anger flooding my body. After a couple of turns, I stopped before him, my arms folded across my chest. "Do you think I would choose to be envious? No one *wants* to live with envy," I said. "It is not something one aspires to. It makes one miserable to compare oneself with others more fortunate, not more sanguine."

Fortunatus swatted at my logic. It was a dismissive gesture, something I would have expected from Maroveus, not from a man who had regarded Radegund as his intellectual equal, and who had never brushed me aside. What had changed? Was he not here for my critique of his work?

"I believe you should worry less about your conditions and more about your soul," he said. "Perhaps you should think less and pray more."

I shook my head and dropped back down on the bench. Was even this champion of the Holy Cross now adopting the church's new attitude toward women?

"What would you say if I suggested you think less and pray more?" I asked.

"But I'm a m— . . . poet." He was about to say "man" but caught himself just in time. If he had said "man," he could claim no credit for his good fortune as a famous and revered member of Merovingian society. After all, no one chose to be born a man. But becoming a poet was a matter of choice, and it required work and study.

I let his assertion fall without comment, and we sat in silence for a few minutes. "The worst of it," I said finally, returning to the subject of our cloister, "is I'm afraid that several of the nuns may decide to leave."

"And go where?"

"They do not know," I said. "But that is how desperate it is here. Winter persists in the air and in our hearts, and it is unlikely to get better soon. Maroveus has sunk his teeth into us now, and he is enjoying his new power over us. But his true aim is possession of our relic."

"You have the instincts of a poet, my dear Clotild," Fortunatus said, smiling. He may have intended to lighten my mood, but I wanted nothing to do with his cheer.

"This is not one of your saintly epics, my friend," I said. "You will never be tempted to write one about Lebover. I beg of you, on my father's grave, to hear me out. This cannot go on, or our monastery will be ripped apart, and that evil sorcerer Maroveus will have destroyed the very legacy you are memorializing with your poetry." I held up the manuscript and waved it in his face.

"He is most likely not evil, Sister." I sensed Fortunatus's change in address from "Clotild" to "Sister" was a signal for me to stop arguing, but when would I get another chance to ask someone for help? I looked to Bertie to back up my story, but she had nodded off on her bench, her mouth gaping open, emitting tiny snores and a bit of drool.

"He *is* evil." I lowered my voice to a harsh whisper. "Maroveus is concerned only about one thing—his power. And he is willing to work with that devil Lebover, even lie for her, to get his way."

"It is not just Maroveus, though, Sister. You will find few in the clergy these days who would support this monastery's continued independence. Especially since the councils have declared your sex and its weaknesses make you incapable of judgment in these matters."

"What do you mean, my weaknesses? My sex?" I took a deep breath and sat back against the hard, wooden bench. I knew he was right. Not that women were weak, but that we had few allies in the church. I did not understand how, in just my short lifetime, so much had changed. "Perhaps Bishop Gregory—" I let the words float, waiting for Fortunatus's reaction. Surely, the bishop of Tours, who had befriended Radegund, visited her monthly, and installed her relic of the Holy Cross, would defend us.

"I doubt even he will take your side now," Fortunatus said quietly, as if to reduce the shock of his news. It struck me that Bishop Gregory had not visited the monastery since Radegund had died.

I felt my face sink and stared at the rough stones under our feet. If I could not depend on Radegund's closest allies in the church, to whom could I appeal on behalf of her sisters? My grandfather, Clothar, had been dead for years. My father was dead, and my remaining uncles were locked in endless, mortal battles with each other over territory. The loss of our blessed independence was not a priority for any of them. We would not get Pope Benedict's help from Rome either. Despite his well-known regard for Radegund, it appeared he approved of this cleansing of women from the church, and further, his health was poor.

"You were shielded once from harm by my father, King Charibert, whom you loved," I said slowly, looking past Fortunatus. "When you fled your own dangers in Italy, he gave you shelter. And as he lay on his death bed, he asked you to find me a home. You chose this one, built by my grandfather and your friend, Radegund, and for that I am grateful."

I shifted my focus to the poet's eyes. "Your life and mine are woven together like warp and woof. I beg of you not to abandon me or the legacy of our founder, about whom you write with such love. You must help hold this monastery together, or the church will rip it apart."

Fortunatus blinked a few times and took a deep breath before standing. The conversation was over, and I had accomplished nothing with my tattling.

"Let me offer you my blessing, dear Sister, and then I must rest for my return to Tours tomorrow," he said. Despite a strong urge to refuse, I bowed my head and allowed him to place his hand on the top of my hood.

It was the last time I would see the great poet.

☩

On a blustery day after our observance of Epiphany, Macco, the Count of Poitiers, arrived at the door of our convent with a stooped, shadowy woman. Bertie called on Lebover and Justina to accept the newcomer, but when she was rebuffed at Lebover's chamber door, she pulled me from the kitchen to meet the visitor.

As I went to accept the woman, Macco attempted to slip into the reception room with her, but I stuck my leg out to block his path. "You cannot enter here," I said harshly. I had never liked the looks of the man. With his aquiline nose held high and his chest thrust forward, he carried himself like an aristocrat, not the errand boy for kings that he really was. Large scars on either side of his face and a jagged notch out of one ear attested to his love for battle, if not his ability with a sword.

"Gregory has ordered this wretched woman to be cloistered

for the rest of her natural life." Macco's voice was as excessively loud as his bearing was proud. "I must see that she has no opportunity for escape." He shoved the woman forward. She kept her head bowed, the canyon of her black veil hiding her face.

"I am quite certain that given the choice between your company and the company of the penitents inside these walls, she had not thought to try." I reached out and put an arm around the old woman, pulling her inside. "You may tell Gregory the Lord's newest bride has been delivered as you promised. Good day." I backed away, still holding the woman by the shoulders, and nodded at Bertie to close and lock the door.

Once inside, the woman raised her head, and I saw she was not as old as she had appeared. As she threw back the veil that covered her wavy, black hair, she straightened her shoulders, and flashed a toothy smile, outlined with full, pink lips. Her olive skin and strong nose hinted at a Roman origin. She was beautiful.

"I am sorry for the intrusion," she said, smiling as if she were not sorry at all and proffering an envelope. "I am Marian. Here is the letter from Gregory. I hope he apologizes for giving you no warning of my arrival. I have not been allowed to read it, so I am not sure what he has written."

I first looked her over. Her traveling clothes were simple, but unlike the nuns' woolen sheaths that fell in a straight line from the shoulders to the floor, hers clung to the youthful shape of her body. I surmised she may have chosen to hunch over and hide her face from Macco to avoid amorous advances from him or any of the mercenaries who traveled with him.

"You are most welcome here," I said. "I am Sister Clotild. I am certain Bishop Gregory would have warned us of your arrival if he were not needed by so many others in the diocese."

She nodded at the letter, apparently anxious to hear what it contained.

"I apologize that our abbess and prioress are predisposed and could not greet you," I continued. "I am sure you know that Gregory's niece, Justina, is our prioress?" It was clear that Marian was impatient for me to read the letter, so I read it aloud:

> *Greetings in Christ, Sister Lebover and Sister Justina, my esteemed and blessed niece.*
>
> *I send my blessings to you and your monastery, in hopes that this letter reaches you in health and devotion.*

I skimmed down the page for the end of the salutations and blessings, looking for the meat of the matter. I found it halfway down:

> *Before you stands a sinner to be a novice, sent to you through Christ's servant, the Bishop of Tours, by the ruling of the Council of Macon, to wit: widows of clergymen who attempt to remarry should have their marital vows revoked and should be cloistered in a monastery to live as penitents and abstinents for the rest of their natural lives. I beg you to accept and instruct this woman in the ways befitting a bride of Christ, so that her soul may be redeemed.*

We at the Monastery of the Holy Cross were aware of the councils' rulings, as they were announced after our daily readings of the *Regula* at the noon meal. This particular ecclesiastical pronouncement had not been surprising—it was the latest example of the church's shift to exclude women from clerical positions and prohibit us from assisting in the sacraments.

"Marian," I said, folding the letter and replacing it in the envelope addressed to Lebover and Justina, "are you aware that this is a life sentence? That you may never leave this place?"

Marian dropped her smile and looked beyond, into the chapel behind me. I sensed an arrogance that thrilled me. It was so rare in women who were ordered to surrender their lives to the cloister. "It is my penance."

"For what sin?" I asked. The council had rendered its opinion of her attempt to remarry, but did Marian agree with that judgment? The sin, if God really believed it was a sin, was one of wanting to love again. It took nothing from the church.

Marian returned a puzzled gaze. "It does not matter what I think, does it?"

I shook my head. No, it did not. It was not my place nor Marian's to question the wisdom of the church councils. Even if they were wrong about how Christ judged their actions, it made no difference. "And your dowry?" In offering ourselves as brides of Christ, we had to relinquish our worldly possessions, both to prove our humility and asceticism, and to help fund the convent.

"I was married to a clergyman, Sister Clotild," Marian said with a sly smile. "I have no possessions that the church has not already taken from me." She paused. "Including my work in the church and my sex."

I decided I was going to like Marian. She spoke plainly and honestly, claiming less loyalty to church doctrine than to her own mind.

"Sister Clotild!" Lebover's voice boomed from the corridor, and we turned to see the abbess stomping her way toward us, cane first, then one foot, then cane, then the other foot. Huffing laboriously, Lebover made her slow approach, the frown on her face deepening the closer she came. "Sister Clotild, who is doing your chores? Have you been relieved—?" As she rounded the corner and looked up to see Marian, she doubled down on her reprimand. "You have no authority to meet guests. Have you found it unnecessary—?"

I took advantage of the abbess's ambulatory struggle to excuse myself. "I was just on my way to the kitchen. Your newest novice has just arrived." I handed the letter back to Marian, nodded at Bertie, and strode down the opposite corridor.

NINE

Over the past six months, our lives, in many ways, had gone from plain to grim. The arrival of Sister Marian was a much-needed boost to our morale.

With Lebover sequestered in her chambers with her eunuch and Justina, and with Maroveus apparently weary of visiting our somber cloister, the mood started to turn. Marian was not tainted by the sorrow we had felt at Radegund and Agnes's deaths, or the change in atmosphere that accompanied Lebover's ascension. Basina, in particular, took to her, and they stuck together during the Hours and moved their cots closer so they could whisper at night. I was glad for them. Ever since my run-in with Lebover and Maroveus, I had avoided Basina so my ill repute would not rub off on her. She needed a new friend.

Immediately upon her arrival, Marian dove into her chores—the ubiquitous sewing and cleaning—and joined me in the kitchen most afternoons to take over the baking of our evening bread so I could focus on foraging meals from our meager supplies of root vegetables and barley. She seemed to generate more energy the more she expended it. Her joy was infectious, even though no one else in the monastery spoke her German dialect, which came from the Languedoc region. Her Latin, however, was impeccable, probably due to her first husband's service in the church.

I watched her for a couple of weeks, cautious not to get too close for fear that Lebover might notice our friendship and turn against her for it. But Marian's effervescence eventually wore away at my reserve, and I finally abandoned my intention to avoid her.

"Are you happy here?" she asked me one day, her apron covered with flour and her fingers deep into sticky dough.

"Yes, I am," I said. I paused a moment to check the validity of that answer. I was happy—not as happy as I remembered being when Radegund was with us, but then, how could I be?

"But you are the quietest of all," Marian said, and I paused to think about that as well. Had I allowed Maroveus and Lebover to turn me taciturn and reclusive? "Why is that?" Marian asked, echoing my silent question.

How much should I tell her about my troubles with Lebover and Maroveus, and the threats held over my head that evening in the chapel, I pondered. "I am under more scrutiny than most of the sisters," I finally said. "I had aspirations to Lebover's position, and so I am watched carefully."

Marian nodded and continued to punch and turn the dough. She worked efficiently, and it occurred to me that she had likely been a good wife. I wondered what sorrows she was hiding behind her good nature.

"You seem to be getting along well here," I said. "I am delighted by your constant cheer."

"I am simply grateful to finally have work to do and women

to do it with," Marian said, flipping the dough over and over to form a tidy loaf and dropping it into a greased pan. "Marriage to a clergyman is a lonely life."

"And your new husband?" I knew I was treading over dangerous ground. It was what had condemned her to the cloister, and was a subject for confession, not for idle chat.

Marian looked over at me, solemn now, as she carried the loaf pan to the oven. She paused at the oven door. "I did not love the man, but he would have provided me with a home and a bed. Otherwise, I would have been doomed to a life of poverty and squalor. Or the monastery." She chuckled.

"It seems then that you did not have much choice."

Marian threw open the heavy iron door, and a blast of hot air blew over us.

"Ahhhh!" I said unguardedly. The oven's heat was one of the benefits of kitchen work, but expressing physical delight was sinful. It could be tolerated from novices, perhaps, but was discouraged, especially under Lebover, after we had taken our vows.

Marian laughed. "I now know why you spend so much time in here. It is the warmest spot in the monastery."

"Yes, it is, but it is also the warmest place in the summer. You will discover why many of the sisters prefer the laundry in a few months. At least they get to take the sheets outside to hang them. Why do you like the kitchen?"

"I love the heat, yes," she said, returning to work another lump of dough. "And the fragrance!"

"And the wine?" I asked. I had not spoken so brazenly in months. Marian was clearly having an effect on me, but I knew this could get us into trouble.

Marian threw back her head and laughed with an abandon I

had never seen from anyone in the cloister, even during the happy days of Radegund's tenure. I smiled even as I shushed her.

"Lebover will prohibit you from working in here if she hears you," I whispered. "She hates joy."

"Do you think God hates joy?" Marian asked, straightening out the laughter in her face and lowering her voice.

I smiled. "I am certain He does not."

✝

I wish that short-lived improvement in the goodwill and cheer at our monastery had made me optimistic about the future—my soul could have benefited from the respite—but a cynicism that colored my humors muddied even my best moods and especially my most anxious ones. I would be listening to the clever banter of my sisters, their heads bent over the stitches of their wool work, and feel a creeping gloom sneak up on me like the draft from an open door.

Maroveus avoided our monastery until a month after Marian arrived, which should have been a relief for all of us, but I never doubted he would return to refresh our misery. When he did come, early in March, blowing through the front door like a cold gale personified, he did not disappoint. He met with Lebover in the reception room, and the rest of us were ordered to stay away so that we would not hear their discussion.

Before then, Lebover could not have told him much about what was happening at the monastery, other than the fact of the arrival of Sister Marian. She was spending nearly all her time bedridden by her gout in her chamber. Near the end of his visit, Maroveus hailed Bertie to bring Marian to the reception room.

Our novice talked with him only a short time before whooshing back into the kitchen and retreating to a corner near the pantry where she sat on a stool, sobbing into her hands.

I looked around the kitchen. The other cooks had gone to the dormitory to rest before None. Although I was certain we were alone, I whispered. "What is wrong, dear? What did he say to you? Why are you crying?"

"What a horrible, horrible man!"

"Shhh!" I admonished her in a whisper. "You do not want anyone to hear you say that!" I wished I could speak her German dialect—the better to keep our conversations from reaching Lebover's ears.

Hearing her call the bishop a man, I suddenly realized how different her recent history was from mine. I thought of him as a man about as often as I thought of him as having two arms and two legs. Yes, those things were true, but they were also irrelevant. What mattered was his tyrannical greed for power over us. Seeing her reaction to him, I wondered if I should have told her more about the upheaval he had caused over the past year. Perhaps I had foolishly protected her too much. I enjoyed her cheer, and for self-ish reasons, I did not want Marian to sink into the despair the rest of us were slowly starting to shed.

But had not her late-night talks with Basina touched on this? No doubt they had, but now I could see that Maroveus was an evil force someone had to confront to fully appreciate.

"Does everyone not know it?" She sputtered through her snif-fles. "Does everyone not see it?"

"Yes, we do," I said. "But you do not want him or Lebover or Justina to hear you. They are just waiting to punish you for sins they only imagine. Do not give them real ones."

Marian sat up straighter and let the tears flow down her cheeks.

"What did he say to you?" I asked.

"He said I was not humble enough. I do not bow my head in his presence. He said I was tainted with the 'smell' of my marriages. He said the word *marriages* like they were a shameful, dirty thing. I was so ashamed! I tried to beg—" Another round of deep sobs prevented her from continuing.

"I am so sorry," I said. I wanted to put my arm around her shoulders, but feared the abbess, the prioress, or the bishop himself would follow Marian into the kitchen. It was against the *Regula* for us to embrace. "You cannot let—"

"What made him such an ogre?" she interrupted me. "You would not believe the things he said about your founder, Radegund. I had no idea he hated her so! Why has the church allowed this cloister to exist if she was so sinful?"

I thought her questions were fair, and I considered giving her my thoughts about them. As I saw things, Maroveus had never enjoyed the friendship that Radegund had established with the Bishop Pescentius, his predecessor, or with bishops from other sees. Maroveus was staunchly committed to the local cult of Saint Hilary, and with Radegund's reputation for miracles and saintliness continuing to blossom even after her death, she was a serious rival for the town's affection for the saint. His allies, however, argued that his only concern was that the relic be accessible to all who worshipped Christ, and as it was sequestered in the monastery, the *Regula* prohibited others from entering and beholding it. I had seen the hatred in his eyes, though, and I believed his affliction was simple envy that Radegund had achieved a status in Poitiers that far surpassed his own.

Marian was new to the Holy Cross, and she did not know

about the bishop's refusal to celebrate the arrival of the relic at the monastery. And there was still more to Maroveus's animosity that I could have told her. At a saint's day celebration a dozen years before, when Maroveus was a local priest and before he had been named our bishop, Radegund provided a seat of honor to a foul-smelling hermetic monk named Junian, treating Junian as Maroveus's priestly equal. To anyone else, it would have seemed a minor oversight or a generous gesture, certainly not something to hurt Maroveus, but he chastised her for it. It was one thing for Radegund to continually upstage Saint Hilary in town. But upstaging Maroveus battered his self-esteem. Anyone who remembered that incident knew that if someone was guilty of arrogance, it was not Marian—it was Maroveus.

But answering Marian's question about Maroveus required far more background than we had time for in that moment. Marian needed comfort, not explanations, and comfort was in short supply in the new Holy Cross. I decided the best thing for her would be a quiet cry in the dormitory. I pulled a hand from her face and led her off the stool. "Please go to your cot for the rest of the afternoon," I said. "I will tell the cook you are ill. Do not come down for None or Vespers. Lebover or Justina may look for you, but I will distract them."

As soon as Marian shuffled down the hallway toward the dormitory, I went to find Basina. She was in the sewing room with a dozen other sisters, and I beckoned her to follow me into the hall.

"Marian has been reprimanded by Maroveus."

Basina squeezed her eyes closed. "I am not surprised."

"I wonder if you could go to the dormitory and sit with her for a while." Still concerned about Lebover's spies amongst us,

I whispered what had happened. Even then, in the late afternoon stillness of the monastery, I could not be sure no one could hear me.

Basina glanced up and down the hallway, lowered her eyes, and headed for the dormitory.

Back in the kitchen, I channeled my anger into punching and kneading the bread that was Marian's regular afternoon responsibility and wondered how to explain Bishop Maroveus to a newcomer like Marian. Given that she had already become victim to the disregard with which the church now beheld women, I thought it would be easy for her to see Maroveus in that context.

But my immediate concern was not explaining Maroveus's behavior. It was how to distract Justina from looking for Marian at None. The bell had rung for the Hour, and I was certain the prioress would be watching Marian for proof that she had taken her chastening seriously. I had to keep her from noticing our new sister's absence.

I need not have worried. Just as we gathered in the chapel, the big brass bell at the front door rang, and Bertie ran in to pull Justina away. Apparently, we had another visitor.

TEN

My Aunt Brunhilde had arrived at the monastery, and by the time Justina accepted her at the door and pulled me out of None, Lebover had limped out to the reception room to chaperone us.

Brunhilde—Hilda, as I had always called her—was first married to my father's brother, Sigibert, who had been King of Austrasia. Hilda and my mother had much in common, and even though my aunt was much younger, they had grown close. They had both been born outside the kingdom—my mother in Thuringia and Hilda in the Goth's territory south of Gaul—and were hauled to Merovingian courts by Clothar. They both ended up in royal beds, although Hilda's bedding had been with the benefit of marriage, while my mother's had been as a slave and concubine.

Hilda's higher status, however, had not gone to her head. She was kind to her nieces, including Basina and me, and loved my mother, but she hated her sister-in-law, Fredegund—the woman married to my Uncle Chilperic, my cousin Basina's father and King of Neustria, the northern region of Gaul. We called her Freda.

My extended family's story was as complicated and intriguing as could be expected, given royal proclivities for polygamy, murder, and war. Our kings' alliances were brittle and short-lived, and their rivalries vicious and long-standing. My great-grandfather Clovis slaughtered his sibling rivals to the Merovingian throne and united much of Gaul under his reign, only to have his sons tear it apart and start their warring—and whoring—all over again. Out of that nasty nest, my grandfather Clothar rose to vanquish his brothers and assume sole authority over the Merovingians, at his death leaving my father and his brothers to once again claw at each other's throats over territory. Their queens, more often than not, were just as guilty as their husbands of homicidal, if not adulterous, behavior, and deaths of Merovingian relatives were nearly as common as births. Sustaining the family legacy in progeny relied on the contributions of concubines and the influx of foreign-born wives.

Most of my own half brothers had been murdered, mostly by their stepmothers, and my cousins had thinned out considerably since I had entered the monastery.

Freda had killed my Uncle Chilperic's first two wives—Hilda's sister, Galswinth, and Basina's mother, Audovere—out of jealousy and avarice, coveting the inheritance of the kingdom for her son. Not yet done with her mischief, Freda ordered Chilperic's soldiers to rape Basina, her stepdaughter, who then fled to Hilda's villa.

I had not seen Hilda in years, not since the day she escorted Basina to the monastery for protection. As always, she was well dressed and groomed, her hair piled impeccably atop her head, as if she had not spent days traveling the mean highways of the kingdom, although she looked much older than I remembered, and her posture betrayed her fatigue. She had sent no message that she was coming, and once I heard what she had to tell me, I knew she had kept her visit a secret—again because of Fredegund.

Despite the ongoing prayer Hour of which she should take part, the abbess insisted on sitting with us. I could hear the sisters singing and reading the prayers and Psalms of the Hours in the chapel, and I kept glancing in that direction and then at Lebover, hoping she would join them, but once she settled her bulk between my aunt and me, I knew she would stay with us unless the monastery caught on fire.

After we exchanged cheerful greetings and sat down on the wooden benches along the wall, a more serious Hilda led me through the news of the kingdoms as they affected our families. "A decade ago, after your father died, my husband consolidated your father's kingdom with his," she began in vulgar Latin, an emerging dialect of the country that most in the convent understood but was discouraged within our walls. "It was not easy, and I fear it cost the lives of many men and their wives and children, who starved when they never returned home. My husband was murdered too, just hours after he was raised on his shield by his soldiers to celebrate his military victories in Paris."

So Fortunatus had told me. "God bless his soul," I said, bowing my head.

Hilda acknowledged that with no more than a sad smile. Such murders were commonplace, almost to the extent that they were expected. Her voice was steady as she talked. I considered how brave she had to have been in the face of all she had suffered. She was only a few years older than I was, but now I noted how the web of wrinkles around her eyes and the deep frown lines in her olive skin made her look much older. I despaired for her once strong, handsome face.

"I am sorry you have lost so many and so much," I said. "I have prayed daily for Sigibert, my father, and their men. Surely, they are with God."

Hilda brushed off my ersatz religious sentiments and continued, but now in the German of my father and her husband. "Once my husband was killed, I was imprisoned at Rouen, but Basina's brother Merovech rescued me, and we were married there."

This was news to me.

"Sigibert was Merovech's uncle, so it is considered incestuous to some, although we were not related by blood."

I had no comment. What could I say that would not sound like pandering or accusing?

"My news today is that Merovech has committed suicide," Hilda added.

I swallowed hard and blinked. "Oh! God bless his soul." This was shocking. It would be horrible news for Basina, and I grimaced, thinking that I would have to be the one to deliver it.

"Everyone knows that Freda plotted Sigibert's death and was also the cause of Merovech's suicide, yet she continues to escape sanction. Then she murdered her own husband, Chilperic, as well, and now she rules as regent for her son Clothar, who will be king when she thinks he is ready."

I sat back to take it all in. The violence and murders kept multiplying in the kingdoms of Gaul as if we Merovingians were, as a people, bent on our own annihilation. "Why are our kings never satisfied with their own territory, their own good fortune?"

I asked, not expecting an answer. "Why do they each think they need to reign over all of Gaul?"

"It is not just our kings, my dear niece," Hilda said, her face as sad as her tone. "It is the way of the world of men. Mortality is nothing to them—especially the mortality of others."

"Sigibert was well regarded by his troops," I said. "I had been certain they would protect him."

"Humph." Hilda shook her head. "It is easy to find spies and traitors in a kingdom where a few Roman coins or even a Celtic broach will buy enough loaves of bread to allow a soldier to slip away from the garrison and back to his family before starving."

"True. So now only my Uncle Guntram stands between Freda and her son's dominion over all of Gaul."

"My son Childebert rules Sigibert's old territory of Austrasia," Hilda corrected me. She shifted on the hard wooden bench. "But you are right; Freda will never lose her imperial sieges. Before his death, Chilperic had been pursuing military adventures in Burgundy and Thuringia—as far as Noricum and Pannonia. Likewise, her ambitions have no limits."

I noticed Lebover was starting to fade, her chin dropping lower with every nod, her eyes closing and barely opening again in slow rhythm. The fraternal battles of the Merovingians probably would not have held her attention, even if she could have understood my family's German. She had never demonstrated much interest in what was happening among the Franks, as she had entered the convent from the Celtic region of Breton.

For a moment, I reflected on my good fortune to be inside a cloister—however claustrophobic it had become under Lebover and Maroveus—where physical contact, let alone physical violence, was unthinkable. Even when our rations were small, we were better off than those in the countryside where disease and hunger were more common than good health or long lives. I was safer now than I had been in my childhood.

Lebover exhaled a deep snort, drawing me from my thoughts. She had lost the battle to keep her heavy eyelids open, and her chin was resting against her chest.

Hilda lowered her voice to a whisper and reached for my hand. "And how is your cousin Covina? I must find time to visit her as well someday."

"Covina is strong and healthy. She is a wonderful sister in all ways."

"But you look very thin, my dear niece," she said. "Is the cloister running out of food? Should we order the bishop to send you more supplies?"

"We have plenty of food," I replied. "It just does not always get to the table."

"Why?"

I nodded toward Lebover. "She does not understand our German, but we must be careful. I will write to you when I can find a way to send a letter that she does have Justina read first," I whispered. "But I cannot imagine you made the hard journey from Metz just to bring me up to date on Gaul's endless turmoil, and to see if I am eating well. Is there news from *my* family? Is my mother well? My grandmother?"

"Ah, yes. It is not your family that brings me here."

"What then?"

"Basina."

I was momentarily confused. If the news was for Basina, why had Hilda asked for me? "What about Basina?"

"We hear that Freda has arranged for Basina's marriage to a

chieftain in Burgundia—someone she supposedly wants in an alliance against the Goths in Aquitaine."

"Where did you hear this?"

"From an emissary within Neustria. As you can imagine I have spies in all corners of Gaul."

"But Chilperic tried this before. He wanted her to marry the Goth Reccared, remember? Back when he wanted the Goths as allies?" I said. "Radegund refused to let her go."

"Yes, I know." Hilda looked over at Lebover. "But we hear that the new abbess is easier to persuade." I followed her eyes. As if awakened by our glances, Lebover's lids flickered open, and she struggled to push herself upright against the back of her chair.

"I am certain our dear abbess will protect all of our sisters' virtues, regardless of what the king wants." I spoke in Latin now, projecting my words so that there was no chance Lebover would miss them, however sleepy she was. If there was one thing I knew she would stand behind, it was that no nun should ever leave the monastery. I spoke louder. "No one can force a cloistered nun to abdicate her vows. Basina will stay."

"If she leaves, she will die." Hilda had taken my cue, switched to Latin, and raised her voice as well. "I believe Basina is in mortal danger if she leaves the Holy Cross. Fredegund will employ every ruse to eliminate heirs to compete with her son. I know she will murder your cousin the moment she leaves Poitiers."

"No one is leaving this abbey." Lebover struggled to force a gravelly voice through the phlegm in her throat. She coughed harshly and waved a flabby hand at us. I was not sure if she wanted us to continue to talk or go away, and I threw her a puzzled look. "Go on . . . go on with what you were talking about," she managed to say between hacking fits.

Under the cover of her wheezing, I lowered my voice and asked in German, "Why not talk with Basina herself about this?"

"I fear she would not trust me," my aunt whispered back. "Freda has blanketed the kingdoms with lies and rumors about me, although it is hard to see how she has any credibility, given her propensity for intrigue and murder."

"What is this gossip with which you pollute this monastery?" Lebover had caught her breath and leaned in to catch our words.

"We were just finishing with our visit," Hilda replied, switching back to Latin. She rose and turned to me. "I hope you are finding great satisfaction in your love for Jesus Christ. I will take your blessings to Guntram, whom I visit next. He will be pleased to hear that you and Basina are thriving here under Abbess Lebover."

I said goodbye to her, lowered my head, and walked back to the chapel.

✝

That evening, as we stripped down to our shifts for bed, I motioned to Marian to switch places with me so I could lie next to Basina. Still stunned by Maroveus's rebuke, Marian barely raised her head to acknowledge me and merely shuffled over to my cot. Basina looked surprised, but I put my finger to my lips. "Later," I whispered. She nodded, and we pulled our rough blankets over us.

A few hours later, while soft snores surrounded us, I reached over to gently wake Basina.

"What is it?" she asked. "Did Hilda bring news?"

"Yes," I whispered hesitantly. "And not all of it is good."

"I do not expect it to be."

"Hilda was imprisoned by Freda after Sigibert's death,"

I started. Then I told her about the marriage to Merovech, his short-lived quest for the throne, and his suicide.

Basina gasped. I could not see her face for the darkness, but I heard her choke back a sob.

Now that Merovech was dead, Basina's only surviving sibling was her half brother, Clothar, Freda's infant son. Freda was ruling Neustria from Soissons as his regent until he was old enough for the throne.

That was enough bad news for one night, but she had to know about Freda's attempt to woo her away from the monastery for marriage to a Burgundian, so I continued. I reached for her hand.

"Lebover said she will not let anyone take you away," I said in the most soothing tone I could muster. "She said none of us would be allowed to rescind our vows. And I will not let it happen either."

But could I keep that promise? Did I have the power to resist anything Maroveus decided to do to Basina, or to any of us for that matter? I felt my failure as a leader hover over me like a dark cloud that left us all in its shadow. I saw my half brothers taunting me as I stood helpless. Most of them were dead now, killed by jealous siblings or cousins while I, a *bastardis*, was still alive. And I had yet to do anything to be worthy of the breath I took.

Basina did not speak, but I could feel her sorrow as I held her hand. At that point, I thought I knew her well enough to feel her strength as well. It turned out I had no idea how she would react when things got tough. But then, neither did I know how tough things were going to get before we parted ways forever.

ELEVEN

If I had any faith in Maroveus's commitment to the sanctity of our monastery, I lost it the next week when he came to take Basina away.

Bertie slipped into the kitchen that afternoon, her soft sandals making no sound. I was slicing bread for the evening meal and I jumped, the big knife flying out of my hand and onto the floor with a clatter. "Bertie!" I cried. "You should not sneak up on people like that. Someone could get hurt! Especially when some-one is holding a knife."

"I'm sorry," the old nun whispered, her eyes cast down. I wiped my hands on my apron and lifted her chin. "I should not be so jumpy. Do you need me for some reason?"

"The bishop is here. He is talking with Lebover about Basina. I thought you should know."

I smiled. Bertie's decision to come for me indicated my status among the nuns had not eroded totally. Then I frowned. Why would Freda send Maroveus to demand Basina's release instead of one of her soldiers? Were she and Maroveus in cahoots?

Despite his lofty ecclesiastical position as Bishop of Poitiers, it seemed that Maroveus's loyalty to the Merovingian rulers was greater than his commitment to protecting Christian lives. Here he was, demanding on behalf of one of the bloodiest and cruelest of the Merovingian queens that Basina be released from the monastery so she could marry the Burgundian. How, I wondered, did that amount to serving God?

As muddled as my own faith was, I held it with higher regard than loyalty to kings and soldiers—even those related to me. I knew that when it came to divvying up kingdoms and territory, there were no principles at play. At least, the ideal Christian life comprised self-lessness, generosity, humility, and other fine qualities I espoused.

"Thanks, Bertie," I said, pulling off my apron and brushing the flour off my shift before running out of the kitchen toward the reception room. I did not think about what I was going to say, nor about what punishment Lebover or Maroveus would impose for my intrusion.

The bishop stood in the middle of the room, waving his arms and shouting, his back toward me. Lebover sat on the bench, her swollen legs stuck out in front of her like wooden posts, shaking her head.

"No," she insisted at the end of each of the bishop's statements. "No."

"You have no choice!" the bishop declared. "Your survival depends on the beneficence and tolerance of the kings. If you lose their patronage, your monastery will be shuttered, and you will be thrown to the streets."

It was the same threat they had leveled at me not four months before, and I wondered if the irony of it was lost on Lebover.

"No," Lebover answered, struggling to speak in Latin. As she often did, she leaned on vocabulary from the liturgies. "She will not depart. She has taken her vows, and her marriage to our Lord is sanctified. That marriage cannot be torn asunder."

"You would trade this monastery's future for the sake of one sister? One whose innocence was forsaken years ago?"

Mention of that overcame my intent to be silent. "Are you referring to the rape by Chilperic's own men?" I interrupted. "The rape that was directed by the very woman who is now demanding Basina's release?"

The bishop jumped at the sound of my voice and turned toward me. He nearly stumbled over the floor's rough stones. "What are you doing here?"

I could not prevent the smirk from forming on my face. "I *live* here. So does Basina. We have no other home and we desire no other husbands than Christ."

"This does not concern you," he said, pointing his fat index finger at me once again. I had come to know it well over the past six months. "This monastery has been a snake pit of iniquity since its inception. I never understood why Pescentius, that weak and incompetent bishop, allowed Radegund to evade his authority. I will not make the same mistake. This monastery will do as I say, or I will shut it down."

I knew Maroveus hated Radegund. She had been successful in repelling his heavy hand by befriending the likes of Gregory, Fortunatus, and Caesarius, the composer of the *Regula*. But I was surprised to hear Maroveus besmirch his predecessor as well. That was a breach of protocol I had not expected even from such an unprincipled character as he. It was not an argument I needed to get into with him though. "This does concern me, not Radegund or Pescentius or any other servants of God to whom you show disrespect," I said. "Basina is my cousin. Our fathers were brothers."

"You have no father! Your mother is a whore!" Spit flew from his flabby lips with every foul word.

My heart pounded against my ribs, and I put a hand over it,

as if to calm it down. I was not hurt by the insults—I had heard them since childhood—as much as I was angry that he thought they mattered. What did we know of his mother and father?

"My birthright is not in question here," I said, pressing my hand against my chest. "The question is whether this monastery deserves the church's protection, or if it is simply the property of kings and queens. Whether Basina's duty to her stepmother is higher than her duty to her savior. As a man of God, I would think you would want her to answer to the highest authority."

"Get out!" Maroveus thrust his arm out to wave me away, throwing his weight into the gesture, and for a moment, I thought he would topple over onto his face.

"No!" Lebover was struggling to stand up. Her face burned red with the effort. I reached over to help her rise, and steadying her over her feet, I placed her cane in her hand. She faced Maroveus. "No, to you and your adulterous queen!"

Surprised at her outburst, I snapped my mouth shut.

"I am glad Clotild is here," she said as I continued to hold her upright. "No less than I, she and Basina are nuns. They are not daughters of kings or brides of warriors. Their vows either mean something to the church and its bishops, or you should leave us and never return. Your hypocrisy and your hubris are the greater sins in this room and they should not disgrace us further."

She had told Hilda that Basina would not be allowed to leave, but I had not expected her to stand up to Maroveus when the time came, and to speak with such polish. Had she learned this articulation from her time with Justina? Of course, I never expected Maroveus to stoop to deliver the queen's orders himself. Now I had to give Lebover credit: she was stronger than I thought. Perhaps there was hope for our monastery after all.

Maroveus stood, his arms flat at his sides, steaming with anger. His lips trembled as if he could not control them long enough to form words. Finally, he sputtered, "You will regret this. You will pay for your insubordination." And with that, he stomped toward the entry hall. I watched as Bertie hurried to open the door and stood aside to allow him to rush back through it.

Lebover shook loose from my support and dropped heavily onto the bench. "Go get Justina," she ordered.

"Thank you for—" I started.

"Do not thank me. You have no right to thank me. I am doing the Lord's work, not yours. Basina is no more your cousin than she is Fredegund's stepdaughter. She belongs to this monastery and the Lord."

I was impressed with her sudden loquaciousness in Latin. From now on, we would have to speak our German dialects around her if we did not want her to understand us.

"Go. Summon Justina," she spat at me. She waved for me to leave, and so I did.

☩

Basina had been saved from expulsion by Lebover, and Gregory, the Bishop of Tours, had backed her up, which no doubt further incensed Maroveus. I had been pleasantly surprised that Lebover found the nerve to stand up to him. But I did not expect that finding ourselves on the same side of an argument would lead to a truce between us, and it did not. Still, the incident softened my attitude toward her, and I did my best to try to see her in a new light.

The abbess herself, however, apparently came away from our battle with Maroveus with a different mission: to make sure I could not profit from our agreement in the matter. She not only continued to target me with extra chores and insults, but anyone who could be suspected of being my friend also suffered her wrath.

Marian had never recovered from her tongue-lashing with the bishop, and our community grew wretched again as she withdrew. I began to wonder if she had been truthful when she said that she never loved her second husband, that she liked her new duties at the monastery, that she enjoyed this community of nuns. Was any of it true?

I could feel her spirits continue to plunge as Lebover sent Justina looking for her daily to reprimand her for one failure or another—all petty and insignificant.

"The abbess believes your eyes were not cast humbly enough at None," I heard Justina report to Marian in the kitchen one day. "The abbess suggests that your bread contained too much salt yesterday," she relayed in the sewing room the next.

I wanted to intervene, to tell Justina to back off, but I was afraid any interference by me would only increase Marian's mistreatment. Still, I worried. And I wondered: Why did I stand up to protect Basina but continue to let the other nuns down?

The only sister whom I could befriend unconditionally was Covina, who spoke the same Frankish German as I and Basina. A *bastardis* of one of my long-passed uncles, she was as cynical as I was, and she also had been one of Radegund's favorites. I often wondered if our founder was partial to us because we had been fathered by royalty and yet rejected by our privileged families. It mirrored her own rejection of King Clothar as her husband. It was Covina, then, who became my confidant and to whom I shared my ideas for getting us out from under Lebover, and for eventually fomenting our rebellion.

TWELVE

Even during Radegund's reign, some nuns just never adjusted to the ascetic, cloistered life. One such nun named Agnes—not our dear, late abbess—fled the cloister by shimmying down a rope hung from a dormitory window in the middle of the day. Maroveus's predecessor, Bishop Pescentius, recruited townsfolk to return her to the convent, which he made her reenter the same way she had left—by climbing back up the rope. Lucky for Agnes, her arms were strong enough to pull herself up without too much humiliation. Even so, it had been excruciating to watch her be dragged to the monastery by rough men and ordered at sword point to ascend.

The first church council at Macon showed no mercy on Agnes's soul, ruling in her case that her attempts to bribe the Bishop Pescentius to let her stay in the outside world condemned her—and anyone who had accepted such a bribe—to excommunication until death.

In a matter of days, she became ill, and within a fortnight, had died—presumably of the plague, which she supposedly contracted while outside. But her demise was sudden and short, and I suspected something else: poison she had smuggled back to the cloister.

I feared that Marian would try something similar. Either she would escape—perhaps by bribing Bertie to look away as she went out the same door she had come in—or she would commit the doubly mortal sin of suicide. Her demeanor, under Lebover's constant ridicule, had changed from cheery to dispirited. I no longer heard her hum as she worked, and she no longer lifted her voice above a whisper when we sang in the Hours. The skip I envied in her step was gone, and now when she walked into the kitchen, she stared at the floor. Her smile had vanished.

Eventually, I decided that since she was already subject to Lebover's ridicule, it would be better for me to befriend her than to leave her struggling with her anxieties alone. Although all of us slept together, ate together, worked together, sang together, and prayed together, doing nearly everything in unison, loneliness hid amongst us as a silent killer. With so many rules, so many prohibitions, and so few opportunities for spontaneous interactions, the close friendships that did form among us grew slowly. With Lebover's strict interpretation of the *Regula*, I could not befriend Marian as I had bonded with Covina under Radegund.

In the kitchen one afternoon, I put down my knife, dropped the beets I was peeling into a pan to soak, and walked across the kitchen to where Marian was kneading a large ball of dough. Her anemic punches and tentative rolls paled in comparison with the way she had wrestled with the flour and water when she first arrived.

"I feel spring coming, do you?" I started, slowly wiping my hands dry with one of the frayed rags we used for kitchen towels. It was a lie. Winter was stubbornly ignoring the calendar, and March was even colder than our miserable February.

Marian looked up, her eyebrows knitted as if I had confused her with my simple question. "The days are longer, yes." She turned back to her dough and gave it a feeble poke with her fist.

"I was hoping maybe you would be willing to help me with the garden this year." I sat next to her pastry board on a three-legged stool and rocked slightly back and forth on its uneven legs. "Sister Deuteria helped me the past couple of years, but her legs have grown too weak to dig. I am thinking perhaps you might like the chance to get some more fresh air."

Marian nodded but did not look up.

I plowed ahead. "We grow some root vegetables and herbs, and if we can get the seeds, we will plant some greens. None of the townsfolk like them, so they rarely donate any, but occasionally, an emissary from Rome will come through with them. Peas, of course. We always grow peas. They seem to like our soil and the cool spot right below the chapel wall."

"Yes." Marian's voice was barely audible. She punched the dough a little harder.

"I thought, given how rarely Lebover ventures outside, it would also give us more opportunities to talk and get to know each other."

Marian shook her head just enough to communicate dissent.

"What? You do not want to talk?"

"No, I want to," Marian whispered, still focusing on her work. "But Justina has told me Lebover is watching me and says I am too friendly. I fear that idle chatter is not something the abbess allows, and friendship is not something she encourages. Are we not supposed to be talking to God and befriending Christ?"

"Yes, we are."

"Then perhaps you should return to the beets, and we should quit gossiping."

This stung, but I let it pass. "Yes, I know you are right. Still, can I count on your help in the garden?"

"Yes. If the abbess will approve," Marian replied. She still refused to look at me, but I thought I spied a small smile on her face. I watched her work for another minute, believing my proximity would somehow start rebuilding a bond between us. By the time we convened for the evening meal later that day, I sensed a smaller cloud over our heads.

Either the improvement in her mood did not last, or I was wrong.

☩

Two days after our brief talk in the kitchen, Marian sliced her wrist.

I had just finished my preparations for the evening meal and was heading to the sewing room to get a little embroidery done before Vespers. Marian was cleaning her pastry boards and sweeping the floor while waiting for the loaves to finish baking.

"Are you all right here?" I asked. "Do you need any help cleaning up?"

"No," she said. "I have it all in hand. You go ahead." When I paused at the doorway, she pleaded for me to go. "Please."

I thought the smile she gave me looked insincere but I had been so worried about her moods those days that I convinced myself I was overreacting.

When she did not show up at Vespers, I talked myself into believing she was still occupied with her duties. But after the Hour, I scurried back to the kitchen.

She was hunched over the three-legged stool I had sat upon earlier, her face nearly touching the floor.

"Are you ill?" I shouted. Before I reached her, though, I saw a pool of blood spreading under the stool and the pastry table and soaking into her linen shift. Suspecting what she had done, I lifted one of her wrists from the floor where it hung limp, and saw the dark, jagged line running from nearly her elbow through to the palm of her hand. The knife was laying a couple of feet away. How she had managed to cut such a long wound in the face of the pain it must have caused, I could not fathom.

I had to move my feet to avoid the spreading pool of blood on the floor. I felt Marian's neck for a pulse, but it was already cool. Apparently, she had commenced her own murder shortly after I left that afternoon. She knew no one would find her soon enough to save her life.

I heard the rest of the kitchen staff approaching and held up a hand in their direction. The cook, Veranda, yelled for someone to check the ovens. "It smells like the bread is burning." I had not noticed.

"Please, come no closer. Someone bring Ingund." Although I knew the infirmarian could do nothing to help Marian now, she was more accustomed to death than the rest of us, and she was responsible for collecting the body and confirming the death to the bishop.

"Oh, Mary, Mother of God," murmured Covina. I looked up into her face, white as the apron she had donned on the way into the kitchen. She covered her mouth with her hand, turned, and ran back out of the kitchen. I heard her vomit in the corridor.

Veranda stepped up beside me and knelt. "I sent the others away. They will bring Lebover," she said quietly. She put her hand on my shoulder. I started to shake it off but stopped. Lebover could not chastise us for comforting each other under these circumstances, could she? Veranda wiped a stream of tears off my cheeks. "I know she was a friend," she whispered.

"We are all friends, are we not?" I sobbed despite my efforts to steady my breath.

"Go to the dining room and tell the sisters we will not sup tonight," she said, pulling me off the floor. "I will deal with Lebover when she comes."

"But I do not want to leave her," I said, hanging onto Veranda's arm, unsteady on my feet.

"You are not leaving her. She has left us," Veranda said. "You can do nothing here. Go now."

As I limped to the dining room, I felt helpless and weak. I had held myself up as a leader of our cloister, and here I was, depending on others to calm me and make decisions. But it was true. There was nothing I could do for Marian now.

Basina! Suddenly, I thought of my cousin. She was still reeling from her brother's death, and Marian's suicide was going to devastate her. Her constitution was tenuous already. One moment she could talk bravely about standing up to Lebover; the next, she would cower and grovel in the abbess's presence. She and Marian had become confidants, their cots pulled so close together they could have shared one sheet and a rough blanket. My heart sank at the thought of how she would take the news.

By the time I hobbled into the dining room, Marian's death had already reached the sisters, who sat huddled together on the long benches with red eyes and wet faces. They looked up at me, not a single question on their lips. What was there to ask? I glanced around for Basina, but she was not there.

I took my regular spot on one of the benches, bowed my head, and closed my eyes. I knew how to look like I was praying; I had practiced it for more than twelve years. I did not want to talk. I had no advice and no authority to give any. I was less than the weakest among them; I had encouraged them to depend on me, to look up to me, and now I had nothing to offer them. No hope, no comfort, no leadership.

✛

There was no fool amongst us when it came to Marian's death. We all knew what had happened, and we all suspected something of why it had happened. Still, in officially announcing her passing at Compline that evening, Lebover described how Marian had slipped while cutting the dough into loaves and suffered a mortal wound. No one raised any objections to the abbess's story. I guessed it was the version she was prepared to share with the bishop.

Marian's death was more my fault than anyone else's. In trying to distance myself from Lebover's further cruelties, I had ignored her for too long. On the other hand, her sadness was not my doing alone. She had come to us with enough misery in her past to fuel prolonged melancholy. But still, I had failed her. I had failed the others too, in that I had not stood up to Lebover's abuses and Maroveus's interference. Even confronting the bishop over Basina's departure deserved no badge of courage: I had Lebover on my side in that argument.

As I expected, Basina took the news the hardest. For the next couple of weeks, I heard her crying in the night, and she spoke no words to me or anyone else. At the Hours, her voice never rose above a whisper. I worried that she would decide to leave and marry the Burgundian, thinking it would be better to risk death on the way to a miserable marriage than stay cooped up in our gloomy cloister.

We slouched through the motions of Marian's vigil by her bedside and the requiem. When the bishop and his emissaries arrived to cart her off to the cemetery not far from our cloister, we stood along the passage from the infirmary through the door she had entered, not three months earlier. The whispering gossip in the dormitory at night stopped. In its place were cold silence and fear.

Under Radegund and Agnes, we had found joy in our work and our Hours. Lebover had taken so much from us, and now Marian's suicide had sealed our hearts against any hope we would ever get it back. I worried for the rest of the sisters, and for our beloved home, the Monastery of the Holy Cross. Marian's melancholy haunted us all.

It took another unexpected visitor two weeks later to finally pull me out of my darkest despair, and while eventually nothing worked out the way I expected it would, it set me on a journey to end our desperation.

THIRTEEN

If I had ever expected to see another visitor, it would not have been my grandmother. As I was approaching my twenty-eighth year, my grandmother was getting close to her sixtieth. I had never known anyone that old.

She arrived on our first warm day of April, the day I had started working the soil in my herb garden. My little patch lay on the south side of our chapel, just far enough from our monastery's outer wall that the sun could peek over it for several hours a day by midspring.

I struggled with a spade to turn the dark muck, laced with roots and stems from years past, thinking about how strong my grandmother had been back in the garden at the villa. I had just stood up to ease the pain in my back when Bertie appeared around the corner of the chapel, her face flush with excitement.

"You have a visitor, Sister Clotild!" Bertie was frailer than ever, and I feared for her safety as she hurried across the uneven garden toward me. "It is your grandmother."

"My grandmother?" I dropped my tool and wiped my hands on my heavy garden apron. I had not known whether she was still alive. Through watering eyes, I watched Bertie trip and grab the branch of one of my ten-year-old apple trees to catch herself.

"Stop!" I yelled. "I am coming. It is not safe to run through here. There are snakes and roots and stones."

"Hurry!"

"What is the hurry?"

"She is very old."

I chuckled for the first time in months. Bertie worried that my ancient grandmother would die of old age before I got inside.

A tiny old bag of skin-covered bones sat on the hard bench in the reception room, and although her emaciated body shocked me, I recognized the round hump of her back and the long beak of a nose from a distance. I threw off my apron, tossed it to Bertie, and ran to embrace her.

She looked up to me with cloudy eyes and a toothless smile, her face a web of deep wrinkles—but it was hers. I was surprised how much she still looked like herself despite the savage markings of time.

"Grootmoeder, dear! What a joy to see you!" I took her gnarled hands in mine. "What a hard journey you must have had! Why have you come?"

She worked her mouth for a few moments before words finally came out in a harsh whisper. "I have news for you, dear Clotild."

I nodded. I did not want to talk over her; every word she uttered cost her precious energy. I waited, smiling through tears and holding her hands gently.

"Your mother has passed," she said. I felt my heart plunge,

but I held my smile. I knew my mother had been ill, contaminated with the worms that enter the brain and steal part of our being. This latest news was sad, but it was not unexpected.

"She wanted me to come tell you if I could." My grandmother formed the words slowly. The trip from my father's villa near Paris had exhausted her. "I waited until spring so I could make the journey. She died on the Nativity," Grootmoeder continued.

"I am glad you came to tell me." I leaned forward and kissed her papery cheek. "Do you still have a home? A place to live?"

"No one bothers me." I could see a sparkle through the mist of her eyes that reminded me of how spirited she had been when I was a child. She had not lost all of her mischief. "I still live in the garden cottage, but no one comes to the villa anymore."

"Are you alone? How do you live?"

Grootmoeder looked amused at my concern. "It is quiet and peaceful. I do my rituals, talk to the goddesses. I have whatever apples the worms do not get first, and every year, the peas return and bless me with their abundance."

"But are you going back? Are you traveling alone?"

"Why do you talk of my departure already, Clotild? I just arrived."

I realized that I needed to find a way to keep her at the monastery for a few days to rest before she started the arduous journey back home. Overnight guests were not allowed, according to the *Regula*, but certainly, there had to be compassion for such a traveler.

I turned to Bertie. "Does Lebover know that my grandmother is here?"

The portress shook her head and smiled. She must have had the same thought I did.

"Of course, Grootmoeder, you can stay with us as long as you like," I said.

"Good." She looked satisfied, even pleased with herself. "I have so much to tell you."

Over the next two days, the old woman took Marian's empty cot at night, and leaning lightly on my arm, walked out to the garden to watch me work during the day. During Hours, she either sat nodding tranquilly on a bench I fashioned for her in the sun by the garden or slept in the abandoned dormitory. My work in the kitchen had been trumped by my work in the garden, so it was easy to avoid Justina and Lebover—neither of whom ever stepped outside into the fresh air.

While I dug and broke up the heavy, black loam, my grandmother relayed her version of my mother's last years. Once my father, Charibert, died and I left, the villa had been abandoned. At first, my Uncle Sigibert had kept some of the slaves working at the fields, but as the soldiers from Rome disappeared from the territory, and the roads to Paris and Tours sprouted weeds and washouts, those who were left slipped away in the night. The house gave purchase to slim trees and vermin, and soon, large sections of roofs and walls fell inward into piles of rubble.

"And my mother? What did she do during this time?" I asked Grootmoeder.

"She and I tended our own garden and chickens for several years. The winters were hard and lonely, but we scavenged candles and wood from the villa. She started to forget everything years ago. In the end she was difficult, but she was too weak to wreak much havoc. And when she passed, the old tenant who lived clos-est to us helped me bury her," Grootmoeder told me.

"You have been very strong and very brave."

That seemed to amuse her. She chuckled, nearly tipping off the bench. "The countryside is nearly empty now," she continued. "Only a few families remain, and even they leave one by one. I paid one of them to bring me here on his way to Aquitaine."

"Paid?"

"With silver from the villa. I recovered much of the treasure. No one else knew it was there. I had polished that silver for Charibert for years. I knew right where it was hidden."

"And how will you go back?" I asked her.

"I do not expect to. Hilda has made plans for me to join her family in the south. In Aquitaine, where the Goths rule. She came to see me on her way back from visiting you. She was heading to Chalôns-sur-Saône to see Guntram. They have grown close."

I was surprised at how clear my grandmother's mind was. My mother had started to forget names and places long ago; it had started by the time she made her only trip to see me. I could tell how confused she was from the letters she sent after that.

Two nights later, before she left the Holy Cross to live with Hilda, my grandmother and I snuck out to the back garden and sat under a full moon, our backs resting against the trunk of my sturdiest apple tree. She lit a rock of incense in a small saucer, and I was transported to the garden in the villa of my childhood. I closed my eyes, and my grandmother murmured chants to Máni, the moon goddess. I followed along with my lips, voicing nothing, afraid my memory would fail me and cause me to ruin her incantation.

As I listened and breathed in the vapors of musky incense, I looked up to the moon rising over the horizon, as big as the chapel's bell tower that loomed dark beside it in the night sky. I breathed deeply and felt my body relax as it had not in months.

The rhythm of my grandmother's voice was a massage for my soul. I was at peace and I felt as if I had come home.

As she finished, my grandmother closed her eyes, and for a moment I thought she had fallen asleep. But as I watched, her eyes flickered open and met mine. Their intensity frightened me a little, but I did not look away.

Grandmother reached through the collar of her heavy shift and pulled out a dark metal amulet hanging from a thin leather cord. She wound it up over her head slowly, her stiff, thin arms resisting the motion, and pulled it free from the knot of hair at the nape of her neck. She held it out to me. "You must keep this, Clotild," she said, her voice husky from chanting in the cool night air. "I know you are a Christian now, but I beg you to remember the goddesses of your people. There is not one god. You know that in your heart."

Her voice picked up energy as she talked, and I stared at the pendant in my hand, intimidated by her rising passion. "How can one god watch over all peoples?" she asked. "The kings fight against each other, one wins one battle, one wins another. The gods determine their fates, and yet, the kings turned their backs on them. They have forgotten how to worship, how to appease them. No wonder there is so much blood in the kingdom."

Her voice was older but it was still the voice I remembered in the garden of my childhood when it rose up to greet the Valkyries, the goddesses, and the gods. She had been a priestess back in Thuringia; even then, the old traditions and faiths were under attack by the angry Arian priests.

"I see you among your sisters," Grootmoeder continued. "I know you are strong, but there are forces in this kingdom and in your church that want to suck the strength out of you. They want to suck the strength given by the goddesses out of all women. You must wear this amulet and preserve its powers so that they are not lost to the world."

I nodded but I had no words. The small metal pendant was of the Yggdrasil, the Y-shaped world tree where the gods and goddesses gather, whose roots extend to the nine worlds of the universe in my grandmother's religion.

The conflict between Christianity and the pagan rituals of my youth welled in my chest, and I shook my head and folded my fingers around the amulet. How could I reconcile these faiths, and yet, how could I shed either of them?

"I have seen your future," Grootmoeder whispered. "The goddess of my childhood brought it to me in a dream—a dream in the middle of the bright day. The blood of kings that flows in your veins and the blood of the goddesses from which we all come will mix like poison and terrorize you with their quarrels, but it will also give you unworldly strength. I have seen your destiny, child. You will be the link back to the goddesses that have given women the strength to survive, to bear children, to tend their gardens." She stopped and closed her eyes, and her body hunched forward, as if the energy that had powered her soliloquy had been spent.

I waited a few moments as her breath slowed and a peace settled over us. "Grootmoeder," I whispered. "We must go inside now. You need to rest before your journey."

She blinked, and after a few moments, obliged me by holding up an arm. I gently pulled her slight frame to her feet, and one tiny step at a time, we went inside and snuck back into our cots without waking a single sister around us. I wondered if they had been lulled into a deep sleep by my grandmother's incantations.

FOURTEEN

My grandmother left the next morning between Matins at two o'clock and Lauds, an hour before sunrise. She and I waited with Bertie until we heard the knock, and once I was certain it was Hilda's emissaries who had come to retrieve her, I helped her slip out into the dark morning and into the waiting wagon. The full moon was still bright on the cobbles and it shone off the slick hides of the draft horses. We could afford only a quick embrace and kiss before I retreated into the abbey and closed the door.

I felt like a different woman after my grandmother's visit. Perhaps it came from the power of the quiet ceremony for the goddess Máni that we had shared, or perhaps from the courage the amulet gave me, but I began to worry less about Lebover's threats and trust my place as a leader of the sisters. My confidence grew as I embraced the rites and goddesses of my youth.

Already I had been enjoying a resurgence of authority at the Holy Cross, which had, of course, no official sanction. I merely filled the vacuum left by Lebover's increasing immobility and her demand that Justina stay within a whisper's carry. A church council was keeping Maroveus in Lyons; no doubt the bishops were considering more ways to chase women from church leadership. I did not care what they ruled as long as they left us alone to take care of ourselves and savor our peaceful daily routine.

As the nuns came to me for advice and to share their problems more often, I realized how devastating the past year had been to them. Many of us had entered the monastery to escape bad marriages or our families' homicidal sprees, and we had found peace in the rituals of prayer and hymns, and camaraderie in our shared circumstance. Maroveus's dispiriting presence and Lebover's creeping perfidy, however, had tainted our compliance, and I wondered if our servitude and our prayers for the souls of the departed advanced the work of Christ or abetted the worst instincts of men. But what could we do from inside the monastery to promote the higher aims of the Christian faith?

No more than twelve hours after my grandmother slipped out of my life for the last time, Covina came to me for help.

I was working on a manuscript, enjoying the new light of the waxing spring sunshine with Sister Desmona, whose own sadness had lifted a bit with the warming temperatures and strengthening sun. It had been a week since I had to ball up my fists and blow on my knuckles to warm them enough to hold the quill. We had received a request from a monastery in Avignon, one with its own strong tradition of female independence, for a copy of the letters of Paul.

Our celebration of the resurrection of Christ had passed with gloomy solemnity and a meager feast a couple of weeks before, but now, excited to return to the sweet work of scratching ink on parchment, Desmona and I hummed one of the glorious Easter hymns in unison, almost subconsciously.

Covina paused at the door to the scriptorium until we noticed her presence and stopped humming. "The cellarer has bad news." Covina approached me and whispered in my ear. "She has told everyone in the kitchen, and we are worried."

I had been out of the kitchen for most of a week, working on the manuscript and in my garden, and Covina had added most of my culinary duties to her own. "Let us talk elsewhere," I said under my breath. I did not want Desmona's emerging cheer ruined by whatever Merofled, the cellarer, had shared with Covina.

We walked to the chapel, empty between the Hours of Sext and None. The afternoon light was filtering through the high windows, and it struck me that it had become the setting for far too many distressing conversations and requiems. It should have been a joyful place, resonating only with the prayers and hymns of the Hours. Covina kept glancing back, as if afraid someone might be following us. "We are running out of food," she whispered once we had settled into a front pew, far from the light of the doorway. "Merofled is worried that we will run out of flour for bread before the end of the week. And Lebover told her we must cut back on our portions."

"Why does Merofled not order provisions?"

"She says she has no money."

"But the sacristy contains many valuables, all that was donated by our novices and their families."

"Apparently, much of it has disappeared."

I did not need to ask where it had gone. There was no one other than Greta and Lebover who had access to the treasures. I had no reason to suspect Greta, who had been for decades a most humble and obedient sister. Lebover was either collecting treasure for herself or for a niece's lavish wedding celebration she was planning. But where would she be hoarding it?

"Has Veranda talked to Lebover?" It was the cook's responsibility to ensure we had enough flour to make our daily bread and tubers to make our modest stews.

"Yes." Covina's eyes shifted right and left. Why was she so worried about being overheard?

"And—?"

"Lebover told her to fix it."

"Fix it? How?"

Covina shrugged. "She also said not to share the situation with the rest of the nuns."

"How does Lebover think we will not notice? An empty table is not a thing you can hide."

Covina shrugged again. "Veranda thinks you should talk to her."

"Me? Why me?" As soon as the words were out of my mouth, I realized how disingenuous—even cowardly—I sounded. Why was I pretending like I did not know why anyone thought the threat of starvation was my problem?

It was time for me to step up and try to get Holy Cross back on an even keel.

☩

As I knocked on the abbess's chamber door, I tried to think of something I would hate doing more at that moment. Over the past couple of months, Lebover's temper had risen along with her physical ailments. She wore a permanent scowl, and I felt sorry for Justina, whose life must have been as hellish as it could be for a cloistered nun.

Justina opened the door a sliver. The light that slipped through into the dark room shone on little more than her nose. "What?" she asked.

I had never envied her, and hearing the strain in her voice, I pitied her. "I would like to speak with the abbess."

Justina turned away and closed the door. I could hear muddled voices through the heavy wood but I could make out no words. Then there was a long pause, and I felt Lebover's heavy tread vibrate through the floor stones.

"I have nothing to say to you." The abbess's hoarse voice preceded her appearance. She opened the door, but her frame blocked entry. I glanced beyond her to see Justina and a large hooded figure standing a few feet back as if ready to catch her if she fell.

"I need to discuss the condition of our larder," I said, struggling to keep my tone neutral and without incrimination.

"It is none of your concern." Lebover started to close the door, but I stuck my foot in its path. It hit my ankle just above my sandal, and I winced.

"It is my concern if there is not enough for me or anyone else to eat."

"If there is a concern about provisions, Veranda will manage."

I snorted a laugh. "She cannot make bread from air."

"Talk to Maroveus. It is he who has cut back our supplies."

"I doubt that." I knew I had as much as accused her of theft with those three words. And Lebover took my bait. She swung the door open, nearly losing her balance in the act. Justina stepped forward and steadied her with a hand on her back. I did not know how the tiny prioress thought she could support the heavy abbess by herself, but the other person in the room did not step up to help.

I took advantage of catching Lebover off balance and stepped inside the dark chamber.

"You cannot—" Lebover started to say, but a coughing fit stopped her. Suddenly, with me in the room, her attitude swung from arrogance to fear. I realized how much she depended on Justina and Maroveus—and perhaps her extant male companion—to project her illusion of power. Perhaps her gluttony was less driven by conceit and more as compensation for her meekness.

"You cannot be in here!" Justina shouted. The other figure—man?—shrank away from us.

A fire burned in the hearth across the room even though the morning had been warm enough that the fireplaces in the rest of the abbey were not lighted. The room smelled of illness and acrid bodies.

I looked around as my eyes adjusted to the dark interior. A candle would have been more practical than the fire. But quickly, I espied rows of silver chalices and candlesticks along one wall, a pile of fine woolen fabrics in a corner, and wooden boxes stacked to the ceiling in another. Was this where Lebover was keeping her stolen goods? Why would she risk keeping them here, right under our noses?

"You must leave immediately!" Justina yelled again as Lebover doubled over, leaning on her cane so heavily I could see it bend. "You are upsetting the abbess."

"The abbess should be disturbed and ashamed! Look at this room! Why is all of this not in the sacristy where it should be? Why are we not trading it for flour and lard?"

Suddenly, two large hands hit my chest, and I stumbled backward. "Out!" yelled the shadowy creature. The voice was deeper than any nun's and it was certainly not Maroveus's. A dark hood covered both head and face down to the nose. I could not see the eyes, but the dark hairs on the chin were unmistakable. So the rumors were true. The abbess was keeping this man in her room.

Before I could fully recover my balance, he hit me again, and I fell back into the hallway. The door slammed shut, shaking the wall on either side and the floor below me.

If I aspired to grab the reins of the Holy Cross, I had failed right away.

Justina came to dinner that evening and announced that the abbess had taken ill and would not attend dinner, Vespers, or Compline that night. She did not meet my eye or anyone else's. She stared at her feet while she talked, her voice barely rising above a whisper. Then she took a plate, heaped it with bread and stew, and left the dining room.

I looked around the room at my sisters. More than half of them were looking back at me, anxious frowns meeting my eyes, pleading for assurance. But a few were looking down at their laps, as if they were saddened by the news of the abbess's health. I studied them so I would know who would be with me and who would not, whatever I decided to do.

FIFTEEN

"The Lord will provide," Greta offered. I envied her faith but I disagreed.

"I am certain that is true, but the Lord first helps those who help themselves," Merofled answered Greta's assertion. Her practical nature was what made her a good cellarer.

I had called Merofled, the cellarer; Veranda, the cook; Ingund, the infirmarian; and Greta, the sacrist, to the dining room between Matins and Lauds the next morning while the other sisters returned to their beds for two more hours of sleep. I invited Basina to join us, simply because if I did not, she would be angry with me. And Veranda invited Covina, who had been asked to help solve the problem of dwindling kitchen supplies. I chose not to meet in the chapel as I wanted to taint it no further with our troubles.

Maroveus was due back from Lyons in a week, and we needed to decide as the leaders of the convent what to do about Lebover's thievery and our own dire situation before he returned. I expected that the abbess would summon him as soon as possible and make the case for getting rid of me and any other troublemakers. If we were evicted from the monastery, it would be with the curse of excommunication, and none of us wanted to suffer that any more than we wanted to subsist on herb-flavored water.

"We must contact our families and request offerings," Ingund said.

I nodded, as did the others. "I will ask Hilda to send some assistance from her son Childebert's court," I said.

Except for Basina, the others also offered to request wine, pork, or other barrels of provisions from relatives. Basina's royal family was plenty prosperous, but her deadly stepmother, Freda, was more likely to send us poison than victuals.

"We still have the problem of a thief and a coward hoarding the wealth of our monastery," I said. "We have to solve that ourselves. I am quite certain that Maroveus will take Lebover's side. I am also certain she will not invite him into her chambers to see her stash."

I described what I had seen stacked along her walls, and no one doubted my story. We all had known for some time how mendacious Lebover was, and how reluctant the fear-ridden Justina would be to betray her.

"Still," I continued, "we will have to start by appealing to Maroveus. If we try to skirt around him, he will throw the entire heft of the church at us. I suggest we all—"

"Perhaps begging from Lebover and Maroveus is not the answer," Basina interrupted.

I stopped and nodded for her to continue.

"At some point we have to appeal to a higher authority. Maybe the archbishop or the Pope. Maybe one of the kings. Poitiers is still in Guntram's territory, is it not?"

"Yes," I said. "But going over Maroveus's head will have consequences. I would expect the archbishop to agree with him, and he is most likely to see us as rebellious and troublesome nuns."

"Perhaps that is what we are," Covina said. "And perhaps that is what we should be. Rebellious and troublesome."

Jolted by her audacity, I waited a moment to see if anyone wanted to talk her down. Basina was nodding her head enthusiastically, but Merofled, Veranda, and Ingund looked as surprised as I was. Greta's face was blank.

"Rebellious and troublesome?" I asked.

"None of the inflictions we have suffered for the past year has come from Maroveus alone," Covina said. "For decades, the church councils have ruled against our independence, against women in the clergy, against women, period. What chance do we have of success appealing up the ranks of the church? I think we must throw ourselves at Guntram's mercy."

Covina was right. Ever since the Council of Orleans gave power over the church to the royal families, the kings were the supreme authorities over its policies. They convened the church councils, which had taken away our rights to be ordained, then prohibited us from administering or assisting in the sacraments. The rule that doomed Marian's second marriage had come down four years ago. No doubt more bad news would come out of Lyons.

"I agree," Greta finally muttered. She spoke so quietly, I wondered if she was afraid to say it. "Guntram's our only hope." As the sacrist, she oversaw the treasury as the silver and other precious objects disappeared, and she would be accused of the theft if Lebover denied her larceny and could hide her booty from Maroveus.

I let this soak in and waited to see if anyone else wanted to agree or disagree. "I believe we should consider that only if we cannot convince Maroveus to listen to us," I said. "And if we are refused an audience, we can decide then what to do next."

I was reluctant to go to my Uncle Guntram for help. Guntram was the least warring, the most reputable and least duplicitous of my father's brothers. But the way the political winds could shift in the kingdom, you never knew from one year to the next who would be friend or foe. If we aligned ourselves with Guntram, and he was overthrown by Freda or his nephew Childebert, we could end up on the wrong side of their lethal dispute.

Furthermore, I knew that whatever we decided to do, not all the sisters would be with us. In fact, they might undermine anything that threatened their safe, albeit hungry, existence. They had joined the monastery, after all, for the peace and stability they could find nowhere else in our kingdom.

✝

I had never considered Lebover a particularly astute woman, let alone a capable abbess, but it still surprised me when she sent Justina to Vespers to make an announcement. It was brazen.

"The abbess has sent her blessings." Justina's tiny presence at the front of the chapel barely registered in the dark Hour. No one breathed as we struggled to hear her. "She has decided that we will not observe the feast of Pentecost. We will hold the vigil and the celebration of Christ's ascension, but we will not serve the feast itself."

At that, the room exhaled, and the sisters moaned. The feast was still a couple of moons away, but we were already salivating at the promise of meat and vegetables.

We had just finished our recitation of Psalm 111, which ironically extolled the Lord for providing food and all else for his faithful:

> Praise God! I will give thanks to God with my whole heart,
>> In the council of the upright, and in the congregation.
> The works of God are great,
> Pondered by all those who delight in them.
> His work is honor and majesty. His righteousness endures
>> forever.
> He has caused his wonderful works to be remembered.
>> God is gracious and merciful.
> He has given food to those who fear him. He always
>> remembers his covenant.
> He has shown his people the power of his works, In giving
>> them the heritage of the nations.
> The works of his hands are truth and justice. All his precepts
>> are sure.
> They are established forever and ever. They are done in
>> truth and uprightness.
> He has sent redemption to his people. He has ordained his
>> covenant forever. His name is holy and awesome!
> The fear of God is the beginning of wisdom. All those who
>> do his work have a good understanding. His praise
>> endures forever!

This Psalm always had a special meaning for us, as we had been, under Radegund and Agnes, the beneficiaries of a kitchen made famous throughout Gaul for its epicurean splendor by Fortunatus's gushing poems.

And now, piling disappointment onto our general dissatisfaction, Lebover was denying us the summer feast that had always been one of Holy Cross's most celebrated and anticipated. Our community had suffered enough over the past year, and I feared that this additional blow to our spirits threatened to send more of my sisters into an emotional slump.

I had been ejected from Lebover's chambers once and I did not want to try again to approach her, this time to argue the feast need not be canceled for lack of food. We were short of flour for bread, but my garden had already produced a bounty of early vegetables, and we expected to receive several barrels from our families in the next week. Our entreaties had been well received, although we knew that we could draw from our families only so often before we were rejected as larcenous leeches.

Merofled had volunteered to be the next to try to talk to the abbess. As the cellarer, she could announce herself with the good news that the shipments were expected any day.

"She refused to discuss it," Merofled reported that afternoon. I was back in the kitchen helping Covina and Veranda prepare the evening's stew. "She said she will not rescind her decision to cancel the feast, and that—" She paused and looked worried.

"That . . . ?" I prodded.

Merofled continued slowly and reluctantly. "That you must stop interfering with her leadership, or Maroveus will exact new punishments on you and—" She stopped again.

"And?"

"And the rest of the sisters."

I took that in with a deep breath. So he wanted to make me the scapegoat for the monastery's misery. But what more could he do to us than he had already? Intercept our supplies and keep them for himself and the fat priests who suckled greedily at the church's breast? Perhaps we should not have told Lebover the shipments were on their way.

"Well, we will see about that," I said, keeping my voice low. I began to realize that we were unlikely to get anywhere fighting from inside our cloister. In order to raise our voices, we would have to aim higher, as Covina had said.

"We will see," was all I said then, but I had already started to develop a plan. A dangerous, risky plan.

SIXTEEN

I was not sanguine about our choices of either obediently suffering the indignities of Maroveus and Lebover, or begging for help from our relatives, the kings. I did not want to go over Maroveus's head without warning, so I had written to him that I was appealing to the kings and the archbishop. I got no answer.

"Will Maroveus share your letters with Lebover?" Greta asked.

"He might," I acknowledged. I had considered it likely even, but the abbess had become immobile. All she could do would be to ask Maroveus to eject me from the monastery and perhaps excommunicate me. That, I expected, would probably be the result of our rebellion anyway.

I wrote to my cousin, King Childebert, Hilda's son, and to my uncle, King Guntram, describing our misery and Maroveus's interference, and received polite but unhelpful responses. "Pray to the Lord for your deliverance," Guntram had responded. "If your cause is just, He will provide the answer."

Another letter to Archbishop Godesigel, Maroveus's superior, had been refused and returned.

Clearly, these letters were making no impression. I decided that we had to do something they could not ignore. I sent a message to Uncle Guntram in Chalôns-sur-Saône and Bishop Gregory in Tours, telling them that we were coming to ask for help in resurrecting the health of our monastery. I wrote to Hilda, asking her for transportation and an escort to take me from Tours to Chalôns-sur-Saône during the summer. Then I called another meeting of the sisters to describe my plan and secure agreement.

Leaving the cloister would be one of the worst violations possible of Caesarius's *Regula virginum*. This powerful document had fortified our monastery under Radegund and Agnes, but it offered us no protection from Maroveus's malevolence under Lebover. Caesarius, after all, had been as guilty as any of the other church leaders of expecting blind obedience—especially from women.

Since we first entered the monastery, none of us had traveled beyond the front door for more than a few steps, and then, only to accompany an elderly visitor to transport. Leaving our cloister and walking all the way to Tours would be frightening. I had no idea what to expect from our journey, but I hoped our status as nuns would be recognized by all of Gaul's citizens as much as it was by God. And as a group, we would be safe. The scariest part of the journey would be my solo travel from Tours to Chalôns-sur-Saône. It was a much longer voyage, but Hilda had promised me a wagon and an escort.

Over the final fortnight before we planned to leave, I prayed to the goddesses of my grandmother as well as to Jesus Christ for wisdom and courage to find a way to recover the peace and love we had once enjoyed at Holy Cross.

Justina pretended not to notice the brewing insurrection, but it was a poor act. Lebover may have thought she was avoiding outright rebellion by ignoring me, but she did not know how much she was abetting it. When I received no reaction from her, nor response from Maroveus, we set our date.

"Are we certain we will receive sanctuary in Tours?" Covina had wondered aloud at one of our clandestine midnight meetings in the garden. She was my strongest sister, both tall and hearty, and I knew she would encourage and help others on the trip, as long as she believed we had any chance of surviving and succeeding in our mission.

"I expect so. The Council of Lyons, the same convocation that condemned our dear sister Marian, forbade anyone to remove by force a Christian who enters a church for sanctuary," I answered.

By then, forty of our sisters were committed to the plan, but I was glad we had a chance to talk it over many times while we waited for an answer from Maroveus. I wanted no defectors along our way.

The only sister who worried me was my own cousin, Basina. She was embracing our rebellion enthusiastically, but I knew that as ardently as she believed in something, she could, in a matter of days, turn in equal measure toward the opposite view. I envied her passion, but I feared her capriciousness.

During these planning meetings, held between Compline and Matins in the dark shadows of my garden, I frequently touched the amulet beneath my linen shift for strength and hope but made sure no one else saw it. It would not be good if my sisters saw the holes in my Christian faith.

✝

We left after Compline, in the dark of a moonless night, a week after the vernal equinox. Bertie let us out the front door and bid us a safe and successful journey. Too frail to make our arduous trek, she stayed behind to bar the door after us, and to try to keep Lebover clueless about our departure for as long as she could.

"May God bless you with an answer to our problems. Travel with Him," Bertie whispered.

When I heard the heavy bolt fall into place, my heart thumped in my breast. We could have turned back right then, and Bertie would have let us back in. I hesitated but none of the others noticed. In turning and heading down the dark cobblestones, they were binding their fates to each other, and I had to put my faith in them.

We had decided to start walking just before midnight, after the ground had frozen. As we walked into the day, we expected the roads would turn to mud. If we kept up a steady pace, our journey would take twenty-four hours. Walking twenty miles each day and resting at night, we believed we would make it to Tours on the evening of the third day.

We left twenty women behind. These were sisters too weak to walk out the door, as well as those who felt our mission was foolhardy. I knew it would not be long before Justina would question them about our disappearance, but even though they lacked the courage to join us, they had assured us they would resist her prodding. I hoped they would—at least for a time.

Waiting outside for us was Angelica, Covina's cousin, a young woman skeptical of all religion, having long been physically abused by her husband, a deposed priest who had died of syphilis not long after losing his post. Excommunication for assisting us meant nothing to her; she had rejected Christianity and returned to the Celtic rituals of her ancestors long before.

Angelica knew the city streets, and she supplied us with a map of the countryside that her husband had used in his travels to church councils and meetings with the bishops. I was the only one who had ever read a map, and even for me, it took a few days of study to get the lay of the land in my head well enough that I could make use of it.

As we passed the Poitiers city gate, Angelica stopped and pointed the short way toward St. Hilary's basilica, and ten sisters unable to make the long trek to Tours waved silently and split away. They would enter the church and ask for sanctuary. Desmona went with them. I would have liked to have had her company on our journey, but she had been too sickly to make the trip to Tours.

The thirty of us who were strong enough for the twenty-league walk took off down the road. Other than Desmona and Bertie, my closest sisters were all with me: the perpetually giggling Vivian; my closest friend, Covina; my cousin, Basina; our infirmarian, Ingund; our cellarer, Merofled; our cook, Veranda; and our sacrist, Greta. We, too, would request sanctuary at the basilica of St. Martin once we entered Tours.

If we entered Tours.

If we stuck together.

If no robbers or storms or soldiers thwarted us.

We had no guarantee of anything. But the resistance that had started with our Christmas feast months before had blossomed into outright rebellion, and we were staking our lives on it.

SEVENTEEN

As the sun rose on our first day, our legs were already tired, but our spirits were high. We had rested twice during the night, first about the time we would have been observing Matins back in the monastery and then again when we sensed it was time for Lauds.

Each time, we recited our Psalms and prayers from memory, as we sat on rocks, stumps, and logs until we were so cold that we preferred walking again.

I was not sure how far we had traveled, as we had not yet reached any of the landmarks on the map, when light gradually brightened the horizon and the birds launched into their morning trills.

"We should make it to where the Le Clain river meets the Vienne by nightfall," I told Covina, with whom I was sharing the itinerary in my head. If I were to be injured and could not continue to lead our unlikely pilgrims, she would step up and lead our party forward. "If we do not, I think we will have to readjust our expectations."

Covina and I were sitting with our backs against a solid oak tree and our feet straight out in front of us. I had felt a thrill all morning simply from having no roof over my head, no wall around me, not even the garden's stone enclosure blocking my view. I kept turning my head to take in the woods, the sky, and the fields. My eyes followed distant birds with a wonder I had not felt since my childhood.

I was twirling my ankles and flexing my toes, afraid that the cold would conspire with their fatigue, and they would be stiff as boards if I did not keep them moving. How was I going to walk another half a day? How were any of us? Every other sister was either lying back and moaning about sore legs and feet or sitting up and massaging them in a most immodest manner. I guessed that we had made it about halfway to the rivers' confluence in six hours of walking. Another six seemed almost too impossible to contemplate.

"Do you think we are foolish?" Covina asked, pulling a foot up onto her thigh for a vigorous rubbing. "Maybe we should see if we can beg a local Christian for a ride on a wagon."

I shook my head. "There are no farmers for miles," I said. "And we are too many to fit in a wagon. We would need three or four. I doubt there are that many left in all of Neustria's countryside."

My grandmother had told me that our part of Gaul, which only a few generations ago had been populated with thousands of farmers prospering on the demands of hungry and well-funded Roman troops, now lay largely abandoned. We were seeing proof of this. If we had been worried about being discovered and forced to return, or pursued and molested by strangers, we had lost that fear in the vacuum of this countryside. We had yet to meet another pilgrim, farmer, or tradesman on our journey.

We passed field after fallow field, surrendered to native grasses and shrubs that grew thick with neglect. Barbarians from east of the Rhine had swept through here more than a century before, murdering peasants, their wave of terror chasing others to the cities, where most of them starved. The Romans had retreated at their advance and never returned, even after the barbaric tribes passed on to Aquitaine and farther south. Eventually, the emperor ceded control of Southern Gaul to the Goths and the rest of Celtic lands as far north as Belgica to my own Merovingian Franks.

I gnawed at the crumbly biscuit that would comprise half of my day's sustenance. We had saved up for the trip, squirreling away biscuits and storing some of the peas and carrots I had harvested in a bin we sunk into cool garden dirt. As in the monastery, Merofled was responsible on our trek for doling out the rations, although the younger sisters shared the literal burden of carrying them. We were already thin from our meager meals of the past few months, and I suspected that by the time we arrived in Tours, the local priests would take pity on our gaunt selves.

Some of the sisters slept, their heads resting on heaps of leaves and moss. Others murmured prayers for our safe passage, for forgiveness for our sin of rebellion, for their fellow pilgrims. My eyelids grew heavy, and I dozed off to the soft hum of their voices.

Covina shook me awake, and I jerked upright. I had been dreaming an updated version of a recurring nightmare. My cousins and half brothers were circling around me chanting, "*Bastardis! Bastardis!*" In this dream, Maroveus broke through the circle and pulled me away. The cousins had faded and disappeared, but he took up the chant, squinting at me with his puffy eyes, and pointing his fat finger in my face.

"You were shaking," Covina said. "Are you cold? Perhaps we should get back on our feet."

"Yes." I shook myself to clear the haze in my brain. "Yes. And no, I am not cold. But it is time to move on."

We stood, and with a little prodding, our pilgrimage returned to the frozen road and continued north. Before long, the spring sun had melted the frost off the tops of the ruts in the dirt, and slowly the hard mud turned soft, so we sought easier footing in the grasses on the sides. I started us off in the right direction, and then I stepped aside and watched my sisters pass, tossing encouragement toward the frowns, and returning smiles.

I turned in to follow the last sister at the back and took in the sight of my sisters walking ahead. The sun rose and lighted the empty fields around us. In the distance, dark woods swept along the horizon, giving the land a soft edge that reminded me of the fringe we sewed onto the bottom of the priests' vestments we were assigned to produce each year.

The road headed toward the trees and then dipped to the banks of the Le Clain, where we stopped just long enough to drink the cold, clear water. Wordlessly, we returned to the road, now surrounded by forest.

I noticed a few sisters had started to limp. I hoped it was due to blisters and not some more serious ailment of muscles, joints, or bones. Blisters could fester and hurt but they would heal once we were sequestered in the basilica in Tours. Ingund, our infirmarian, brought ground nahcolite, which we would mix with a little water to make poultices, but that treatment would do little good until we could stay off our feet.

We reached another clearing, blanketed with a riotous show of colorful wildflowers. The green foliage with its dots of orange, yellow, and lavender hosted what seemed like thousands of hopping and swooping birds enjoying a morning feast of crickets, flies, and caterpillars.

I thought how sad it was that we had been cut off from this outside world. The cloister—except for the narrow confines of my garden—had denied us the splendors of nature. Except for the pastoral Psalms and the illustrations Desmona sketched into our manuscripts, the Bible described only a frightful and bitter wilderness. Wild and barren, uninhabited lands harbored hunger, loneliness, and the desire for deliverance. Deserts and impassable mountains dominated the Biblical landscape. Perhaps that was what the Hebrew homelands were like. But what I saw before me could never be described as a desolate, dreary desert.

Once, a wild pig snorted in the woods that ran between us and the river, and several sisters shrieked and ran to the far side of the road. Early in the morning and as we approached the confluence of the rivers at dusk, herds of deer leapt in front of us on the road and then bounded out of sight, with not so much as a glance to acknowledge our passage.

This, I thought, was the world of my ancestors—the lands north and east of the Danube and the Rhine. I felt my chest swell with pride—pride in the poems and the prayers of my grandmother and mother—poems and prayers that worshipped this wonder and beauty and allowed that even trees and springs could be sacred.

Dusk settled in a pool of cool air around us. The wide Vienne, shown as a ribbon of waves teeming with fish on the map Angelica had given me, flowed lazily north. The diminutive Le Clain streamed into it, barely causing a ripple. We chose a small clearing surrounded by dense shrubbery for our dormitory, albeit one without the comforts of our meager cots.

Merofled divvied up a third of the peas, carrots, and onions, as well as another biscuit for each of us. Back at the monastery, such skimpy fare would have elicited grumbles, but as the fog rose up to us from the river's banks, and the clouds above us sank to meet it, no one complained about the humble picnic.

Free of the restrictions of the cloister, the sisters chattered as if they had stored up words for conversation and gossip for years. I listened to the rhythm of the sentences and the rise and fall of their voices without trying to follow the meaning. I realized how much the Psalms and our hymns had trained their tongues in cadences of the liturgy. I was certain it was more beautiful and fluid than the cadences of the peasants, the nobles, or the soldiers we had left behind when we accepted our cloistering. Wherever they had come from, my sisters were more like each other now than they were like their siblings and cousins. Getting our monastery back for them was my only goal, and it was vital. They would not be happy anywhere else, I believed.

I was wrong about that and many other things, it turned out, but believing it was enough to sustain me—to sustain us all—over those three arduous days of our walk. As the insects, birds, and plants closed in on themselves, and the soft evening turned to a hard, cold night, we recited the Psalms and prayers of Vespers. Forgoing the observance of the Hour of Compline in favor of rest, we settled down alongside each other like the spoons in Veranda's neat kitchen drawers, and my sisters fell asleep as one contiguous, exhausted heap of flesh.

For a few hours, probably up to the Hour of Matins, I lay awake, imagining every soft sound in the woods as an approaching wolf or bear. I felt guilty for lying in the middle of our pack; the riskier spots were along the edge of our rough circle. Finally, convincing myself that even a hungry wild animal would never approach this mass of humanity, I dozed off.

The dream of my childhood torture returned. Only this time, the cousins' menacing circle was broken by my grandmother, and I woke at dawn feeling calm and refreshed.

EIGHTEEN

In the freezing morning air, I pulled myself to my elbows, trying not to disturb the two bodies closest to me, Covina on one side and Basina on the other. I looked around at the lumps that comprised my fellow sisters, covered with thin wool cloaks and the few blankets we carried, and it struck me how ridiculous it was for such vulnerable and peaceful women to be branded as the devil's handmaids by the church.

As the others shook themselves awake and wandered into the woods, two by two, to relieve themselves, I walked among them, assessing wounds and swollen ankles. Ingund retrieved a buttery salve and clean cloth to wrap the most severe abrasions and blisters. Even as they grimaced with the sting of the applications, the sisters assured me they would continue without complaint.

"How are you feeling?" I asked as I finally reached Vivian. There was no doubt she was our weakest pilgrim. As small as she was, she still endured the monthly curse that had, thank God, abandoned most of us when we grew too thin. We were accustomed to her preternatural silliness and giggles, but now, moans from her cot at night testified to the pain she suffered for the sake of a fertility she would never need. Twice on the first day of our journey, Vivian had stopped by the stream, pulled the blood-soaked rag from between her legs, and washed it out. She replaced it with another and hung the wet cloth from the twine around her waist to dry. We gave her the privacy we would have wanted for ourselves, turning our backs to her, and waited patiently until she was ready to resume the walk.

Back at my blanket, I nibbled at my biscuit and studied my map. Where could we find a sanctuary for Vivian between here and Tours, if we needed it? Two or three dots suggested the possibility of towns between our camp and the intersection of our road with the road to Chinon, which I hoped to reach by dusk. Whether the towns, like so many other dots on our map, had survived the exodus in the wake of the barbarians, I had no way to know.

As the night fog started to lift, we pulled our small bundles of blankets and supplies onto our backs and returned to the road. Basina and Covina walked with me in the middle of the frozen trail in silence. Clear of the smoke from the wood we burned in our monastery, the air was fresh and cold. The murmur and tinkle of the Vienne retreated and approached as our path meandered along its ancient course. From the back of our flock, I marveled at the strength and determination of my sisters. They were risking their lives, their community, their shelter, and their sanctum in this rebellion. If it turned out that we were wrong— that I was wrong—and instead of sanctuary and succor, what we encountered in Tours was reproach, punishment, possibly even excommunication, where would they go? With few exceptions, their families would reject them, ashamed of their wickedness and perversion. Not for the first time, I pondered what would become of us. What was our plan in the face of failure?

Deep in thought, I nearly stumbled over the nun in front of me. Those at the front shrieked, and the group came to an abrupt halt. Ahead on the road stood three large men, bearded and long-haired Goths, dressed in ragged trousers and tunics. They looked young and wild. One's arm had been cut off at the elbow, and the other two had large, pink scars across their faces. Holding a large dagger in one hand, the tallest was speaking to his companions in a language I did not recognize as he surveyed our group. The two men guffawed beside him and slapped him on the back.

I pushed to the front, Covina on my heels, and stood facing the brutes with my hands on my hips. I hoped I looked fiercer than I felt. "You must let us pass," I announced, first in our usual Germanic language, and then again in Latin.

The men exchanged mirthful glances. The leader spoke again in his strange tongue.

I trembled, the mean-looking trio not ten paces away from me. I turned to Covina and then to the other sisters. "Does anyone recognize those words?" I asked, fighting to stay the nervous flutter in my voice. Twenty-nine heads shook no, their eyes wide with fear.

I turned back to the men, who were now grinning with amusement. As I held the eyes of the big man in the middle, I could feel the veins in my neck throb.

The leader waved his big knife in a circle, as if to indicate he could kill us all, and shouted out another string of foreign gibberish. I knew many Germanic words, and I was familiar with several Germanic dialects, but this one was new to me. As the man's companions chuckled at his oration, my mind raced over the possible outcomes of this scene. We were thirty, they were three. Surely, they would not try to attack us all, and if they did, they could only reach some of us before we overcame them with our sheer number of arms and legs. But, on the other hand, my sisters might hitch up their skirts and run, each for her own safety. Either way, I was not about to surrender even one of us to these brutes.

I held out a hand behind me, signaling I wanted stillness. Our only hope was our solidarity. I knelt, crossed my hands at my chest, and started to pray. "Father in Heaven," I began. I heard the soft swish of the sisters' linen as they knelt behind me. *Good. They understand. This might work.* It had to work. I had no other ideas. "Fifty days have celebrated the fullness of the mystery of your revealed love." Immediately, the sisters joined me in the prayer that we recited every year on the morning of the Pentecost. Among our morning prayers, it was special, and everyone had it memorized. "See your people gathered in prayer, open to receive the Spirit's flame. May it come to rest in our hearts and disperse the divisions of word and tongue." That was the phrase I hoped would deliver us, and I heard my sisters' voices strengthen as they recognized why I had chosen this prayer out of all our liturgy. "With one voice and one song, may we praise your name in joy and thanksgiving. Grant this through Christ our Lord."

As we recited the words, the men's faces grew quizzical. The two who flanked the leader leaned in to whisper in his ears. The man in the middle smirked and then, as I introduced Psalm 34, his expression turned to confusion.

"The angel of the Lord encamps around those who fear Him, to rescue them," I announced. Immediately, the chorus behind me joined in:

I will bless God at all times. His praise will always be in my mouth.

My soul shall boast in God. The humble shall hear of it and be glad.

Oh, magnify God with me. Let us exalt His name together.

I sought God, and He answered me, And delivered me from all my fears.

They looked to Him and were radiant. Their faces shall never be covered with shame.

This poor man cried, and God heard him, And saved him out of all his troubles.

The angel of God encamps round about those who fear him, And delivers them.

Oh, taste and see that God is good. Blessed is the man who takes refuge in Him.

Oh, fear God, you His saints, For there is no lack with those who fear Him.

The young lions do lack, and suffer hunger, But those who seek God shall not lack any good thing.

Come, you children, listen to me. I will teach you the fear of God.

Who is someone who desires life, And loves many days, that he may see good?

Keep your tongue from evil, And your lips from speaking lies.

Depart from evil, and do good. Seek peace, and pursue it.

The eyes of God are toward the righteous. His ears listen to their cry.

The face of God is against those who do evil, To cut off the memory of them from the earth.

The righteous cry, and God hears, And delivers them out
of all their troubles.
God is near to those who have a broken heart,
And saves those who have a crushed spirit.
Many are the afflictions of the righteous, But God delivers
him out of them all.
He protects all of His bones. Not one of them is broken.
Evil shall kill the wicked. Those who hate the righteous
shall be condemned.
God redeems the soul of his servants. None of those who
take refuge in Him shall be condemned.

Halfway through our recitation, the men shook their heads and slouched away into the woods. One of the smaller two made the sign of the cross on his forehead and chest as he slipped into the trees. Whether they were Christian or not, it did not matter. We had just introduced them to the power of David's poem, which he wrote to escape the Philistines, and to the power of a community of women on a mission to save themselves. Once the ruffians passed the first trees, they broke into a run. We watched them retreat but continued our recitation to its end.

We stayed on our knees as the silence of the countryside closed in on us. I heard a couple of sobs and a low whine behind me. I stood and turned to my pilgrims.

"You are brave and steadfast. You have faced your fear and overcome it. I love you all."

The sisters rose and cheered, hugging each other as pent-up tears ran down their faces. I watched and accepted my share of their embraces. We were united and strong. Now I believed we could do anything.

About that, too, I was wrong. But as long as I live, I will remember that solidarity, that sisterhood we experienced that morning on the road to Tours. It is largely what made me who I am today and encourages me to pursue what is now my life's work.

NINETEEN

Despite Fortunatus's warning, I still believed that Bishop Gregory of Tours would accept our plea to intervene with Maroveus on our behalf and on behalf of our beloved monastery. He had visited us often when Radegund was still alive. He had supported her efforts to acquire our relic of the Holy Cross from the church in Constantinople and stepped in to install it at the monastery when Maroveus refused. Surely, he would at least give us an audience.

As our third morning turned to afternoon, I could feel my sisters' excitement for our imminent arrival in Tours. But they grew somber as a lone wagon, drawn by a donkey that looked smaller than its cargo, appeared on the road ahead. An old peasant, possibly the oldest person I had ever seen, walked alongside, rocking from side to side, supporting the steps of his left leg with a rough-hewn branch of oak and his right with the starving animal's back.

Without a word, the man, donkey, and wagon passed through the middle of our group. I supposed that to him, we looked like any of the hundreds of pilgrims who walked to St. Martin's shrine every summer, except that we were all women and it was late spring, before most pilgrimages arrived.

The traffic picked up as we approached the city, some faster pedestrians and horse-drawn carts passing us from behind, and small groups of peasants and carts meeting us from the other direction. Stooped women walked with children, all poorly shod or barefoot, over the cold, wet ruts of the road, not one glancing up to meet our eyes. A man staggered forward with each step, pulling a club foot forward to meet his good one, a large, smelly bag slung over his shoulders. The human rabble grew into a sad parade of ragged clothing, emaciated bodies, and so many crippled limbs. No one greeted us or acknowledged our presence other than to step aside to let us pass. Was this the Gaul our kings were so proud of ruling? Not once had I been outside the cloister walls since I was thirteen years old. But how had I forgotten this? Was our misery at the Holy Cross no different—except possibly less extreme—than that of the rest of our countrymen?

The change in our mood was palpable. Instead of anticipation, dread crept into our steps, and we slowed. Instead of hope, I was now filled with consternation. I did not need to look into my sisters' faces to sense their dismay. It was the same as mine. I was also worried about Vivian. We had left her earlier that day in the care of a kindly priest along the way—a priest who assumed that we were sent on a pilgrimage by the abbess herself.

We spied the peaked bell tower of the basilica of St. Martin rising outside the city walls as the sun's rays cut horizontally before us, and its shadows grew long and chilly. Before we reached the church steps, we were intercepted by an emissary of the bishop and six of his guards, who surrounded us with the efficiency of collies herding a flock of sheep. I had figured that word of our departure and disobedience would reach Tours before we did, although I had not seen a messenger pass us on the road.

The emissary spoke loudly enough that all twenty-nine of us could hear him. "The Bishop requests that you return to Poitiers forthwith," he announced. "You may stay tonight as guests of our generous citizenry, but tomorrow morning, after Lauds, you will be on your way back to your monastery."

A collective moan rose from the sisters around me. We were all looking forward to a few days of rest for our tired and bleeding feet.

"Is one of you Clotild?" the emissary asked, ignoring their groans.

I stepped forward. "I am here."

"You will come with me."

"But where will the others go?"

The emissary looked confused for a moment, and it struck me that news of our imminent arrival had just reached the city, not giving the bishop much time to plan for us.

"Should they continue to the shrine of St. Martin?" I suggested. I was getting more practice thinking on my feet than I liked, but I suspected this would be far from the last time I would have to do so. "As pilgrims, they will not disturb the peaceful citizens of Tours."

"Yes, fine," the exasperated messenger said, waving his hands in the direction of the bell tower that rose above the stick-and-mud-daubed buildings that surrounded us. "Hurry. His Excellency is waiting."

I turned to Covina and lowered my voice. "As soon as I am gone, go to the basilica, tell the priest that the bishop sent you, and once inside, ask for sanctuary. I will join you as soon as I have talked with Gregory."

Covina nodded, having understood all along that we would seek refuge in the basilica. She turned to the sisters with hand gestures that unmistakably indicated for them to wait. Given Basina's unreliability, I was relieved at the way Covina had stepped up to share the leadership of our pilgrimage in my cousin's place. If we succeeded in our quest to get our monastery back, it would be as much due to her efforts as mine.

I followed the bishop's man through the city gate and down a broad, cobbled street, leaving the sisters and the guards behind. After three days out in the open country, the dark shadows of the squat buildings felt constricting, and the smoke of wood fires that streamed from the chimneys stung my nostrils. I tried to take shallow breaths, but the emissary's pace was demanding, and soon I was panting, the acrid air burning my lungs.

Tours had been a major Roman outpost long before the emperors had turned management of northern Gaul over to the Frankish Merovingians. As a youngster passing through the city with Fortunatus on our way to the monastery, I had waited while he soaked in the baths and enjoyed a fine meal and wines in a guesthouse where he was well-received. His fame as Gaul's rising poet had already begun to pave wide entry for him in nearly every town north of Aquitaine. I stayed in the guesthouse dining room, entertained by the scurrying about of the cook and server who had heard of his prodigious appetite, which was already as famous as his poetry, and sought not to displease the bard.

I had no idea where in town that guesthouse or the baths were then or now, as I had been too young at the time to develop mental maps of new territories. As I scurried, sore-footed, after the long-legged bishop's man, I thought of all I had foregone and failed to know about the world by living in the monastery. How much I had missed!

Would tallying the shortcomings of cenobitic life weaken my resolve to win our monastery back from Lebover? I could not allow that. Besides, Gaul was still wracked with political warring, although we had seen little evidence of it on our pilgrimage. All we had witnessed was its destitution. Further, as a woman, the only choices I had were marriage, prostitution, or the cloister.

The emissary led me for a kilometer or so into the center of town, and turning a corner, I saw the fine stone building built by King Charibert, my father, to house the bishopric and appease the church, which demanded donations that proved the kings were sufficiently pious.

A guard in a stiff, heavy cloak thick enough to serve as armor stepped aside, and we entered a great hall punctuated with marble columns that held up a high ceiling. Under the roof, a line of small windows fitted with glass let in the last light of dusk. Even though the contrast with the squalid, ramshackle houses we had passed on the road should have prevented it, my head filled with pride as I witnessed for the first time the grandeur my father (God rest his soul) had commissioned for the bishop. We walked through the cavernous hall, and the emissary knocked on a dark wooden door, a full meter taller than any man I had ever seen. Not waiting for an answer, my guide pushed the door open and swept his arm to usher me inside.

I had seen Gregory with Radegund on the many occasions when I was asked to accompany their meetings and record their conversations. Now, all these years later, Gregory looked much as I remembered. He was wrapped in a heavy robe adorned with colorful, interlocking embroidered images—perhaps it was one we had completed at the Holy Cross. His long beard was salted with silver—this was new to me—but he still sported a thick head of shoulder-length hair. He had grown considerably wider though. I suspected that his sedentary pursuit of writing his history was contributing to the swelling of his body.

Gregory did not look up as I entered. I stood for a moment just inside the door of the darkening room as he scratched his quill across a sheet of parchment. The candles on either side of his heavily carved, dark, wooden desk were unlit. I wondered how he could see well enough in the dimming light to continue.

Finally, with a deep sigh, he put down his pen and looked up at me. "Sister Clotild."

"Your Excellency," I responded in a whisper, bending my knees in a shallow curtsy and lowering my eyes. However I felt about the church, I knew, even then, that I was in the presence of greatness.

I looked up to his impassive face. His eyes held mine without blinking, and it looked like he was trying to make some sense of who I had become before deciding what to say. He waved an arm in the direction of a wooden chair backed up to the wall by the door. I stepped back and sat on its hard flat surface. Unlike the worn seats of the benches and chairs in the monastery, it betrayed no history of accommodating a backside other than mine.

He continued to stare at me over tented fingers. I studied the dark red-and-black woolen rug that stretched across the floor from my seat to well under his desk, its intricate designs reminding me of Desmona's illustrations. I let my eyes pass over the wood-and-leather-bound volumes that lay on shelves on either side of the room. A stack of chests in the corner no doubt held more. How I would have loved to have a few hours alone to explore their stories, their histories, their laws!

"Word has reached me of your sins and insubordination," he finally began. His voice was lower—either due to his advancing age or the gravity of the circumstances. "Perhaps you do not fear the excommunication and damnation you may well deserve, but Abbess Lebover is distressed that you have drawn so many good, pious sisters into this blasphemous enterprise with you. She has asked me to demand your immediate return, and unless you can convince me otherwise, that will be my order."

"Your Excellency," I said. "I understand the abbess's concern, and I assure you neither I nor the others decided to take this journey without serious deliberation and hours in prayer for guidance. But I want—"

He interrupted me. "Do you mean to imply that through prayer, you received God's counsel to execute this shameful trespass?"

I realized I was unprepared for this conversation, as much as I had imagined it and practiced my delivery in my head. He had already taken my words and turned them against me. I felt scrambled and confused as I tried to form an answer. Perhaps the best approach was to ignore the question. I had only this one chance, I guessed, to plead our case against Lebover and Maroveus and I could not allow him to knock me off course. "We came, not on God's command, but on behalf of the monastery that the blessed Radegund founded—may she receive her due sainthood under your enlightened leadership."

Through the darkening space between us, I glimpsed one corner of his mouth turn up in amusement. My flattery humored him, but he was clearheaded enough to recognize it as cheap bribery. "Radegund is not our concern here," he said, losing the smile. "But because you have made such an arduous and dangerous journey, I feel that I should give you the chance to tell me why you have left the monastery that you claim to have such concern for. You have my attention, but I ask that you make efficient use of it."

"We are a pious community of women, and all of us have accepted the limitations and blessings of cloister," I started. I had practiced this part. If I did not get interrupted by more unexpected questions, I was sure it would make an impression on Gregory. "You have visited us. You knew our mother, Radegund, well. You watched and admired her work as she built a monument to God's love and His gift of grace. Over the past year, the sisters who knew and loved her have suffered indignities, including near starvation and unadjudicated punishments, while the new abbess, Lebover, appointed over our objections by Bishop Maroveus, has persisted in acts of thievery, adultery, and gluttony. Our appeals to the *Regula* of Caesarius and to the bishop have been summarily rejected. Our appeal to the archbishop was refused. We have suffered the heartache of a suicide of a dear novice who could not bear Lebover's cruelties. Others have talked of reneging their vows, at the price of excommunication, to escape her tyranny." I paused for a breath and for effect.

Gregory took advantage of it, raising a palm before his face. "I know your family, or at least the family that you claim to be part of," he started. I winced. His reference to the question of my parentage was no surprise. Of course, it was another way he could assert his superiority, although clearly, he did not need to. While my legitimacy would forever be questionable, his was unassailable. At least four of his relatives had been bishops in Gaul before him, including a great-grandfather, a great-uncle, and an uncle. "Your uncles and your cousins continue to wage jealous and costly wars against each other, instead of taking up arms against true evil—the heathens and their shrines they raise to worship their gods." I stifled another grimace. My grandmother and I were such heathens, although I was not exclusively.

He either ignored my discomfort or felt compelled to take advantage of it and express a few more opinions, relevant or not, while I listened. "And despite this, Rome has chosen to elevate the royal houses over our bishoprics, ill-advisedly. Your Uncle Guntram, the blessed man, is certainly an improvement over that Nero, Chilperic, but I do not always support his imperial desires." Gregory seemed, for a moment, preoccupied with this thought. His eyes focused on some abstract point far in the distance over my head, and the tendons of his neck tightened so that they stuck out through his thick layer of flesh.

I knew he was composing a history of Gaul and I guessed that he was, at that very moment, developing a thesis he would explore in comparing my uncles—in his estimation (and mine, to be honest), the good Guntram versus the evil Chilperic. He had argued publicly with the evil king over many things, including taxes levied on Tours and Chilperic's desire to limit the bishop's powers. Gregory had enraged Chilperic by sheltering his son Merovech, who had waged war against his own father. That Chilperic had been murdered seemed to have had little impact on Gregory's enmity.

Eventually, his gaze returned to my face, and he refocused on the question at hand. "I understand that you feel particularly aggrieved because you, yourself, wished to become abbess, but I will let that coincidence pass, understanding and living as I do with the inborn initiative of the ambitious. But I believe the answer here is to be found where you should have been seeking it all along: in God and in prayer."

Taken aback by his knowledge that I had coveted the position of abbess, I wondered who his informant had been. I would not deny that I had such aspirations, and I had the backing of the sisters in that ambition, but I had not expected him to know that. Leading my sisters to Tours, however, now had only that higher purpose—saving Radegund's legacy—and not restoring my own dashed authority.

Gregory continued to lecture me about accepting my role in the cloister with humility, but my focus wandered. I watched his mustache and beard move with the rhythm of his words and heard the far-off sound of speech crossing the room, but I did not recognize words. I knew what I had to do. I had to brave the discomfort and dangers of further travel to see King Guntram in Chalôns-sur-Saône, and hope that, as a member of the family that had both begotten and rejected me, he would feel enough obligation of kinship to listen.

As if he could read my mind, Gregory said, "The kings may be the ultimate political authority in Gaul, but when it comes to ecclesiastical and eschatological questions, you must keep in mind that it is the bishops, not the kings, who know God's will."

I must have looked tired—which I certainly was—because sympathy suddenly crossed the bishop's stern face, and he stood and walked to my chair. I noticed his gait was labored, and I wondered what illness had afflicted him, and how much longer he would persevere under its tortures. Our mutual pity changed the atmosphere, and he spoke kindly. "You have had a long and difficult journey," he said, holding out his hand to help me rise from the chair. "I have reconsidered my orders. You and your sisters should stay here in Tours, at least until the rains and the heat of summer pass. The basilica will grant you sanctuary, and I will canvass my fellow bishops regarding your concerns. But then, you must return to Poitiers and rededicate yourselves to your life of prayer and penitence."

I stood as tall as I could, given the weariness of my bones, and looked him in the eye. "Thank you, Your Excellency. That is all we ask. Meanwhile, as my sisters rest, I will continue on to assure my Uncle Guntram of our good intentions and love for our cloister."

I kissed his outstretched hand and left.

TWENTY

I joined my sisters in the basilica with at least one small victory: the concession of Gregory that we could remain in Tours for a few months and make our journey back to Poitiers once the fall arrived and the air had cooled enough to accommodate our safe passage. As certain as Gregory was that our sins were more important than our mission, he did not want to bear the blame for the death of any number of thirty sisters from the monastery of Radegund.

"You will be assured of food and shelter here," I announced to the weary sisters scattered on the floor of the nave of the basilica. "And I will carry our plea to my Uncle Guntram, as soon as I can arrange for a conveyance."

"Did Gregory listen to you? Did he say he would help us?" Basina knew the answer before she asked, but others, she recognized, did not.

"He listened, but he did not hear," I said. I allowed my disappointment to show on my face. It was better that the sisters realized we risked being abandoned by the very church and religion to which we had pledged our lives than to be misled about certain victory. "I fear that only King Guntram's intervention will force the archbishop's hand."

A couple of sisters moaned and lay back down on the floor.

"Maybe we should not have—" Greta started, but she did not need to finish her thought. I saw a few nods, but I was relieved to see more nuns shake their heads at her suggestion.

"No." Covina spoke up. "This was necessary." She came to stand beside me. "Besides, our three days of discomfort on the road was but a trifling compared with the suffering of our Savior. Let's not forget that He never promised our paths would be lined with rose petals, or that our journeys as Christians would be easy. Remember the true martyrs: Polycarp, burned at the stake, or Saint Agnes, martyred by the Romans while still a young virgin. Our sacrifice is much smaller than the eye of a needle or the head of a pin."

I smiled. I knew Covina's reference to the eye of a needle was from the admonition of Jesus, that it would be easier for a camel to pass through one than for a rich man to enter heaven. I tried to remember the reason one counted the number of angels that danced on the head of a pin, but I was too tired. I felt my legs falter with fatigue, and, trying not to show my weakness, I leaned on my hands against the prayer rail at my knees.

"Let us say our Vespers prayers and get our rest," I said with my eyes closed. I felt Covina's strong arms guide me to sit, and her strong voice led our pilgrimage into the Psalm of the Hour.

☩

One time, when I was still young enough to sit on my father's lap, my Uncle Guntram had come to visit us in Paris. He strode into my father's villa, sporting the same stature and good looks as my father's other two brothers, but his soft eyes displayed none of their arrogance. He and my father embraced with joy, their laughter rang out, rattling the wine goblets that were set out while we were awaiting his arrival. Guntram smiled down at me, the first time any of my uncles had acknowledged my presence, and rubbed the messy curls on my head.

"You are growing up to be a fine woman," he praised me. My face grew hot with a blush, pleased at the compliment, even though I knew I was far too young to be referred to as a woman, and there was no evidence in that room that anything about me was *fine*.

I focused on that early image of Guntram as I endured two days in the wagon Hilda had commissioned to take me to Chalôns-sur-Saône. I was happy to give the blisters on my feet some time to heal, but otherwise, I thought the walk from Poitiers to Tours had been more pleasant, and certainly less jarring to the bones, than riding over ruts and potholes of a sometimes frozen and sometimes mud-clogged road in a mule-drawn wagon.

I left the sisters at St. Martin, calling on one of my father's other daughters, Berthageld, who lived at a monastery nearby, to make sure they had food and cider or beer. Although Berthageld had held herself above me in my childhood, she and I had both ended up cloistered. She, however, had come to it to escape an unsatisfactory marriage, I to avoid murder by her mother, Ingoberga.

The giant bear of a man Hilda had sent as my escort growled at me, as if he would rather have more profitable and less bothersome cargo to transport. "I do not want to hear a sound from you," he spat through his beard. "I do not care if you are comfortable or happy or want to stop. We drive until I decide to stop, and we start again when *I* want to." I wondered how Hilda had managed to get such a disagreeable man to agree to do anything. He pointed to the box of the wagon. Without offering to help, he watched as I put my hands on the side, stepped on one of the spokes of the wheel, pulled myself up, and tumbled onto the hard bed lined with empty grain sacks. He tossed my blanket and my small bag of rations in after me and climbed up next to the driver. The wagon shook back and forth with the weight of his ascent, and I got the first sense of how rough this ride was going to be.

Well after dark the first day, we stopped at one of my uncle's villas, and I climbed out of my berth slowly, my cold, aching muscles resisting any rapid movement. We slept on soiled mattresses filled with straw in a cold and dusty bunkhouse that had at one time housed *foederati*, the barbarians Romans recruited to maintain control over this province of the empire. My escort slept nearby, his rumbling snore so annoying that I slept but a few hours.

The next day, I was delighted to see what I took to be Chalôns-sur-Saône in the distance. I was cold, hungry, sore, and my head felt as if that oaf riding above me were pounding it with the handle of the large dagger he kept lashed to the sash of his tunic. But as soon as we stopped in front of Guntram's big stone house, I leapt out of the wagon and ran to the door. As I clanged the huge brass ring against the lion's head knocker, I noticed how much it resembled my chaperone.

☩

The following three months I spent in my uncle's house in Chalôns came close to changing the fate of our rebellion. The food and the fireplaces might have been enough to dissuade me from returning to the monastery, but the clean, comfortable bed, the soft rugs underfoot, the pretty rainbow patterns thrown on the floor by the beveled-glass windows made me question the ascetic life I had chosen. Of course, that austere existence had been my choice only to a degree; at the time I entered Holy Cross, my other options were limited by my gender and illegitimacy, and the danger posed by my stepmothers, cousins, and half siblings.

King Guntram was not home when I first arrived, although Hilda had advised him I was coming. He had taken to Hilda the same way he had to my mother: enjoying her exotic foreign differences and appreciating her love for his brother, Sigibert. Guntram had adopted their son Childebert as his own when Sigibert was killed. And, like Hilda, Guntram harbored no love and had no time for Freda, whom he knew to be homicidal and unprincipled.

I slept the first night as soundly as I had slept in months—no, years. I did not rise for Matins or Lauds but slept right through until the time I would have been reciting the prayers of Terce. I did not wonder if the Christian God would notice my absence at the Hours, which should have been a signal to me that my practice of the church's liturgy did not prove my devotion to the faith. It was simply ritual and, as in my childhood's pagan rites, I had found comfort in Christian ceremonies. But I did not need them.

I woke to a soft knock at the door well after the sun had risen over the rich gardens east of the palace. I sat up and looked around the room with blurry eyes. I knew where I was immediately, but it was the first time I saw the room in daylight. The sleeping gown covering my body was clean and soft enough to cause my breath to catch with pleasure. I closed my eyes and pushed the miserable trip in the wagon out of my memory. I wanted to savor the luxury without concern for the return trip. "Come in," I called out in answer to another, more insistent knock.

A young servant entered carrying a tray with a steaming cup of liquid. She was dressed in a shift not unlike those we wore at the monastery, and suddenly, I wondered where mine might be. What was I going to wear once I shed this luxurious nightgown?

"The king wishes you to join him to break fast," she said.

"He is here?"

"Yes, he arrived before sunrise. He asked me to wake you."

I clutched at my neck, relieved to find the amulet still secure there on its cord, and looked around the vast bedchamber for a crumpled pile of clothing. "But where are my tunic and my cloak?"

"They are with the laundress. She will have them ready for you for your return to Tours."

"What will I wear?" The woman pointed to a dark wood chest, covered with intricate and incongruous carvings of angels and soldiers, an amalgam that conflated the triumph of Christianity and the strength of the empire.

After the servant left me alone again, I rose, took a sip from the mug of hot cider, and examined the contents of the chest. The half dozen woolen dresses that were folded there were far more elaborate than the simple shift I had worn ever since entering the monastery, adorned as they were with embroidery and jewels. I ran my fingers over a colorful flower on the breastplate of one, its intricate stitches as fine as any we produced on the priests' vestments back in our sewing room.

I pulled the nightgown off over my head and washed in the warm water the servant had brought in a pitcher. A boar's-hair brush lay next to the wash bowl, and painfully, I pulled it through my tangles before securing my hair atop my head with the pins I had extracted the night before. I glanced up into the shiny metal plate hanging on the wall and saw my mother staring back at me.

For a moment I was fooled, thinking it was her portrait painted on pewter, but the face moved with mine. It was the first time I had seen a reflection myself as a woman. I was a younger but thinner version of that woman I had left in my thirteenth year, with the same dark eyes and high cheekbones. I stared with pride at my handsome face, and then turned away with shame for my vanity.

I chose a slim slip from a pile on a shelf in the wardrobe and slid it down over my body. It was soft, and when I turned, it swung freely, its silk like a breeze caressing my skin. I chose one of the gowns, and struggled into it, pleased that when it settled over me and I fastened the hooks on the side, my small breasts fit comfortably in place and the neckline hung low enough to frame my amulet. Shyly, I glanced in the pewter again, but I could see no more than my face. Perhaps I would catch a glimpse of my complete visage somewhere else in this grand house.

As I pulled open the chamber door and descended the gleaming marble stairs, I wondered if I had to return to Tours, but immediately felt guilty for my thoughts. My sisters were back at the basilica, sleeping on cold dirt floors. Of course, I would return, and when fall arrived, we would return to Poitiers and reclaim our monastery for the memory of Radegund.

Or would we?

✝

I found my uncle in the conservatory that looked out onto manicured gardens. He was seated at a small marble table, studying a document. He looked up as I walked in. "Clotild! What a blessed pleasure! Come to my side!" He rose and held my fingers lightly in his hands, studying my face, which he had last seen before I left my father's villa. Much older than when I had seen him last, he was nearly a stranger.

I was unaccustomed to this strange way of dressing and watched his eyes to read what he saw as he gazed at me. His expression was inscrutable, but his next words were kind. "You are of your mother's beauty and your father's strength," he declared. "I am proud to have you in my home, dear niece. Now sit and tell me about your journey."

Spread out on the table between us were plates of thinly sliced, dried meats; a pewter pitcher of milk with a thick layer of cream floating on top; and a basket of breads. A huge dish of figs and dates sat on a sideboard an arm's length away, and at one end, a bowl of apples—enough to feed all the sisters at the Holy Cross. As I surveyed the feast, the servant who had brought hot cider to my bedchamber entered with two more steaming mugs.

I sat speechless, wondering how to partake of such abundance. It felt like larceny or, at least, gluttony. My face must have shown my dismay, and Guntram rescued me.

"Forgive me," he said. "You must be famished after your journey, but I imagine you are not fed like this in the monastery. Your stomach must adjust. Please, take your time. Start with the cider and a biscuit."

"Uncle, you are kind." I glanced down at my bare neckline. "I am not accustomed to this dress, the servants, any of this—" I waved an arm to take in the room and everything beyond it. "It is beautiful and yet also frightening. I fear I have little experience at life as a royal daughter."

"Although you are one!" He bellowed a hearty laugh. "Your father was my favorite brother, and the only one I would show my back to as I walked out of a room. Most of your brothers are dead, and your sisters have been married off or cloistered. For years, I have seen no hint of my Charibert in a single face." He paused as he held his stare. "Until you."

I felt my face flush. To avoid his eyes, I focused on the hot cider, its sweetness coating my tongue, and reached for a biscuit. It was soft and warm. I marveled at how fine the flour must be in Chalôns, how much more refined than the crude grain we pulverized on the grinding stone in the monastery. "And your sons?" I asked before biting into the spongy biscuit. "Are they well and thriving?"

I knew Guntram's three wives and his first two sons had all died from plague or murder by my uncle's enemies, but I had heard nothing of his sons Chlodomer and Clothar.

"Taken from me by sickness," he answered slowly, sadly.

I regretted having asked; my sympathies were late and worth little, and I struggled to think of what to say next. I noticed that he was enjoying nothing of the feast before us. "Are you not hungry, Uncle? Have you already broken fast?"

"I fast many full days now, Clotild," he said, looking down at the mug of cider he held but did not lift to his lips. "I have sinned too much for too long, and God has punished me by taking my wives and my sons. These days, I pray and fast, but I do not expect God to grant me His forgiveness, which I do not deserve, however great His mercy."

Now I noticed how thin he was—much thinner than Gregory or Maroveus. As religious as the bishops were, they did not appear to have ever embraced the ritual of fasting.

"But it is known that you give to the poor, and you have built monasteries and churches," I said. "I am certain you deserve God's grace."

My uncle looked up at me and smiled. "I appreciate your kind assessment, Clotild, but the judgment will be God's, not ours."

I nodded and finally bit into the sweet, soft biscuit. I closed my eyes, savoring its buttery, rich texture and wondered how, with access to such bread, anyone could fast.

"And now." Guntram retrieved my attention. "You must tell me of your quest. Why travel halfway across Gaul to see me?" He watched me finish my biscuit and reach for another. "Although now," he said, "I see perhaps it was for my biscuits."

TWENTY—ONE

My cousins were back, circling around me, taunting me with their chants of "whore" and "bastard." But this time I was wearing one of the dresses from my uncle's wardrobe, and the low-cut neckline showed the bare tops of my breasts. Grabbing at me, they tore the amulet from my throat, and I screamed.

I sat straight up in bed, a cold sweat soaking through my nightgown, and blinked until I had erased the image from my mind. I fell back against the feather pillow and stared at the ceiling. The moon was bright, almost full, and the room's rich furnishings cast shadows against the wall.

I had been at my uncle's house for nearly three months. As summer steamed through the countryside, I had quickly grown accustomed to the comforts of his home, and the longer I stayed, the more I dreaded the trip back. With no food to prepare, laundry to tend to, or texts to copy, I found the idle days lusciously long, and tried to push the inevitable return of long winter nights in the monastery's dormitory out of my mind. My uncle forbade me to return to Tours in the heat and demanded that I stay with him until fall. But honoring the vow I had to renounce the world and its temptations, he kept me inside, as if in the cloister, and I do not deny that I longed to see the baths, the Colosseum, and other grand buildings left behind by the fading Roman empire in Chalôns. I wrote frequently to my sisters in Tours, sending my letters in care of the Bishop Gregory. I did not tell them about my luxurious surroundings, but I explained my uncle's orders to stay until cooler weather. I bid them a pleasant stay in sanctuary and reminded them of the reason for our rebellion.

"My uncle is considering our request for assistance," I wrote each time. "I am praying for his sympathies, as I am certain you are." As time passed, and I began to fear that my uncle would not intervene on our behalf, I began to add, "We must have faith that God will aid our righteous quest to preserve our monastery."

Of the comfortable hours I spent in my uncle's house, my favorites were those with Hilda, who arrived a few days after me. Almost unheard of in the history of the Merovingians, my uncle and her son Childebert had formed an alliance to rule jointly over their two territories in Gaul. Now Hilda and her son spent most of the time in Chalôns with Guntram. I was lucky to have her as my companion. She knew my mother like no one yet living in this world, other than my grandmother (if by some miracle or charm she were still alive). Hilda brought me small embroidery projects, which we worked on while she chattered about my uncle's politics and my cousin's military campaigns. When she had no sewing projects for us, we read aloud the plays of Aeschylus and other Greek masters from books my uncle had yet to purge from his library since his rededication to Christian piety. Hilda was one of the few women I knew who could—or would—read anything but the Scriptures since Gregory had pronounced the ancient texts to be demonic, damning fables.

In spite of the gentle way my uncle treated me in his house, and his promise to talk to the archbishop and Maroveus about conditions at the Holy Cross, he declined to align himself with my sisters and me against the church's wishes for Lebover's continued rule. As he had pledged himself to a new life of piety and abstinence, he found my complaints too worldly for sympathy.

I was gaining weight and starting to fill out my borrowed dresses like a mature woman, and as I laid and stared into the moonlit room, I wondered if that had something to do with a new recurring dream. In it, I was lying next to a man, listening to him breathe, wishing he would turn to me and pull me atop his broad chest. He never did, but I awoke each time with my heart pounding and breath short.

I had never been comfortable thinking or talking about the affairs of marriage. The only instruction I had in such matters were the whispers and gossip of the sisters, most of whom had as little experience—that is none—with a marital bedroom as I. I had never allowed myself to imagine an attachment—physical or emotional—to a man. But as my body became softer and more feminine, I felt an emptiness in those dreams that I could not erase by reciting the Psalms or prayers.

One cool, late summer morning, I was stoking the cooking stove when I heard someone clear his throat behind me, and I startled, knocking the iron to the floor with a clang. The man with his helmet in his hand behind me was one of my uncle's top lieutenants, a man who commanded several legions. Yet, there he stood, looking shyly at the floor, perhaps embarrassed for having come upon me stooped over, my newly rounded backside projecting toward him.

I felt my face flush. It was not the first time I had noticed him.

His broad shoulders and narrow hips formed a silhouette nearly the opposite of mine. I had seen him walking with my uncle in the gardens, their heads bowed in serious conversation, and his had become the figure I imagined lying next to me in my dreams. Was it the return of my monthly bleeding that brought about this awareness of the shape of men's bodies?

"I beg your pardon—"

I realized he was trying to figure out what to call me. "Sister," I filled in for him. "Sister Clotild."

At that, his eyes rose to meet mine, and I saw an amused grin spread across his clean-shaven face. "Yes, of course. Sister," he said.

My hand flew to the cool skin of my bare décolletage, and I blushed. "Do you need . . . Can I help—?" I could not decide how to address him either or what to offer. I had no experience to fall back on. The only men I had spoken with were priests, bishops, the poet Fortunatus, my father, and my uncle.

In my confusion I turned to run from the kitchen and collided with Guntram. He looked down at me, then across the kitchen at his lieutenant, and frowned. "Sister Clotild," he said—the first time he had addressed me as such instead of "my dear niece." "Please leave the lieutenant and me to discuss our affairs. It is probably time for your hourly prayers, is it not?" His eyes were focused on the bareness of my chest, and I believed it was the first time he noticed me as anything other than the young girl who sat on my father's lap and danced around the garden with my cousins.

Even though my uncle had taken new vows of piety and abstinence, his bed was still warmed by the presence of his concubine, whom he had acquired after his third wife, Austrachild, had passed, and his choice for his fourth bride, Rusticula, had declined to marry him, preferring instead her life as an abbess in Arles. As I ran to my room with embarrassment, it struck me that his judgment was unfair. Why did men have a right to pleasures of the heart and body, while women had none? Why would God punish me and not him? At that moment, I realized I had forgotten my pledge at the monastery to join myself in marriage to Jesus Christ. Had I more than forgotten it? Was I ready to abandon it altogether?

My shame burning in my face, I tore off the gown, slipped my nun's undergarment and shift over my head, and tugged them down over my breasts and hips. It had been nearly three months since the night I had arrived and taken them off. I looked down at my shapeliness, wishing again I could see a reflection of the length of my body as I had seen my face in the pewter.

I sat down on the bed and cried into my hands. It was shameful to be so proud, to care about one's appearance. Who was I? I once had known myself as a cloistered nun, but as my Christian faith wavered, as I wallowed in this luxury, I had lost a sense of myself.

I retrieved my uncle's Bible from his library and searched for lessons in humility and abstinence to refresh my desire for the lifestyle of a penitent. I wished I also had a copy of Caesarius's *Regula* to refresh my dimming memory. I knew it was time to get back with my sisters and talk to Covina, Basina, Greta, and Merofled about our next move. I was accomplishing nothing in Chalôns, and, even more worrisome, they had never responded to my letters.

Guntram and I spoke less often after that collision in the kitchen, in part because he had started planning his spring military maneuvers with my cousin, but I knew he was also avoiding me, even when he had time to join me at my breakfast or dinner. I mourned the sudden change in our relationship and realized I did not belong there, luxuriating in his royal lifestyle. Once I had pledged myself to an ascetic life devoted to Christ, even though I had secretly reserved part of my soul for my grandmother's gods, and here I had been eating, dressing, and socializing like a courtesan.

Two weeks later my uncle gave me a cool parting hug at his front door and retreated into his house. I felt like something valuable between us had been ripped away over the last month. But Hilda was waiting and she hugged me warmly and handed me a large sack of biscuits, dried meats, and dried figs and dates.

"Travel safely, dear Clotild," she said, stroking my cheek, tears gathering in her eyes. "I hope your pleas are answered by the bishops and your monastery can feel like a home to you again."

The road back to Tours was as rough as it had been three months before, but this time, I had the roof of Hilda's covered wagon over my head, and my compartment was cushioned with layers of wool blankets. We stopped overnight at another abandoned army outpost, but my new, courteous escort helped me down from the wagon and honored my privacy by taking an adjoining bunkroom. I was eager to get back to the rituals that had filled my days at the monastery and fell asleep reciting prayers from Compline. I was anxious to share these with my sisters again.

In my uncle's house, I had set aside my vow to live a life of austerity, and for a short period, I had even contemplated abandoning my sisters. The temptations of aesthetic pleasure had lured me into complacency, greed, and gluttony. It slashed at my love for my sisters, threatening to sabotage our mission to save our community. I remembered my grandmother's prediction: that I would be a link to the goddesses of our ancestors who gave women the strength to survive, bear children, and tend their gardens. My sisters needed me, and for that reason, I needed them.

✝

I had heard nothing from my sisters in Tours since I left. Gregory had not communicated with me either, so I was unprepared for the chaos that I found at the basilica when I returned.

We arrived late in the evening, well after the sun's last light faded overhead. Guntram's kind servant helped me dismount from the wagon and waited until a monk opened the door of the basilica before wishing me God's speed, doffing his cap, and backing away into the dark street.

Walking into the narthex, I was confused by the silence in the chapel. It was the Hour of Compline, and I had expected to hear twenty-eight voices raised in Psalms and prayer. "Where . . . ?" I turned to the monk. With his hands in the pockets of his robe, he walked down the side of the nave toward the north transept. I followed, not knowing if he meant me to, and saw a small gathering of my sisters, their heads bent in prayer, sitting in a tight circle on the floor. I recognized our leaders, Covina, Greta, Basina, and Merofled. Eight others were with them. Our quiet approach had not interrupted their prayers, and I stood, watching. I had missed these women, and I wanted to kneel and embrace them all at once.

But where were the others? The twelve sisters on their knees on the floor accounted for fewer than half of the pilgrims I had left behind. I had paltry news for them. And now, if only these dozen sisters were still with me, I realized the prospect of our mission's success was even lower than I thought.

I placed my bag of food on the floor and knelt outside the circle. I said my own prayer, silently, asking for forgiveness for my sloth over the past three months. I would fast and pray until I felt absolved and deserving of my sisters' faith in my leadership again.

TWENTY-TWO

My sisters raised their heads from their prayers and slowly rose to their feet. Covina was the first to notice me kneeling behind them. "Sister Clotild!" She ran and wrapped her arms around me as if to lift me off the floor. She had no idea how much weight I had gained in my absence and she grimaced as my knees stayed planted on the stone tiles. "My, you have eaten well, my dear sister!" she whispered, laughing quietly.

The women surrounded me and begged for news. "Is Guntram going to help us?" "What will happen to us?" And from Basina: "Is our uncle going to save our monastery?"

As the others swarmed around me, Covina's comment on my weight gain took on greater significance. Their lean fingers were like spikes, their nails broken and untidy. They threw bony arms around my neck, sharp elbows poking me painfully. Their sunken eyes looked wild with hunger. Had Berthageld not provided for them?

"Let me rest first," I said. I was shocked by their appearance, more afraid now that my unimpressive report would add injury to their obvious misery. I wanted everyone to get a night's sleep, including me, before we discussed what little progress I had made. And I needed to know what had happened to them and to the missing sisters before we could begin to consider our next move.

"Yes, of course," Greta said. "I imagine you are tired from your journey. The summer heat does not seem willing to give up its hold on Gaul this year. It must have been miserable out there."

They led me to a dark hut next to the basilica that smelled of unwashed bodies and urine. A bucket in the corner of the mud floor was half full of human waste, and I fought the urge to hold my nose. Greta's sympathy for my "miserable" trip took on new irony. This was far worse than anything I had experienced in my two-day trip back to Tours. Was Greta being sarcastic?

Covina pulled me aside. "We do not rise for Matins," she admitted, looking sheepish. "None of us has the energy anymore. Please understand. The past few months have been hard."

I had just enjoyed more than three months in inexcusable luxury, never rising for Matins or Lauds, and missing more Hours than I observed. They were living in this sty and apologizing for missing one. Horrified and ashamed, I shook my head, glad for the darkness that hid the tears in my eyes. "Of course," I said. "Let us all sleep and have a long discussion in the morning. God bless you all for your patience with me."

☩

The news I had to share with my sisters was tepid but it was less dreary than the tales they had to share with me.

We gathered around a makeshift table set up for my sisters

outside their hut, away from the room's stench. It would have been simple for the priest to give them access to the kitchen after our brethren had finished their meal and scattered to their daily chores, but he had refused.

I opened my food bag and spread out the figs, dates, dried meats, and biscuits in the middle of the long table. I looked around and recounted. There were thirteen of us, counting me. "Where are the others?" I asked. My question was innocent; at that moment I guessed they had gone back to Poitiers.

"They are gone." At Covina's answer, the nuns all bowed their heads and murmured blessings.

"To Poitiers?"

"No, *gone*."

The finality of the word horrified me. "Did they die here?"

"No," Covina answered again. "They left."

"Do they intend to come back?" I asked. Maybe they joined Berthageld's monastery, the one nearby that was founded by Ingoberga, her mother.

"Sister Clotild," Greta said with a tone that foreshadowed the grave news to come and barely concealed her impatience with my ignorance. "Some have taken husbands, and some of them are with child. Others may be in Paris or Avignon, for all we know, or possibly we will never know what becomes of them."

In my absence, hunger, cold, and the misery of their living arrangements had worn down their tolerance, even though they had been accustomed to an ascetic life. Like me, many of them had ended up in the monastery for its security, sustenance, and freedom from marriage, not for their piety. Now that security and sustenance was less than assured, marriage seemed like a reasonable alternative. More than half of those I had left behind in Tours had departed the basilica to join relatives outside or take their chances on the streets, all breaking their vows of cloister.

But then, I realized, we all had. Leaving the monastery in the first place was against the *Regula* and a violation of our vows. But I had thought if it was done to save our community, and we planned to return, we would be forgiven. Now, I was not so sure. Gregory had given me no such assurance. Would we all be excommunicated? Would my sisters be denied communion and any chance to ever escape purgatory or hell? Even if I did not believe that a priest could decide my sisters' ultimate judgment in the eyes of God, the possibility that I had brought them to such a fate made my heart sick.

I felt nauseous and regretted the fig I had just put in my mouth. I wanted to spit it out, but it would be unseemly to waste food in front of such hunger. My sisters exercised little restraint, grabbing the crusty bread and fruit, piece after piece, and devouring it all quickly. In the silence at the table, I watched them eat greedily, rarely stopping to wash the food down with beer. I wondered how they had survived for three months. Had they received anything more than dry bread and beer?

I forced myself to chew on the sticky wad in my mouth that seemed to grow larger the more I worked it. I finally swallowed the last of it and drank from the pitcher we shared. "Tell me what happened," I said, hoping for some better news.

"We have been hungry," Greta answered first.

Covina added, "And your sister, Berthageld, chose to ignore us. She eats plenty, works none at all, and grows fat and gouty. Even her mother who fought to keep her at the monastery cannot abide her behavior. We understand they fight constantly."

I mumbled an apology, although I knew none of them held

me responsible for my half sister's greed. I should have known, however, that Berthageld, who had joined in torturing me as a child, had not changed. I should never have trusted her.

"You were so long in Chalôns," Greta said. I noticed how the others were now treating her and Covina with the same deference they had once had for me. "Some thought you were not returning."

"But did the bishop not deliver my letters?"

"The bishop has been in *Marseille* himself all summer," Basina said, her tone sarcastic. "Apparently, the heat in Tours does not agree with him. He prefers the sea breezes." The others nodded but they did not laugh.

"But tell us what Guntram said," Greta said. "Will he help us?"

"Yes, in a way." I paused, knowing what I had to say was not what they wanted to hear. "He will call a convocation of bishops to hear our complaints. He understands and sympathizes with our situation and he was comforted to know that we were not asking to renounce our vows." I realized how hollow that statement was, now that more than half of our members apparently had. "He believes that Maroveus has good intentions and will listen to reason, and we can find a way to accommodate one another, Lebover and us."

A dark silence followed my news. I had spent three months away, getting fat and sleeping in soft beds, to return with no more than this. "We will stay here and await the convocation to hear us," I continued into the gloom that had settled over us. "I am certain they will be appalled by Lebover's sins and depose her, returning our monastery to us so we can restore the glory established by our blessed founder."

My optimism and positive speech, however, were as shallow as my uncle's parting words, and they made no impression on my sisters. To break their immediate despair, I suggested that we retire to the nave to celebrate Terce. "The sooner we return to our routine of prayer, the stronger will we be in our arguments with the bishops," I said.

"We cannot," Covina said. "The monks have the basilica throughout the day. The priest says men and women cannot be in the same room at the same time or even lay eyes on each other. We say our prayers here or in our hut. We can only enter the areas of worship after they have said Vespers."

The irony of our situation hit me. Here we were, continuing to recite the liturgy and follow the rules of the same church that was belittling, ignoring, and mistreating us. We stood in silence, our faces pinched with hunger and the mental task of rationalizing our goal—independence—with our strategy to achieve it—obedience and ritual.

We returned to the dark hut and recited our prayers and Psalms without enthusiasm. A wave of sadness washed over me like a sickness. We were approaching the feast day of the Exaltation of the Cross, but instead of fasting before it, my sisters were barely getting enough to eat to stave off starvation. For the monks of the desert, those who lived in isolation and deprivation in wild stretches of sand and wind, the difference between asceticism and suicide was small. But for them, starvation was a choice.

After Terce, the sisters described their life of the last few weeks, focusing—for good reason—on food, or lack of it. When they first arrived, Basina said, cousins and siblings of sisters who had come from Tours and its surroundings donated baskets brimming with breads and cheeses, dried fruit, and even a little salty, dried meat once in a while. But as many of those women left the cloister to return to their families, the rations declined. For the past two months, they had little more than hard biscuits and sour beer. The priest was required by the church canons to provide sanctuary, but he did not interpret that to include sustenance. I wondered if he had been instructed by Bishop Gregory to ensure the nuns paid for their insurrection with a living martyrdom.

Before we came to Tours, I had been disappointed, shamed, starved, and isolated at the Holy Cross, but I had harbored hope that fairness would prevail, and the church would show us the compassion of Christ. Now, anger swelled in my bones, and my ears burned with it. We had given our lives to prayer and abstinence, but that meant nothing to these men. They demanded obedience—even subservience—on top of faith, ritual, and asceticism. It was more important to them to win this battle and break our spirits than to save Radegund's monastery.

If only the church leaders had shown us a little understanding, if the priests and bishops had listened to our stories, if they had made a few simple concessions to our comfort, everything might have ended differently. Instead, my anger grew over the next two weeks, and everything went wrong.

I have nothing to blame but my temper for the horrible sins that were about to be committed, and the blood that would be spilled.

TWENTY-THREE

We waited two more weeks in that miserable hut, and the mid-September feast passed us by, uncelebrated. Our only escape was to the nave for Compline after the monks' Vespers were over. The rest of the time we were either in our hut, or, if the weather was dry, at our table where we gnawed on the biscuits the few relatives were still willing to share with us, delivered by the monk who had opened the door when I first arrived. He dropped the basket outside the hut and knocked loudly so we would know it was there. We returned it empty and awaited its infrequent reappearance. Likewise, we left the bucket of urine and waste outside the door whenever it threatened to spill over, and I felt sorry for him for having to empty it. He appeared to get his revenge by not returning the empty bucket to us for hours and not rinsing it out between trips.

The priest never visited us, and we received no word from Bishop Gregory or my uncle. As miserable as we were, for the first week, we hung onto the hope that our self-imprisonment would end as soon as the bishops came to hear our grievances and announce their findings. But as we rotted in place, I began to understand their strategy: It was to ignore and outlast us. The longer they kept us in our wretched room and denied us basic sustenance, the sooner we would be happy to return to the monastery, Lebover or no Lebover.

Worry and speculation about the women who had left the basilica filled many of our hours. We knew so little of life on the outside of the basilica or outside the monastery. On our trek to Tours, the kingdom had appeared more deserted than I had expected. The few people we saw had looked as hungry and exhausted as we were, and the few inhabited huts we passed over three days of our walk were dilapidated and smaller than the shabby one my mother and I had lived in at the villa. What kind of life did the sisters who left us have?

"Why do you think none of them have come back?" Basina asked one night as we sat with our backs against the walls and our knees pulled up to our chests, waiting for sleep to put us out of our misery.

"Who would want to come back to this?" Covina asked, her voice shaded with derision. She and Basina were not getting along as well as I would have liked. I knew that Basina was not dependable; her moods shifted by the hour, and her commitment to our mission could run hot to cold and back in a matter of days. I sympathized with my cousin, knowing how difficult her childhood had been, but as a *bastardis* of royalty herself, Covina had survived as bad or worse treatment at home, and she was not as quick as I to give Basina slack.

"Murietta married a cousin and is with child," Greta announced. Besides me, she was the only one who could read and write anything but our liturgy. She received the few notes the departed sisters had left for us at the basilica door in the food baskets.

"We must pray for her," Merofled said. The others nodded. Childbirth was dangerous, and we all knew about as many women who had died from it as had lived through it. Even if the mothers survived, few of their children lived more than a couple of years.

"And she reports that Anderitia has fallen to desperation," Greta continued. "She is taking men outside the town walls as the church has forced the prostitutes off the streets." Did it ever tolerate them, I wondered. How little I knew about the world!

"What other ways are there for women?" Basina retorted. "Marriage is a death sentence. Prostitution is ridiculed and forced outside the walls. The clergy will no longer accept us, even those of us who want to pledge our lives to the church. And the cloister is unbearable." She expelled an angry snort.

She was right. It was the way it had always been in Gaul. My mother and grandmother had spun tales of a different life on the pasturelands of Thuringia, where men and women tended the livestock together, and women took part in village management, worshipped their own goddesses, and directed rituals. Those stories may have been improved by nostalgia, but here in Gaul, it could not have been more different. Men ran the church, they performed all the sacraments and led the liturgies, held all the municipal and territorial power, and blamed a woman—Eve—for not just the dangers and pain of childbirth, but for the fall of all of mankind. Women were to worship their God, read their Psalms, and obey their husbands.

But was it possible that our sisters had found something else? "Maybe there is hope for them," I said, unaware I had said it aloud. The twelve heads in the darkening room turned to me.

"What?" Basina grunted.

"Think of this," I said. "The church decreed that any of us who leaves the monastery faces excommunication, but so does anyone who assists them in escaping or living outside the cloister."

"Yes, that is *wonderful*," Basina said.

I recognized a heightened level of sarcasm from her now. But having no reason to argue with her, I continued, "If our sisters had any assistance in living on the outside, those people have lost their access to communion and, far more troubling, they have lost the promise of eternal life."

The others nodded, awaiting the point I was making. "Well, since our sisters have not returned, and I am certain they have not all turned to prostitution, they are getting help from someone. Perhaps Christianity is less pervasive in Gaul than we think. Perhaps many of our countrymen still hold onto the gods and rituals of our Germanic and Celtic ancestors. Maybe women still can find a place in the world out there."

My sisters drew in their breath audibly. "But, as heretics, they are condemned," Greta said. "They will spend eternity in hell. How is that a good thing?"

My face flushed hot as I realized my blunder. I had given the women a glimpse into my heart—into the doubts I had about the patriarchy inherited from the Hebrews and the salvation of mankind by Jesus's sacrifice. For years, I had been proficient at saying the right thing, expressing what sounded like true Christian devotion, even when I did not have faith behind my words. I had hidden my loyalty to my mother's beliefs as well as I had hidden the amulet that hung around my neck since my grandmother's visit. Now if they knew my truth, if they quit believing we were doing God's work by trying to save our monastery, if they believed I had a heretical purpose at heart, they would never follow me back to the Holy Cross, and I would have led them only to excommunication and humiliation.

All the women around me were full of faith, even bad-humored Basina. They had accepted cloister to avoid childbirth, bad marriages, murder, and starvation at the hands of their relatives, yes. But they also had pledged their lives to prayer and worship and were certain it would save their souls.

"True," I answered Greta, trying to recover from my mistake. "I only suggest that perhaps not all of our sisters have faced the ridicule and abuse we assume. Perhaps there are still parents and siblings who accept them and have welcomed them into their homes."

I heard Basina snort again, though with less enthusiasm this time. The others said nothing, and in the poisoned silence, they lay down and settled in for another miserable night on the cold dirt floor.

✝

I slept fitfully—even less than I had any night since returning to St. Martin's. I woke often and stared up toward the ceiling. I accepted that, by leading this rebellion, I had lost any chance I ever had of becoming the abbess at Holy Cross. In my tossing and turning on that cold floor in Tours, I also knew that if I lost this campaign to revive Holy Cross in Radegund's image, I would have proven myself unworthy of that leadership, as well. I was a bastard, an unbeliever, a heretic. Did I deserve any better?

I pledged to myself that I would not give up until I had won the monastery back for my sisters, even if I would no longer be allowed to stay there.

By morning, my sisters appeared to have forgiven or forgotten my heresy. I wondered if they all had experienced doubt at some point in the past three months as even Jesus had in the Garden of Gethsemane.

We waited another week for word from the bishops, the same as we had the week before. But our bodies—even mine, which had stored up plenty of fat during my stay with Guntram—were wasting away. My sisters' shoulders stuck up like those of skeletons, their flesh nothing more than a thin parchment hanging loose over their bones, and their backs had started to hunch in the manner of very old women.

I began to doubt a convocation of bishops would ever happen, but I waited until the end of my second week at St. Martin's to demand an audience with Gregory.

I had no parchment, no ink or quill with which to write a letter to the bishop. I had to talk to the priest, who had avoided us up until then. The only way to find him was to violate his prohibition of appearing with the monks at the celebration of one of the Hours.

I committed my trespass at Matins when no one, not even the most reverent among us, was fully awake. Back at the Holy Cross, we would have passed the Hour shuffling our feet, struggling to stay upright and awake, and murmuring verses with made-up words not even close to their original text. I could not imagine it would be any different for men.

It was easy to sneak into the procession that filed into the nave at the appointed hour. The monks' hoods covered their eyes as much as mine covered my face. My wool coat was the same dark-green wool as theirs, and although I was smaller than some, I was taller than the shortest of the brothers.

I hung back and followed the stragglers into the rear of the nave. As the Hour passed, I mouthed the Psalms and the prayers, not wanting to betray myself with my female voice, although I realized some of the younger men still carried the high pitch of prepubescence. I was more awake and energized than I had ever been at Matins, and my heart pounded in my chest at the possibility of being discovered.

As the Hour came to an end, I held back as the somnambulant monks shuffled out of the chapel and headed back to their dormitory behind the basilica. The priest waited at the altar for the brethren to leave before striding down the center aisle after them.

I stepped out and blocked his path. "Father, forgive me," I said, bowing my head. "I must speak with you."

"Who are you, young brother?" he asked. His voice was kind.

I foolishly took heart in this and pulled my hood back. "I am Sister Clotild of the Holy Cross. I must talk with you about King Guntram, my uncle, and his promise to call the bishops to hear our lament."

He stood a moment, his eyes first dancing with confusion before they turned hard and small. "How dare you pollute our Hours with your presence?" He hissed the words more than spoke them. "Get yourself and your dirty womanhood back to your hut. There is no meeting of the bishops and there never will be. Out now! Or I will eject the whole lot of you from these sacred grounds!"

TWENTY-FOUR

For the rest of that night, I could not sleep. I had told no one of my plans to infiltrate the monk's Matins and confront the priest. Perhaps I had a premonition that it would serve no purpose. But still, I had an obligation to tell my sisters that there would be no convocation of bishops, at least as far as the priest of St. Martin's knew. I waited until we were seated around our outdoor table breaking fast. We were chewing the hard biscuits left from our most recent basket of goods, and when it appeared that our jaws had exhausted themselves, even if our stomachs were still empty, I started my confession.

"I rose last night and confronted the priest of St. Martin's," I said. The sisters' hollow faces turned to me. Their sunken eyes and thinning hair had aged them by twenty years. They seemed as if they had expected my subterfuge. "I now believe we can expect no meeting of the bishops. My uncle's request has gone unheeded."

"But he is the king!" Greta crowed. "He has power over the bishops. They have to do his bidding."

"Apparently, the church is now stronger than the kings." I shrugged, and then regretted it. Looking indecisive, I would never motivate them. I pushed my shoulders back and raised my chin. "We will tell the bishop we want to return to Poitiers," I said, articulating the plan I had formed in the cold, dark hours of the morning. "He will think we have submitted to his demand to return to the Holy Cross. He may even provide us transport. When we get there, we will join our sisters at St. Hilary's. We will request sanctuary there, and with God's help, we will find a way to take back our beloved monastery."

"How?" Basina asked.

"That will be for God to decide," I said. I needed to convince my sisters that I was indeed a Christian who believed in God's ability to deliver us from evil. And before I responded more precisely, I had to figure out the answer to Basina's question.

Around me, there were sighs of resignation. My sisters had also figured out that the bishops' strategy was to ignore us and wait for us to disappear. We would be excommunicated, but our souls meant nothing to them. The anger I had repressed for the past few days returned, now more profoundly than ever. I clenched my fists under the table. My sisters doubted me, and the bishops were mocking us. But I had pledged to myself months before that the priests and bishops would not beat us into submission with starvation and deprivation. They would not succeed without a fight, I vowed. And I was now angry enough to fight.

At least half of the sisters were so weak from hunger and inactivity that I wondered if we could make the three-day trek, so I prayed the bishop would fall for our ruse and provide us with wagons. Staying at St. Martin's was no longer an option. We could either die staying there, or we could die on the road back to Poitiers. And after four months in this dirty, dank room, my sisters were desperate to get out.

I sent a message via the porter to Bishop Gregory, and he agreed to see me. I was received as before, and I sat across the long dark room from him. "We have decided to return to Poitiers," I announced. I had expected that, in his arrogance, he would believe he had won. The conversation was short—he offered no prayer or benediction—and I was back with my sisters in less than an hour.

The next morning, two wagons waited for us outside the basilica door before sunrise, and we headed for them with our blankets and a fresh batch of biscuits donated by the monks, who were delighted to see us leave. We had become an embarrassment to the entire diocese.

I stood at the back and helped the others mount the sides of the wagons as the drivers, respecting our modesty, sat on the forward benches and kept their faces turned away. As my sisters lifted their shifts to their knees, I saw their thin ankles covered with papery skin and the road-weary sandals on their dirty feet. Their linen shifts and undergarments had not been washed in months. I was not surprised that neither the bishop nor the priest had shown up to see us off. If they had, would they have felt any shame for our shabby appearance?

The wagons jerked forward, each propelled by a single, underfed horse that pulled at my heartstrings as hard as it pulled its load. We were underfed and poorly kept as well but were not forced to pull a heavy weight down a rutted road. Our burdens, by comparison, were mental, emotional, and spiritual.

My sisters were alert for the first couple of hours, chattering cheerfully and enjoying the soft, fresh wheat bread from the monks. Once the sun began to warm the air, we dozed, our heads

bobbing with the roll of the wagon wheels. The rough ride brutal-
ized our hips and shoulders but it promised to be shorter than
the walk we had endured. We ignored the passing of the Hours of
Lauds and Prime, but at Terce, we said our prayers and recited a
Psalm, then fell into silence. I decided to wait to discuss our plans
until we got closer to the monastery in Poitiers.

We stopped when the sun was at its apex and scrambled over
the wagon sides to relieve ourselves in a copse of oak trees. Looking
up at the brightly colored fall leaves, I thought of how trees, rocks,
springs, even fields of grass were sacred to my mother. *Natura*
was the supreme being in her view, and gods and goddesses were
merely meddlers in a benign natural world. These deities needed
to be placated and wooed, but it was nature she truly worshipped.

We rested for the night by the side of the road well after dark,
in a place where the horses could graze and drink from the stream.
We stretched out in rows on the floors of the wagons, cushioning
our aching joints with our blankets—the same scratchy woolens
we had dragged from Poitiers that were now our sole possessions
other than our ragged clothing. Whatever we had left behind
at the Holy Cross, we knew, would have been expropriated by
Lebover and her followers.

Midmorning the next day, I asked the drivers to stop at the
monastery where we had left Vivian three months prior. No one
answered when I knocked at the door, and so I slipped around the
small building to the churchyard and cemetery that lay behind it.
I stopped, and forgetting myself, gazed at the landscape spread
out before me. A long grassy meadow sloped down to dark woods
next to the river. I stood in the shade of the church, out of the
bright sun, and wished I did not have to get back in the wagon. I
felt my mother's presence surround me; I imagined her living in

a bucolic place like this before her kidnapping and delivery to my father's villa. In another time, perhaps, I could have had a peaceful life in such a country.

I remembered a chant she sang in our nighttime ceremonies in the villa garden.

As it once was, so is it now.
Women were here and everywhere.
They tied the hands of warriors and stopped the horde.
They will free their bonds and leave the enemy.

Would we break free of our bonds? Could we do that and stay at the mercy of the church? Or was my mother's song right: to escape, we would have to leave our enemy.

I did not plan to suggest such to the women back in the wagons. They were willing to overlook my heresy once, but asking them to reject their God and their faith was out of the question

I heard the wails before I returned to the sisters.

"It was the plague," Merofled muttered through tears as I leaned toward her for the news. "We should never have left Vivian here! This place is crawling with disease."

"We must move on quickly, then," I said as I watched the parish priest who had broken the news disappear back inside the church.

Each wagon took up the prayers for Vivian's release from purgatory. In our wagon, Covina led us as we recited the resurrection promise of Paul to the Corinthians:

We shall not all sleep, but we shall all be changed, in a moment, in the twinkling of an eye, at the last trumpet. For the trumpet will sound, and the dead will be raised imperishable, and we shall be changed.

The difference between the chant I had remembered from my

mother and this passage from the New Testament could not have been starker. In one, women saved themselves from bondage. In the other, we were called to patience—to wait for God to call us from our graves.

As we rode away, we fell into a sad silence. I was angry again at the Christians who had thrust us into this situation for the sake of dogma and dominance. We had entered the cloister to save ourselves, but life there was about rules and patriarchy and power, not the sanctity or intrinsic value of our souls.

I was so absorbed by my anger that it took me a moment to notice we had stopped. The driver in the wagon ahead of us was shouting at someone in the road. He jumped down from his perch and led two men back to me. "I think they want to talk to you," he said.

I tried to think how they might know me. Then I recognized the smaller man as one of the three who had threatened us on the road to Tours four months earlier.

He was the Christian who had crossed himself when he slipped into the woods.

TWENTY-FIVE

By the time we neared the gates of Poitiers midafternoon, I had turned the proposition presented by the two men on the road over in my mind several times. Before we resumed our journey that morning, I had planned to discuss with Covina a strategy I had developed overnight. But since the men's offer held the potential for a significant departure from our plan, I held off. I needed time to consider whether such allies would improve our chances of getting the monastery out from under Lebover, or whether they would doom it.

The wagons pulled up in front of the Holy Cross, and the drivers sat waiting for us to pour out. Believing we were voluntarily returning to the monastery, the bishop had not sent a message ahead for someone to ensure we would. As the sisters and I had discussed before we left Tours, we gathered beside the wagons until we were all assembled, then, instead of heading straight into the monastery, we turned and strode through the city gate into the deepening afternoon shadows to St. Hilary's basilica.

The news of our return had reached our ten sisters at St. Hilary's through Angelica, Covina's cousin, and so when we pounded on the basilica door, we were greeted by their outstretched arms. Their kisses and hugs were like an elixir, soothing our tired joints and relieving our broken hearts. After the joyful reunion, we gathered in the nave for celebration of the Hour of None. With no brethren monastery attached to the basilica, the women had not been quarantined as we were in Tours.

After the prayers and recitation, all of us gathered in the room that had been converted to a dormitory for the past four months.

"No one has left?" Merofled asked the nuns who had stayed in Poitiers.

"We knew you would return," said Gertruda, a tiny, ancient sister who had won the others' respect for her calm and her faith over the duration of their stay. "But where are the others?"

Basina told the story of their stay in Tours without sarcasm or spite. Then Gertruda followed with theirs. The nave of the basilica at St. Hilary's was available for the Hours whenever it was not being used for regular community worship services. Thanks to Angelica's generosity, not only had they been well fed, but they had cots to sleep on. Now that we had joined them, our number had swollen to twenty-two, but our spirits were so high, we cared little about how many beds we had.

"God will provide," said Greta. The difference in our mood was remarkable.

Between Vespers and Compline, we fashioned a circle with the cots and shared a meal of the bread and cheese, dried meat, fresh carrots, dried figs, and sweet wine the monks had given to us. Compared with what I had enjoyed at my uncle's house, it was modest fare, but compared to St. Martin's, it was a feast.

We laid down at the end of the evening with most of the

sisters situating themselves head-to-toe, two to a cot. I piled up a stack of blankets, and Covina and I slept on the floor, but even that was more comfortable than the floor in Tours.

As the snores of the older nuns rose around me, I thought over the encounter with the men on the road. Would I be foolish to call on them as allies? When we first met the three menacing men on the way to Tours, none of them spoke my Germanic language, but the large man the Christian brought to us on our way back from Tours did.

"We will help you," he had called out as he approached my wagon. I climbed down and faced the man, who was larger than anyone I had ever seen. My eyes landed halfway between his abdomen and his neck. With my head tilted back, I could see little other than his voluminous beard. I stepped backward to take in the rest of his face—startling blue eyes, protruding cheek bones, heavy eyebrows that matched his beard, and long, blond hair that he tied back into a tail with a leather strap. I rarely thought of men as handsome or not, but it struck me that he was a very good-looking barbarian. He made the lieutenant in my uncle's kitchen look feminine by contrast. I blushed at my thoughts. Caesarius's *Regula* barged its way into my conscience: *Let no concupiscence of the eyes for any man whatever arise in you at the instigation of the devil.* Was this what *concupiscence* felt like?

"What can you do to help us?" I asked brusquely, trying not to sound intimidated by his size nor impressed with his face.

He did not smile, but his voice was softer than I expected. "We know you have been persecuted by the Bishop Maroveus, and we want to help you."

I was surprised. Had rumors of our rebellion spread to barbarians like him? And if it had, how had this Christian man connected the reports about a group of rebellious nuns with our pilgrimage when we met his friends four months ago? We needed to get to Poitiers before dark, so I pushed those questions out of my mind. "What do you have against the bishop?" I asked.

"He excommunicated my brother," the big man said. "I am Alboin. My brother was Wulf."

"Was?"

"He threw himself on his sword after Maroveus cursed him. To Wulf, excommunication was worse than death."

"What did your brother do to bring—"

"That is not your concern," Alboin interrupted, his voice rising. He seemed quick-tempered, and I moved back a few steps, but he held out a hand as if to reassure me he meant no harm. "But I can bring many men. The bishop would have to bring a legion to resist us. If you want to gain control of your monastery, I can help you."

How did he know we wanted to gain control of our monastery?

"But do you not fear excommunication also?" I asked.

"No. I do not fear the bishops. I fear only the wrath of God if I do not avenge my brother's death."

I was not in my right mind or I never would have listened to Alboin then. But I was angry at the bishops and as angry about the death of Vivian as he was about his brother's. My desire for revenge had taken its place alongside my desire to get the Holy Cross back for my sisters. I had already decided that negotiating with the church—even with the kingdoms—would get us nowhere. The bishops expected us to play nice, and when we did, they simply ignored us. Perhaps our fame as rebellious nuns had spread, but it had not brought us any closer to a resolution. Neither my Uncle Guntram's kingdom of Burgundy nor my cousin Childebert's kingdom of Austrasia was going to accommodate our presence.

The church would not stop subjecting us to abuse because of our protest any more than it would accept women back into the clergy.

So far we had done little to inconvenience either the kings or the bishops in any significant way. Only Hilda and Angelica had done anything to help us, and the priest and monks at St. Martin's had offered nothing but the squalid room in which we were as good as imprisoned.

I held the big German's eyes and considered what he was suggesting. To bring many men to face a legion on our behalf implied fighting. I wanted no bloodshed. I had enough culpability for Marian's suicide and Vivian's death. More blood spilled for our cause was unlikely to turn our enemies into allies and was more likely to harden Maroveus's position.

But then, what did the bishops and kings understand other than war? They fought all their battles with swords and daggers, even those against their own brothers.

"What do you suggest your many men would do?" I asked.

"We would open the monastery's doors by force if necessary. We would remove the offensive abbess. We would resist any efforts by the bishop or the kings and counts to defend her."

"You mean to fight, then. You mean to accomplish this at the tip of a sword."

"Yes, Sister," Alboin replied. "A message delivered by the thrust of a sword is the only language this church understands. And it is the only language their political overlords understand."

I suppressed a laugh. He would be surprised at how much I, he, and the Bishop Gregory agreed on that point. And he was far more articulate than I would have expected.

My instinct was to immediately reject his offer. Engaging in any kind of violence would certainly cement the bishop's judgment of our wickedness. But perhaps the men, if their belligerence could be held in check, could prove useful in other ways. Whatever the case, I knew the middle of the road in the waning afternoon was no place for this discussion.

Alboin stuck out his chest and crossed his arms, as if his patience was wearing thin. "Do you refuse our assistance?"

"If you intend to be an ally and not an army, your offer of friendship intrigues me," I said. "But how do I reach you?"

☦

Later, as I lay on the pile of blankets we had carried across the countryside and back, I found little comfort in a possible alliance with Alboin and whoever did his bidding, even though I both hoped for and feared what our meeting had set in motion. We might hide in asylum at St. Hilary's until the earthly return of Christ for an answer from the bishops. I would be the equivalent of an abbess, but abbess of what? A group of aging and dying nuns with nothing but time on their hands—no texts to copy, no bread to bake, no vestments to embroider—and no support from the kings and bishops?

I tried to weigh that outcome against my goal to get my sisters back to their home, rid us of Maroveus's interference, and replace the evil Lebover with someone who had our welfare at heart—someone who would protect our relic and restore joy in our community. Even that felt like an empty aspiration now. I thought of the crippled and hungry peasants we had met on the road to Tours. How were we, crouching obediently in our monastery, doing Christ's bidding of tending to the sick and poor? How were we spreading His gospel?

We were only praying to save our own souls. Surely, I thought, a woman's life should amount to more than that.

TWENTY-SIX

When we rose for Lauds, I found some relief in the return to our routine. I looked around to see the haggard faces of my fellow pilgrims relaxing and rejoicing in the rhythms of the liturgy. It should have renewed my desire to strengthen my Christian faith but it reminded me instead that ritual as much as theology provided us this comfort. Just as it had done for my mother and grandmother in their worship of their gods and goddesses.

Shaking off those heretical thoughts, I followed the sisters who were now accustomed to life at St. Hilary's as we returned to sit on the cots and break fast with fresh bread and beer. The women chattered happily, old friends renewing their bonds. I mostly listened, the heavy questions of the night still on my mind.

After our meal, the sisters rested to await the Hour of Prime. Those who had traveled to Tours and back looked especially relieved to get back to the regular order of the days. I motioned for Covina and Basina to sit next to me. I had told them—and only them—about Alboin's offer of assistance, but not what I thought it would entail or how I was thinking about it. I wanted their counsel. "What are our options now?" I broke open the topic with the broadest possible question.

"We petition the bishops to hear our concerns," Basina said. "They have to hear us eventually." I was not surprised by how little her imagination allowed her to think beyond that. I loved her still but I included her in the conversation because of her close ties to our royal uncles and cousins, not for her strategic talent.

"Do you really expect that to happen?" Covina challenged her. "After all of this time, do you think they are finally going to, what, come to their senses?"

Basina blinked, and for a moment, I thought she might cry. But she pursed her lips and turned her head away from us.

Covina waved a hand at her dismissively and asked me, "What do you expect will happen?"

"If we petition the bishops again?"

"Yes."

"Nothing."

"That's what I think. We need to set a deadline for them. We need to threaten them with consequences for inaction."

"I am not going to be a part of this." Basina turned back to Covina, her eyes angry. She stood up to walk away. Covina caught her hand and pulled her back down on the cot.

"You already are a part of this, you little mouse," she said. "When you walked out that door with us, what did you expect? Did you think that if we left, if we broke cloister, the kings, the bishops, your precious uncles would come crawling to us and beg us to forgive them?"

"I thought . . ." Basina started. She closed her mouth in a

pout. Her expression was that of a petulant child, even though her face was aging more rapidly than I had noticed before.

"You are *not* thinking," Covina said. "That is the problem. You have been taught not to think. Recite, obey, behave. That is all you know."

"Covina," I said quietly, putting my hand on her arm. "We need each other now more than ever before. We must treat each other with love, not anger." I hardly recognized myself. Who was I kidding? I was the angriest person I knew. When had I started preaching love?

"I am not going to be loving if we stay here any longer," Covina retorted. I was surprised at how agitated she had become. She had seemed as pleased as anyone else at breakfast and at being back to our Hours.

"But we are comfortable here," Basina said. "We have food and cots. We can attend to our Hours."

"Is that enough for you?" I asked her. She shrank away from me. I wanted to calm her, not push her further into retreat. "I mean," I softened my voice, "we have nothing to do here. How can sitting here, eating, praying for our own souls, reciting Psalms . . . how can that be what God intended?"

"What do *you* think He intended?" She spat her words at me.

I paused for a moment, parsing my thoughts so I could say the right thing in the right tone. "I think He told us what He wanted. Through His son, Jesus, He told us. He wanted us to live honestly and sparingly, to give to those who have less than we do, to help those who need help. To pray for others, not just for ourselves. To be kind and judicious and generous. Even Gregory and Guntram say so in their sermons and speeches, although I see little evidence of it in their acts."

"Ha," Basina retorted. She lay back sideways on the cot, her neck bent sharply with her forehead resting against the wall.

I realized that what I had just said was more honest than all the homilies and prayers I had ever uttered. It was what I believed, but not necessarily what I had been taught. It had blossomed out of our experiences on the road, and out of seeing so much suffering, pain, and hunger. Whether God or Jesus, or the pagan goddess Frigga wanted us to spend our lives in prayer no longer mattered to me. I knew it was not what every peasant, slave, and servant wanted from us or their bishops and kings. At that point, I knew that the church and my heart had parted ways. My sisters, whose rock-solid faith had not been shaken by our travails, deserved my full commitment to finish what I had started, even if I could envision no final resolution for either myself and my desires, or for them and theirs.

✝

We had not been back a day when we received a letter from Bishop Maroveus, demanding our immediate return to the Holy Cross and submission to the rule of the abbess Lebover. If we did not return, we would be excommunicated and driven from the basilica by force. Sanctuary, he wrote, was for the faithful and penitent, not for those who persist in their crimes and disobedience.

Not believing it would make a difference, I nonetheless replied to Bishop Maroveus.

Your Excellency,
    We received your directive ordering us to return to the monastery and to place ourselves under the guidance

and rule of Lebover. However, that is not our intent, and you should not expect our compliance. We still demand what we demanded four months ago: the demotion of the licentious abbess; the removal of her male companion; the restoration of our right to choose our own abbess; and the cessation of your interference in the day-to-day operation of our monastery.

Thus started a vituperative exchange of recriminations, claims, and demands between us that stretched through the winter. Maroveus delivered in his second missive a copy of Radegund's Testament, which committed the monastery after her death to control by consensus of the region's bishops. I had copied it for Radegund myself. I knew she had sent my copies to Sigibert, Chilperic, and Guntram as well as to six bishops in Austrasia and Burgundy, including Gregory and Maroveus. But I read it differently. While Maroveus thought she meant that once her soul departed for its journey to heaven, the monastery's administration should come directly under his command, I interpreted her message as meaning: *Do not let Maroveus get his hands on my monastery*. And I told him as much.

We had exchanged three more communiques, each one more pointed and demanding, before I received a letter from Gregory, which I opened in front of the others after None. I scanned it quickly, instantly saddened by its contents. "Guntram has ordered the bishops to remove us from the basilica."

The sisters gasped, but Covina threw her hands on her hips and declared, "Let them come!"

The others turned to her, their eyes wide and mouths open.

"Let them come," she said. "They will rue the day they do. And they'll be sorry they warned us. We will be ready."

"What are you suggesting?" Greta asked. "That we fight them off?"

"Yes, exactly. With candlesticks and knives." Covina towered over the seated nuns and raised her arms theatrically. "We will be ready. We are hardy from our long pilgrimage, and we are no longer afraid of men in long robes."

Stunned, I said nothing for a moment.

Basina, however, spoke up, once again surprising me with her turnabout. "She is right!" Her voice started to waver even as it rose in volume. "We have been chased across this kingdom, given little sustenance and no sympathy. We will stand together and repel them." I had begun to worry about her sanity, and her quavering tone scared me. She had always been mercurial, but now she was vacillating between sanctimony and belligerence at a frightening pace.

Before I could decide what to say, the others chimed in, and pretty soon they were patting each other in solidarity and calling for bravery and fierceness. They were ready for battle!

Who was I to object? I was disappointed by my uncle's treason. His support on which I had gambled so promiscuously had not materialized, and the exchange of words between me and the bishops had led to no resolution either. "So let them come," I said. My agreement was drowned out by the din of their battle cries. I raised my arms and matched their shouts. "Let us get ready!"

☩

Despite their raucous call to arms, the sisters were nervous and slept intermittently and restlessly for the next few nights. Whispered prayers for assistance and forgiveness now filled the night air of the room where we slept, replacing the usual gossip and chatter. We had no idea when the bishops would arrive, so we took turns sitting on guard throughout the night.

We gathered weapons surreptitiously—candlesticks and rods from the sacristy, stools and other light pieces of furniture, anything that seemed heavy enough to inflict pain but light enough that we could hold it over our heads. We decided against hoarding knives as we did not want to draw anyone's blood and we assumed the bishops would not either. We stored the items behind curtains on either side of the nave and hoped that the priest would not miss them or locate our stash before we needed it. We had few of our own possessions to wield, other than our sandals, which we pledged we would use if the other tools failed us.

Although we readied for combat with the bishops, I held my grandmother's amulet in the palm of my hand at night and prayed to my mother's goddesses that it would not happen. I prayed that the bishops would enter, see our determination, and settle down to hear our complaints. I had little hope for that, but I prayed for it anyway.

I would never be the abbess of Holy Cross. Not now. Not after all that we had done and all I would be held responsible for. Now my only hope was that my sisters got our monastery back, and they could choose their next leader.

If it had been up to me, it would have been Covina.

T W E N T Y – S E V E N

The bishops came to eject us in the early evening a few days later, after we had held None and as we were gathering in the chapel for Compline. Their poor sense of timing worked to our advantage: it was too dark inside the chapel for them to see us, but our eyes had adjusted to the low light, and we knew the basilica better than they did.

Maroveus slammed through the front door with his usual bluster, which was our only warning that they had arrived. Five other bishops followed on his heels, unarmed, their hands folded before their robes, as if they were entering to join us in our prayer.

We jumped from our seats, as we had practiced in drills over the week, and dove for our stash behind the curtains. Huddling against the walls, we watched the bishops walk into the center of the nave and look around, their brows knitted in confusion.

"Sisters!" Maroveus shouted. "We are here by order of King Guntram to remove you to the monastery!"

"Go away or you will be chased away!" I called out, the signal to advance.

"Go! Go!" I heard Covina yell. The others chimed in. "Go, go, go, go!" I did not know if they were spurring themselves to battle or warning the bishops to leave, but the spontaneous cries set my heart pounding and propelled us forward.

The bishops stopped, and their hands flew up, guarding their faces as we advanced. We would have reached them in seconds, if they had not turned and run toward the door, their robes flapping behind them. They scrambled outside without one of our blows hitting its target. Their shouts called on God for protection, although some sounded much like taking the Lord's name in vain.

Twenty-two nuns crowded into the doorway, our jeers of triumph speeding their retreat. "Come back when you are ready to help us!" shouted Covina.

We continued to yell after them as they scrambled to gather their mounts. They tripped on rounded cobblestones, fell against their horses and pleaded with the Lord for rescue. More clumsy than skilled, they scrambled up onto their saddles and yanked the reins, pulling their startled horses toward the safety of the city gates. Godesigel, the archbishop of Bordeaux, took off in the wrong direction, heading directly toward the river. We laughed and pointed.

"We hope you know how to swim!" Basina taunted after him.

With the diminishing sound of hooves on stone, it was over. The battle had started and ended in minutes. We stood on the church step, watching the last of them disappear in the dusk, exclaiming our victory and embracing. Tears of relief, summoned by the terror of our own acts, poured down our faces.

"That seemed a little too easy," Covina said. The rest of us nodded. Were the bishops so unaccustomed to physical pain and fear that they were so easily frightened away? Had they not come a considerable distance—most of them anyway—to roust us? Now it seemed obvious they were so weak that they would rush back to their warm bishopric palaces for the rest of the winter and refuse to come back until spring would allow for much more pleasant journeys. We probably would not hear from them for at least three months.

Slowly, we turned and went back inside. We stowed our weapons behind the curtains and, wordless but smiling, we gathered in the nave. With shaking voices, we started our evening prayers.

✟

I knew that our victory in chasing the bishops from the church was hollow, and so did the others. The cheerful hours that followed the bishops' retreat were quickly followed by a cold silence, filled with the recognition that our war could only escalate. The priest of St. Hilary's had not come out of the rectory during the battle, and we had seen nothing of him since. He canceled all services in the church, and an acolyte posted a notice on the front door. If he had known how, I'm sure he would have ejected us. But if six bishops had failed to budge us from our sanctuary, neither could he.

One thing I did not have to worry about was whether the sisters would stay united in our rebellion through the cold winter. Even Basina was, at that point, still with us. I started planning our next move, and I knew it would not be another letter. The bishops would report back to Guntram and Childebert, and the kings could not ignore the humiliation we had caused them.

We passed the next few months in the basilica, which was by no means toasty, but we knew it was certainly warmer than the monastery. We resumed observing the Hours with dedication. Occasionally Bertie snuck a message out of the monastery to us, keeping us informed of the miserable conditions there and Lebover's frequent diatribes about us. From what they wrote, we knew there were many who considered breaking cloister and joining us in the basilica, but apparently, Lebover had appointed a new portress, after deciding not to trust Bertie anymore. Escape had become much more difficult.

As spring returned, our voices and spirits rose, and my sisters were more combative than before. One warm March day, we met in the nave after Lauds to plan our next move.

"What will the bishops do now that they can travel again?" Desmona asked. She was now usually the quietest of the group, and at times over the past year, I almost forgot she was with us, but our wild encounter with the bishops seemed to rouse an element of bellicosity even in her. I glanced at her tiny hands, the hands so skilled at illustrating our manuscripts, and wished she were somewhere else.

"My guess is that they will send soldiers next time," I said. "Sadly, I predict men with swords and daggers, perhaps torches and axes. I have no idea how an army plans to fight twenty women, especially nuns, but they will not be gentle."

"We need Alboin," Covina said from the back row, her voice carrying over the heads of the nuns in front of her. They turned with questioning looks on their faces.

"Who is Alboin?" Greta asked. Everyone turned back to me.

"Alboin," I said, pausing to parse my words. "Albion is a Christian we met on the road back from Poitiers."

"The one who stopped us?" another sister asked.

"Yes. He is angry about his brother's suicide. He thinks he was driven to it by Maroveus."

"No surprise, that!" said Basina.

I acknowledged her comment and continued. "He offered to help us get the monastery back."

"Well, why not? We should find him. Is he in Poitiers?" Greta asked.

"We know how to reach him, but violence is his only talent. We would have to accept that his way will be the way of the sword."

"And so would it be the way of the kings!" Covina said. "We cannot fight the kings' soldiers with candlesticks and sandals. It may be enough to chase off bishops, but not legions."

"Do you think the bishops will just escort us kindly back to the monastery, open the doors, and wish us well?" Basina joined in. "No. We are destined for the dungeons. They will never let us enter Holy Cross again."

I was not sure she was right, but her logic was good.

The anger I felt on the road back from Tours had subsided during our asylum at St. Hilary's, although it started to return with the arrival of the bishops. I could feel it building from a place low on my spine and, as it rose, tightening the muscles in my neck. I never imagined the rebellion I started would come to this: to making friends with mercenaries, with ruffians of the lowest orders, to bringing violence to our community. If only Lebover had been an honest and kind guardian of the Holy Cross. If only the bishops had been reasonable. If only my uncle had listened to me.

This was not what I wanted! One of the reasons I was in the monastery since my thirteenth year was to avoid this kind of ugliness. I knew that ours was a privileged, sheltered existence, and over the years, I never considered giving it up to face the dangers of the real, risky, violent world outside the cloister walls. But if it was what was necessary . . .

"What do you think, Sisters?" I asked the others and watched them turn their heads and look to each other. Slowly, they exchanged nods, and thus, built their consensus. I watched to see if anyone looked willing to voice dissent. I sought Basina's eyes, and when she looked back at me, she smiled and nodded.

I took a deep breath and nodded back. "It will be difficult, and I do not know if we can win, even with Alboin's help, but I will ask him to get our monastery back," I said. "We will have him remove Lebover, and once she is out, we will go back to the Holy Cross, just as the bishops have bid us to do."

"Good!" Covina stood. "Let us get ready to go back home!"

The others rose and left for our dormitory to eat our morning meal. I waited and followed behind them, my anger already dissipating in the face of our plan. Now I was more worried than angry, worried that we had turned a corner from rebellion to war, and I was certain it was a war we could not win. Alboin might recruit a few dozen ruffians to raise their swords and storm the monastery, but the kings had legions and legions. As with any war, it would come down to numbers in the end. Numbers of men, numbers of horses, numbers of swords. And those numbers were not stacked in our favor.

☩

Alboin came alone, which was a relief. I had feared he would show up at St. Hilary's with a phalanx of men with angry faces and rough manners who would intimidate the others. He wore pants and a belted tunic typical of the Germanic migrants who passed through Gaul, now unhindered by Roman troops and of little interest to Gaul's armies, busy as they were fighting each other.

His bare arms bore wide gold bands, and his feet were covered with leather boots.

Through messages delivered and retrieved by Angelica, I had summoned him to St. Hilary's. I did not know where he and his men were camping, but Angelica followed my instructions to leave my message with the local butcher and brewer, a Germani himself, one known to be capable of gutting a cow with one pull of its viscera and carrying a keg of beer on each shoulder without a stumble.

As it had happened out on the road, my body surprised me with its reaction to Alboin's presence. I had so little experience being in the company of any man who was not a relative, a poet, or a clergyman. I had come no closer to Lebover's brothers—the ones who had hopped around in our new bathing pool—than across the monastery's courtyard, and even then, I had covered my eyes and looked away. I knew of flirting, of course, and of the danger women faced in the presence of barbaric men, but I sensed neither of those things would concern me with Alboin. As I watched him walk down toward where I waited for him in the nave, I thought of our sisters in Tours, striking out into the world unprepared for unmediated encounters and unpredictable behaviors of men. How had they fared? Were they surviving? Suffering? Or worse? Much worse?

Alboin surprised me by kneeling and crossing himself before motioning for me to sit down on the floor with him. He must have noticed my puzzled look. "Yes, Sister," he said. "I am a Christian. But an Arian, which in your world is a heretic. I hope that does not cause you great fear."

It struck me that this would be Gregory's worst nightmare: an Arian, not just in his diocese, and not just in one of the great basilicas of the region but aiding us in our rebellion. Of all the heresies that Gregory despised and preached against, it was Arianism that got nearly all his attention. It was a matter of interpretation of the Trinity more than anything that separated Arianism from the Pope's church. But such matters had risen in such importance in our time that Arians were as feared and embattled as the pagans of my mother's Germanic tribes.

Alboin's heresy was none of my concern, as long as the other sisters never discovered it. I wanted to tell him I believed I was no better than he, paying homage as I did to the goddesses of my grandmother, but I had no desire to unveil any more of myself than was necessary. "The world is full of persons of many faiths," I said, which was as much as I had admitted to the sisters. That was enough.

"Have you decided to accept my offer?" he asked directly.

I was relieved to get down to business. "It depends on what you can do for us, and whether it suits our needs," I said.

He answered without hesitation. "I understand you want to depose the abbess, whom you feel has indulged in gluttony and avarice, and return to the monastery to renew your community. Is that not your aim?"

"How do you know this?" I asked. I tried not to notice the quickening of my heart at his clear, well-chosen words. This reaction to a secular man—probably a barbaric warrior, however well he spoke—was ill-timed. Distraction or attraction, whatever it was, could complicate, perhaps even sabotage, our mission.

"Your aunt Hilda was briefly married to Merovech," he said matter-of-factly. "I was one of the men who chose to fight for his honor and his rightful place in Chilperic's kingdom. But as you know, the lecherous Freda and her half-witted son won that battle. Merovech preferred to choose his own manner of death rather than leave himself to the mercy of that demoness."

"But how do you know so much about our struggle for control of the Holy Cross?"

"Many of us who were with Merovech have allied ourselves with Hilda's armies. Your aunt and I have shared loaves of bread and mugs of beer on many occasions."

And, I wondered, what else? I stopped my evil mind from entertaining that mean course of thought. I had no right to question Hilda's morality or behavior, or this man's, for that matter. "And your men?" I asked. "Are they all as fine spoken and familiar with my family?"

A crooked smile formed on his full lips as he shook his head. "No. Of course, you know that. They are warriors of Germanic tradition. They are men who have lived their lives on horses and in the woods. They live for battle; they die in battle. They want or know little else."

"But they follow you? They obey you? Are you the commander of these men?"

Alboin held my eyes, and then shook his head again.

"No?" I asked. Would he be so honest with me?

"They follow me. I am the son of a Germani king, long ago murdered by Chilperic's army, far east of the Rhine. The men followed me here," he said. "But they are rough men. They are unpredictable and ill-mannered. They are my greatest liability and yet my only asset. And I believe now they are yours as well."

My heart skipped heavily. I knew this without asking. If we engaged these men to help us, they would be avenging the death of Alboin's brother first and tending to our concerns second. They would be set loose on the monastery, and no man, not even one as poised and powerful as Alboin could control their worst impulses.

At least, he was being honest. And what other choice did we have? We were stymied at St. Hilary's. We did not have the muscle or the stomach for combat ourselves. If the bishops and kings sent legions to wrench us out of this basilica and lock us in dungeons, as Basina predicted, we would not be able to resist them. And it appeared that would happen.

I heaved a big sigh and sat back, crossing my arms. The specter of a messy battle killed whatever confusion I had felt in Alboin's presence. Now all I cared about was devising a plan of action.

"So where do we start?" I asked.

Alboin rewarded me with a toothy grin.

TWENTY-EIGHT

The next couple of days were odd with their incongruous mix of worship interspersed with preparations for our possibly violent return to the Holy Cross. We kept to our regular schedule of eight Hours of prayer daily, in part to keep the priest from suspecting a change in our plans, and partly to calm our own nerves. As incompatible as prayers and battle plans were, I was grateful for the balancing effect of the quiet, rote recitations and hymns. It was as if we excited ourselves with one and calmed ourselves with the other.

We had to move quickly. The kings would have little trouble pulling a legion together to attack and subdue a group of unarmed nuns.

Covina was put in charge of working with Angelica on the outside to locate a safe house where we would keep Lebover once Alboin's men entered the monastery and captured her. Once we returned to the monastery, Merofled and Veranda would immediately take stock of their prior domains—the larder and the kitchen—and put the nuns who had stayed behind on task, preventing them from engaging in sabotage. Desmona and Basina agreed to take over the portress's responsibilities together. Even if old Bertie were willing, we feared that barring the door would take on an entirely different meaning once we defied the bishops and the legions came to enforce order.

As dusk fell the evening before Alboin's men would enter the monastery and kidnap Lebover, we gathered for Vespers. We expected that by the time we were worshiping Compline, the monastery would be under Alboin's control, and we would start moving through the dark streets to our old beds and chapel.

Of course, it did not work out that way.

✟

The first indication that Alboin's men had encountered trouble came long before we saw or heard from them. We had expected them to return with Lebover by midnight. We waited in the nave, each of us praying our own silent appeals to God (and me to the goddesses), but as the hours grew toward dawn, our concentration wavered. We knew something had gone awry. We mumbled our theories and guesses about what was occurring little more than a kilometer away.

Finally, I could wait no longer. The sun was starting to spread its light through the dense morning fog when I put on my cloak, pulled up my hood, and slipped out the front door of the basilica. I had gone only a few steps up the street when I saw them coming.

I had never met Alboin's men, other than the small one who had brought him to us on the road from Tours, and I was startled at the sight of them. Nearly all as large as their leader, similarly bearded and long haired, they were dressed for battle. Thick leather and metal vests topped their tunics, and the daggers stuck in the lacings over their leggings glinted in the light of their torches. Twenty or so of them tramped up the street with drunken fury, shouting and singing in a language I did not know.

In the middle of their raucous crowd stumbled a nun, her hood pulled low over her face, shackled by the wrists, prodded from behind by men with sheathed swords.

Frantically, I waved my hands to stop the horde, and to my surprise, they slowed and stopped their noisy chant. I looked for Alboin, but he was not among the boisterous warriors. I walked quickly toward their captive, assuming it was Lebover, although this nun was too thin and too mobile to be the abbess we had left behind months before. The pack parted for me, and I reached out to uncover her head.

"Justina!"

The young sister looked up at me, a mixture of fury and fear in her eyes. "It is *you*!" she screamed. "You brought these evil animals to our door! Damn you, Clotild! Damn you and your disgusting horde!"

A shout rang out between us and the city gate. I looked around Justina and the brutes who had been prodding her from behind. A man ran toward us, shouting in the strange tongue of the men. As he grew closer, I recognized him.

"What have you done?" I yelled at Alboin. "This is not Lebover! Your idiots captured the prioress, not the abbess!"

Alboin caught up to us, and stood panting, his arms raised as if holding Thor's bolt over his head, ready to throw it down on his men. The anger in his eyes flew out over the gang, and I could feel their fear, though dampened as it was with beer. He yelled at the men, and one of them nodded, stepped forward, and cut through the rope binding Justina's hands. She stumbled backward, and before I could react, Alboin gestured at the city gate, and the entire horde ran toward it.

They were going back!

"What happened?" If Alboin was angry with his men, he had to see that I was far angrier with him. "They got Justina, not Lebover!"

"I know," he said. "I was securing the women in their dormitory, and when I came out to the chapel, I saw three nuns carrying the abbess to the altar. I realized my men's stupidity and came after them. I am going back."

"But what took so long?" I yelled after him. His footsteps retreated in the dim light of dawn, and I stood alone, furious and miserable.

I could not go back into the basilica with such horrible news. Instead, I waited. If Alboin was able to get the right nun this time, he would have to return up this same street. I would make sure it was Lebover and direct the men toward the safe house we had established for her just beyond the basilica. I wanted them nowhere near the church or my sisters.

I did not have to wait long before I heard them return through the thickening fog of morning, this time, more soberly. As they broke through the mist, Alboin in the lead, I gasped with horror. His tunic was covered in blood, and his hair had fallen from its tether, hanging in blood-wet clumps over his vest. He looked as wild as the barbarians of my childhood nightmares.

Alboin turned to stop the men in midstride. He walked toward me, and I shrunk back, stunned by the sight of him.

"You killed—" I choked out the words. Tears burst from my

eyes, and I covered my face with my hands, not wanting to see any more.

"Yes!" he said. "But it is not what you think. I had to kill one of my men. He raised his sword to cleave the abbess as she lay, partially hidden by the altar. I had to run my sword through him to stop him."

A picture of that brutal scene immediately filled my vision, and I sunk to my knees. "But my sisters?" I pleaded. "Tell me of my sisters."

"They were frightened, but they are safe."

"And Lebover?"

Alboin turned and pointed back to his gang. There were only about ten now, and four of them held Lebover by the ankles and arms. She was screaming the Lord's name, and it was not in prayer.

TWENTY-NINE

The only sisters who had met Alboin before that moment were Covina and Basina, and they had seen him at his best: bathed, dressed in regular peasant clothing, and with his hair tied back neatly. But when they saw him come into the chapel the morning after he and his men escorted Lebover to our safe house, he looked frightful, and their fear was as palpable as the smell of blood on his clothes.

"Can we now return to the monastery?" Covina asked, her voice shaking.

"I would advise that you wait for a day, at least," Alboin said.

"Why?"

Alboin looked pained. "I am afraid I have lost half of my men."

His manner frightened me. "What do you mean?" I asked.

"They left the city to camp nearby. They will not return to our village with me, and they will heed no order to stay away from the monastery. Once they saw the fine objects there, I could see the greed grow in their eyes. I fear they will return tonight to plunder."

"But the sisters!" I stood ready to run out the door to the monastery myself. I could not let those ruffians get their hands on the women still cloistered.

"Do not worry," Alboin said. "They are secure in the dormitory. There is nothing there that will satisfy that gluttonous horde. All they value is silver and gold."

But I did worry. After Alboin left to return to his camp north of Poitiers, satisfied that he had made some progress in avenging his brother's death, the sisters and I discussed returning to the Holy Cross despite his warning.

"But who are we to stand against brutes with swords and daggers?" Desmona pleaded with the others to wait until the next morning as Alboin had advised. I agreed. If the nuns at the monastery were blockaded in the dormitory, as Alboin said, then they would be safe. There were no windows for egress, and even if the horde set the little furniture we owned on fire, nothing much else could burn. The stone floors and walls would prevent the flames from entering the dormitory.

We suffered a restless afternoon nevertheless, and None failed to relieve our anxiety. I covered my head with a scarf, and with my face turned down, I walked briskly to the small wood house Angelica had secured for Lebover's imprisonment and knocked on the door.

The small peephole in the door opened, and Basina's steel-gray eye blinked at me. She stepped back and raised the timber that secured the door.

I stepped into the hut, and Basina dropped the heavy bolt in its socket. It took a few moments for my eyes to adjust to the dark of the damp room. Lebover sat in a chair against the wall, her girth even more impressive than when I had seen her last, nearly a half a year ago. There was no need to shackle her, I could see. She was not capable of moving her large body herself. I wondered if Justina and her male guest had been carrying her around whenever she wanted to join the Hours or supervise the nuns who remained in the cloister. Or perhaps she had just stayed in her bed, exercising her authority by barking orders and accepting reports from the prioress.

"You!" she hissed with spittle flying from her puffy lips. "You will rot in hell for this! There is no bishop or king in Gaul who will find justification for the ruin and death you have brought about!"

"God bless you too," I said, realizing as I did that my sarcasm was unlikely to register. I turned to Basina. "Have you had any trouble? Has anyone approached?"

"No," she replied. The tone in her voice worried me, and I saw her eyes meet with Lebover's. Would my unreliable cousin falter and let the bishop or his lackies rescue the abbess?

I hid my concern and turned away to survey their quarters. The hut was sparsely appointed with two cots in the corner, the chair Lebover more than covered, and a small table. The shutters on the windows were secured with metal rods. The only light came from a single candle that shared the table with a pitcher of water and a bowl. For a moment, I felt guilty for keeping Lebover in such a miserable prison. But it served her right—she who had so lavishly furnished her quarters at the Holy Cross with riches from our treasury—to finally live the cenobitic life the rest of us had endured for years. And it was still better than the smelly hut where my sisters had spent the months in Tours.

"We will send over bread and dried fruit for you as soon as I return to the church," I said to Basina. "I trust you will share some with your prisoner. But it looks as if she could benefit from some abstinence for a few days."

Lebover hissed again, this time without words. Her angry eyes were but slits in the folds of her face, the candlelight flickering off her dark pupils. It was evil, but I enjoyed seeing her misery. It had been her decision to conspire with Maroveus and turn our warm, loving community into a hellish monastery of austerity. Many times since her inauguration, I had thought I saw a glimmer of hope, a possible shred of humanity in her. But I had stopped looking for it.

As I walked back to the church, I thought about the relic at Holy Cross. If it was still there—if Lebover had not surrendered it to Maroveus already—would the ruffians leave it alone? I believed little of the superstitions that held that tiny pieces of the saints' bodies and Christ's cross were magical, capable of performing miracles, healing the sick, and bringing the dead back to life. But I understood its significance to my sisters, for whom the relic was a source of great pride.

As soon as I saw Covina in the basilica, I pulled her aside. "I am concerned about Basina," I said. "You know she has always been unpredictable. Her allegiances shift faster than the phases of the moon. I want to send a couple of sisters to guard her and Lebover, to make sure no one releases our captive until we are safely back in control of the Holy Cross."

Covina agreed and set out to the dormitory to choose two of the healthiest and strongest sisters to send to the safe house with food and beer. We would rescue them from their duties as soon as we secured the monastery and turned Lebover over to the bishop for his care.

The rest of us tried to put aside our worries for recitations of

Vespers and Compline. As we lay down for the night after our final Hour of the day, I made myself dizzy imagining the horrible scene conjured by Alboin's warning. I knew I was not the only one; the tension in the sleeping room was thick as fog. We skipped our regular night chatter and quieted our breath, our ears tuned to catch any sounds from outside the city wall.

Shortly after midnight, the ruckus began. There was crashing and splintering, the *whoosh* of flames, and the unintelligible shouts of men. We sat up on our cots and blankets, too afraid to move, and dreading what we would encounter in the morning. The noise settled down after only about an hour. I imagined whatever plunder the men aimed to achieve had not taken long. The clatter of wagon wheels on the cobblestones and the men's bellicose cries and laughter approached from the direction of the city gate, which they must have breached easily. For a few tense minutes, my heart pounded, as I feared they would extend their raid into our sanctuary at St. Hilary's, but they turned on the street in front of us and retreated toward the city center.

I had heard no women's screams, and I prayed to the Christian God and my grandmother's goddesses, begging to find my sisters safely barricaded in the dormitory in the morning.

We waited until the sky was bright enough to light our way, gathered our few belongings, and walked quietly into the street and out the city gate. I did not expect the bishop to call out his guards in response to the plundering in the night, given how little regard he had for the Holy Cross. And yet, as we turned the corner toward the monastery, I breathed a heavy sigh of relief at the empty road ahead of us.

My relief turned to horror as we approached the monastery. The heavy front door lay in jagged chunks and splinters of wood on the front step. The frame around the gaping hole where it should have been was charred, and detritus—rags, broken benches, and shattered pottery—from the night raid lay scattered in the road.

Where was Bertie, I wondered. I worried that her fragile body had been injured during the capture of Lebover. Alboin had mentioned no casualties among the nuns, but it would have been hard to tell, given the taciturn nature of nuns in pain and the chaos of the moment.

As we approached the facade of the Holy Cross, the nuns around me walked faster and finally ran with what seemed to be a mixture of fear for what they would find and jubilation to be home. I kept up with them, although I had long ago accepted that the Holy Cross could no longer be my home. My return was only for my sisters' sake, and soon, to ensure their survival, I would have to leave.

THIRTY

We poured through the broken door of the monastery and swarmed down the corridor to the dormitory, nearly tripping each other in our scramble.

"Sisters! We are here!"

"We are back!"

"Open up!"

"The men are gone!"

At first, the room behind the bolted door was deadly silent. Covina pounded on the wood. "It is me, Covina. I am here with the rest! Open up!"

As she said her name, a cry replied, and then several more joined it as the bolt creaked and the door cracked open. Six or seven heads leaned out toward us.

Shouts of joy filled the monastery as the door swung open and the women spilled out, their arms outstretched. Crowded into the narrow hall, we exchanged hugs and kisses. The nuns threw their arms around each other and danced, and others tumbled to the floor in mad reunion. I had as many tears in my eyes as the others; for me, they were tears of gratitude. We were being welcomed back, not as traitors or infidels, but as sisters of the Holy Cross. And Bertie, to my great relief, was alive and among them.

Our celebration was boisterous but short-lived. Once we had embraced, cried, and wiped our eyes, we made our way back to the chapel to see what damage the barbarians had done. The few benches we had were smashed to little more than slivers. The thieves had pulled away the altar cloth, taken the candlesticks, and ripped the crucifix off the wall. A jagged gash from an axe had left the altar in halves that balanced precariously against each other. A pitched cask from the storehouse had been dragged to the center of the room and set afire to light the plunder. It had burned itself out, leaving a charred hulk and a sooty stain on the ceiling.

As the sisters picked their way through the debris, stooping to gather up anything that looked worth saving, I headed for the kitchen with Veranda. The shelves that once held our dishes and mugs had been swiped bare. Only a few pewter mugs and plates that the men must have found too crude to carry away lay scattered on the floor. Axes had burst open sacks of flour and kegs of beer and cider, leaving a slippery mess that we tiptoed around. The vegetable bins lay splayed open and empty under our work counters.

Two of Veranda's assistants came into the kitchen, and I left them to begin cleaning what they could. I walked to Lebover's chambers and found Greta already picking through the broken mess.

"There is not much left," Greta mumbled. "They have taken everything of value. Whatever Lebover had taken from the sacristy or the treasury is gone."

"Have you checked the storage rooms yet?" I asked.

She shook her head. "I do not have the heart to look. But Merofled has gone to see what remains." I leaned forward, put my arms around her shoulders, and pulled her close. We stood silently, rocking slightly side to side. We had been through so much in this effort to reclaim Radegund's legacy. We had little to start with, but now, we had nothing but the blankets and cots of our dormitory.

I walked with Greta to the storeroom where a bewildered Merofled stood, hands on her hips. The shelves were empty, but it did not look as if that was due to the raid. I had expected to see split sacks of flour and barley and broken barrels of beer. It appeared as if the larder had been emptied long before we returned to Poitiers. What were the sisters surviving on? Now their joy at our arrival was making sense. I started to wonder if Maroveus was trying to starve the sisters out of the Holy Cross, in the same way Gregory had tried to rid St. Martin's of us at Tours. But why? Would acquiring the relic be so important to him that he would destroy a celebrated monastery?

"The relic!" I shouted. "Did they disturb the relic?"

Greta and Merofled took off before me, and we ran toward the crypt below the floor at the altar. Did the men have any idea what was there? Why would they?

I flew past the sisters and the rubble to the altar. "Come help!" I yelled. Covina and three other nuns joined us. Covina wielded a large piece of wood and together, we wedged it under one of the big stones in the floor to uncover the cavern that hid Radegund's cache. I shrunk to my knees and peered into the hole. The cement box holding the relic was undisturbed. I looked up and nodded. The others closed their eyes, relieved.

I worried what I would find in the little space where Desmona and I had once copied manuscripts, or in the infirmary, the treasury, and the sacristy, where the items used in worshipping the saints' days and celebrating the sacraments had once been kept. I found them as expected: the infirmary and manuscript room were undisturbed, but the sacristy and the treasury were empty.

I stood in the treasury and thought of the beautiful things our sisters had brought to the monastery as their price of entry. Now it was all gone, and we would have nothing to sell or trade to sustain ourselves.

I shuddered at the realization of the disgrace I had brought upon Radegund's monastery. But it had not been my doing alone. It had been Maroveus, Lebover, and I fighting to this horrible conclusion. We more than opposed each other. Our skirmish represented much bigger battles: the war against women in the church, a disagreement over the proper location for relics, a conflict over the role of bishops in female monasteries. And nothing had been settled, although much had been ruined.

As our search reached its conclusion, all of us gathered in the chapel for prayers, standing amidst the rubble. The first Psalm of Terce rose from our lips, and I closed my eyes and saw the chapel the way it was before, long before, with Agnes leading the Hour and Radegund up in front, her chin held high and a beatific smile on her face. The sisters standing in rows behind her, their voices strong and sure, their faces turned up to the crucifix over the altar.

Lebover was there too, thin as the rest of us back then, and next to her, Justina . . .

Wait! Where was Justina now!

I opened my eyes, and the words of the Psalm faded into a distant mumble as I tried to locate the prioress among the sisters. She was not there, I was certain. But I had seen her head back up the street after the men had removed her shackles. Where could she have gone?

There was only one place I could think of: to Bishop Maroveus. He would protect her, and probably send her to her uncle, Bishop Gregory. If it were not already obvious, I then knew that it would be a very short time before the bishops sent the legions to quell our rebellion.

I waited until the Hour was finished and then looked around to find Covina. We needed to think ahead. What would we do when the bishops' men arrived? Instead, a large figure moved into the open doorway, blocking nearly all of the light. The sisters around me gasped and rushed to the farthest corner.

I walked through the shattered chapel to the hulking figure and stopped with my arms folded across my chest in front of him. "Hello, Alboin," I said. "I hope you have come to help us clean up your mess."

THIRTY-ONE

Alboin was not well received at first.

"Sisters!" I commanded their attention. "Do not fear this man. He is here to help us. We cannot repair our door or our altar alone, and there is none other on whom we can call."

"But is he responsible for this?" one of the nuns cried out. I saw several of my fellow sisters point to the mess, in case he had missed the char, the broken furniture, the butchered altar.

"Yes," he said before I could answer. I was going to deny it, but I decided to let him explain what he meant. "My men, half of those who fought under me on behalf of Sigibert and Merovech, did not heed my orders. I failed as a leader and as a friend to you, and therefore I am responsible for this mess. I came to do what I can to repair the damage."

"And our valuables?" Greta spoke up. "Are you going to get them back?"

"I am certain they are well on their way to Burgundy or to the trading houses of the Huns by now," he said. "Humbly, I ask your forgiveness. Perhaps the good citizens of Poitiers will recognize your poverty and provide funds for replacing those things."

Greta sniffed. She had no more faith in the citizens of Poitiers than I did.

"I understand your anger," Alboin said, speaking directly to Greta. "I will do what I can."

It struck me that this rough warrior, returning to the scene of the crimes committed by his men, was more Christian than Maroveus or Gregory in that respect. He was helping us, whereas they would not. But they would think he was a sinner destined to burn in hell simply because, as an Arian, he disagreed with their theology.

Hearing no more arguments, he turned to me. "I will start with the door. You will be needing a strong barrier against the Count Macco and his mercenaries."

"Macco?" I asked. "Is it Macco they have assigned to subdue us?" I had not seen nor heard of the count since he arrived with Marian in tow the year before.

"Yes, he is Maroveus's count now," Alboin said, as he bent over to sort through the debris, picking out several large pieces of wood and collecting them in his arms. "Gregory and Childebert have put him in charge of the attack."

"Do you have any idea when he is coming?" I followed him to the front door where he dumped his load. I jumped as it crashed to the floor. Just thinking of our next battle set me on edge.

"I would expect them by tomorrow evening," he said. He turned back to the chapel for more wood.

I followed, full of questions and not knowing which he could answer. "Do you think we can hold them off?"

He stopped and looked over at the sisters, a few now busy collecting debris and piling it by the side door to the courtyard.

Others had headed to the kitchen or the stock room, and the other rooms that needed attention. "No." He bent and pulled a length of metal rod out from under a dirty cloth that looked like a torn sleeve of a man's tunic. "But if I could find a dozen of these, you could probably keep them from coming in the front door."

"But then they will come over the wall."

"Yes, they will."

I looked over my shoulder out the open door to the courtyard. The stone wall that separated my garden from the countryside was only about three meters tall, and less than a half-meter wide. A decently sized battering ram thrust into it by a half-dozen men could probably knock it over. "What chance do we have, then? Why even fix the door? Why not just let them in? 'Come on in, Count, say a prayer with us. Then haul us off to the dungeons.'"

"Because that is not how you do things," he said. I looked back to see him smiling down at me, his eyes seeking connection with mine. The intensity of his gaze froze my limbs.

"What do you mean? What do you know about how I do things?"

"You have come this far," he said, still smiling, "on guts and fearlessness. If I had been facing you instead of that murderous Freda out there on the battlefield, I might have surrendered." He paused. "For lots of reasons."

I ignored his last statement. Was he flirting with me right in the middle of this disaster? "I am not fearless," I said. I held out my hand. "Look! I tremble."

To that, he threw back his head, and his hearty laugh startled my sisters as it echoed off the chapel ceiling. He leaned forward and tilted his head toward mine. "Yes, but *why* are you trembling?" he said in a low, husky voice.

I had to get away from him and straighten out my head. I was not some young princess who could be won over by a flashy smile and a good pair of arms. I turned so quickly I nearly tripped over a heap of splintered wood and headed for the kitchen.

"So are you and 'Primi' Alboin plotting our deliverance or your elopement?" Merofled looked up from the floor she was sweeping and teased me as I walked in. He was no *primi*—a high officer in the Roman army—but I got her inference.

"What are you talking about?" My face was already hot, and now my ears burned as well.

"He is one handsome legionnaire," she said.

"And I am a nun," I retorted. "Let us not talk like this. We must get ready. Alboin says we should expect Count Macco and his mercenaries to arrive by tomorrow night. We have to figure this out. I want no more blood on our hands."

Merofled straightened up. "Maybe your *primi* has some weapons he can lend us."

I grimaced at her taunt but knew she was right. It was possible he could arm us with a few swords and axes, and perhaps we could hold the mercenaries off for a while. But, in the end, we could not win. I could imagine Covina wielding a sword in the face of a charging legion, but Desmona? None of us knew anything about fighting. I considered the possibility that instead of inflicting any wounds on the advancing soldiers, we would more likely cut off our own fingers and toes—or worse. I had backed us into a corner. What did I think would happen?

I walked across the monastery, looking for Covina, whom I found by the bath Lebover had built, the one her brothers and cousins had used. When she saw me approaching, she leaned against the tank and pulled off her sandals. Then she reached up and pulled off her shift. It took me a moment to realize what she was doing. She heaved herself up on the concrete tank wall in nothing but her undergarment and then dropped in.

"Oh! It is cold!" she screamed. "And wet!"

"What did you think?" I laughed at her.

"But it feels great. Come on in!" She threw handfuls of water at me.

I twisted to duck the splash and saw Alboin approaching. When he saw Covina, he turned and walked briskly away.

"Look, you are scaring him off! Get out of there. I need to talk with you. And I am not coming near you until you have dried off."

I followed Alboin back into the monastery. He stood with his arms on his hips, as if admiring the progress the sisters had made in cleaning up the debris. "I need your help with the door," he said. "You need to hold it while I reattach the hinges. But you need some help."

I found Greta coming out of the storeroom, just finished with her cleaning. After years of lifting sacks of lentils, barley, and flour, and kegs of beer and cider, I knew she was strong enough to hold up her end of the task. As we fell in step, I asked her about arming ourselves.

"I think we have to be prepared for everything" was her surprising answer. I had expected her to reject the idea, mainly because I was so certain it was foolhardy. "Perhaps we will not have to use them, but a sword in hand might limit our abuse."

I reached for her arm. "Is there any possible ending here that is positive?" I asked. I wanted someone to talk me out of my despair.

She said nothing for a moment, but I could tell she already knew the answer. She just did not know how to say it. "No," she said, with a simple finality. "None."

I nodded, and we walked out to the front and lifted the new door in place with Alboin.

THIRTY-TWO

An hour later, a wet-haired and rejuvenated Covina joined Greta, Merofled, and me at one of the dining tables, which had been spared by the raiders probably because of its monstrous size. Only half of the benches remained, but with our numbers now reduced to about thirty, they would accommodate us once we had food to eat. We had left Alboin to work on shoring up the storage shelves in the larder, in case we could find some supplies to load in there.

"Greta thinks we should ask Alboin for weapons to protect ourselves," I started.

"Yes!" Covina answered immediately. "Of course! Will he do it?"

"But wait," I said, holding out my hands, palms down to slow her. "Think about this a moment. Do any of us know how to use a sword? How many of us could lift an axe? How many of us would be able to thrust a dagger in someone's heart? That is something you must do up close, you know. It is not like shooting an arrow from across the room. And can any of you do that?"

Silence descended at the table. My sisters squinted their eyes as if looking for answers. No one had them.

"But if we do not arm ourselves, we might as well just unlock the door and sit and wait for them," Covina finally responded.

"She is right," Greta and Merofled answered in unison.

I eyed each of them, one at a time. Did they really know what this would be like? Had any of them ever seen a battle firsthand, let alone been in the middle of one? My heart sank, and I folded my hands on the table. "Well, then we had better start praying," I said. "We are going to need all the help we can get."

I stood up to find Alboin. At the door, I nearly ran into the two nuns we left to guard Basina and Lebover. They looked frightened, their eyes wild and their breath short. "The bishop . . ." one of them started but had to stop to catch her breath. "The bishop . . ." the other picked up her message, nearly as breathlessly. "The bishop came by and told us that if we do not release Lebover, he will not say Easter mass for the community . . . He told us to tell you . . . He sent us away. We came as fast as we can."

"Who is guarding Lebover?" I asked.

"Basina is with her," said one of them, her words tumbling out as fast as her breath would allow. "Should we go back?"

"Yes, and quickly! And tell the bishop his Easter mass is not our concern."

The nuns nodded and turned. I yelled after them, "And kill anyone who tries to free her!" I knew they would do no such thing, but I wanted them to know how important our captive was to reaching a resolution that was something less than total defeat.

They started to run back toward the front door of the monastery but they had to stop for lack of breath. They were in no condition for this, I thought. None of us were. How were we ever going to hold off a legion of Macco's army?

Now I had another worry. Basina was too unstable to be trusted alone with Lebover. I wondered if the bishop would have already spirited the two of them away before our guards got back. But I had other worries right then.

I found Alboin in the larder pounding a thick timber into place to return a shelf to level again. "Can you give us some weapons?" I asked, getting right to the point. "We need to have some way to protect ourselves."

He gave the wood a final whack with his fist. "I can," he said. "But what will you do with them?"

I shrugged. "I have no idea. But my sisters have followed me all this way into this war, and I will let them decide what our final battle will look like. It is their monastery, and they want to fight for it."

He pursed his lips and looked at me seriously. "Yes, I will bring some this afternoon. And then I will go back to my camp and pray that someday I will see you again. And that you will have two legs and two arms and a head that still sits on your shoulders."

"We cannot win this, can we?"

"You already know the answer," he said.

"It would be ironic, would it not, if we do not survive this? If we lose our heads fighting for a monastery that we will never be able to live in again?"

Alboin had only known me for a few days, but he understood. He nodded. "Do you want me to bring some men? We cannot hold them off forever but we could give them a fine battle."

"No." I shook my head vigorously. "This is our fight, however lopsided. Your presence will only make it worse. Our best hope is that they settle for a standstill, that they recognize our fight as hopeless. No one should die."

He stepped forward and pulled me against his wide chest. No man had done so since I sat in my father's lap. I did not lift my arms to embrace him, but I let him hold me, which was as much a violation of the *Regula* as anything I had done so far in this fight.

It felt nothing like sin, and at that moment, I let go of my allegiance to the church's code of morality. From then on, I would have to figure out my own path to redemption, and I would have to decide what redemption meant.

Before Alboin left, I had thought ahead, beyond the inevitable battle with Macco and the trial that would determine my fate afterward—assuming I lived through it.

"Do you still have spies within Freda's court?" I asked him.

"Of course." He smiled conspiratorially. "One of the six bodyguards who always attends to her is my man. And I have a few well-placed allies in her army as well."

"How would I find them if I need your help at some point in the future?"

"If you need my help, I will know," he said.

"Then I have another favor to ask of you."

He followed me to the altar and helped me lift the stone over the relic. It had taken three of us women using timbers as levers to lift it enough to peek in, but he removed it with ease. I reached down and opened the plaster box. I had only seen the splinter of the cross once, when Radegund had it installed by Bishop Gregory, but I knew which of the cloth bundles held its protective sleeve.

I pulled it out, carefully setting it on the floor, and Alboin replaced the lid on the box and set the stone back atop the crypt. I could feel Alboin's eyes on me as I unwrapped the cloth around the precious wood. I wondered if he believed in the power of relics, and if he knew that I did not.

"Why?" he asked, simply.

"I hold no hope for relics to heal or win battles, but my sisters do, and Macco's men probably do too," I said. "So perhaps it will tip the balance for us if it turns out we need it."

He knelt beside me and watched me lift the metal box out of the cloth and open it. The fragment looked unremarkable, and I touched it, surprised at my trepidation. If I had no faith in its power, why did it intimidate me? I wrapped the relic in the cloth and handed it to him. I stashed the metal box by the altar.

☩

When Alboin left that afternoon, the truth of our friendship struck me. The only way I would ever see him again would be if my life was in danger, and I needed to call on him. Otherwise, we had parted for the last time.

He returned a couple of hours later with two men, each carrying a collection of swords and axes wrapped in wool blankets. They dismounted and dropped their bundles on the front step, knocked loudly, and left.

Covina and I waited until they were out of sight, quickly gathered the weapons, and bolted the door. Only twenty of us planned to make the armed stand against Macco and his men. We discussed our plans—who would guard which door, and who would stand behind them to help if the men appeared intent on inflicting harm. I would stand by the altar, blocking access to the crypt, which the other nuns believed still held the relic. The older nuns would barricade themselves back in the dormitory, with

Desmona in charge. She would decide when to open the door to reveal our fate. We hoped the men would leave them alone—that perhaps they would not even know they were there.

Our twenty warriors gathered in the reception room in a wide circle and looked warily at the pile of weapons as if they were snakes that might come to life and jump up at any moment. I stepped forward and picked up a heavy sword. The late afternoon sunlight glinted off the long blade. Whoever owned it took pride in his possessions. I felt badly that he would lose it. "I hope that I never have to use this," I said as my sisters moved in to choose their arms. They held axes in two hands and tested their balance. Those who chose swords stepped away from our circle and practiced slicing the air in front of them, getting a feel for their heft. Little smiles replaced worry on their faces, but dread washed over me.

"I should have had one of these a long time ago!" Covina chortled. "Just think what I could have done to those cousins!"

I recognized her sentiment; I certainly was not the only young girl tormented by young cousins who were given free rein to insult and assault. The others swung their weapons around, relishing the *swoosh* and *whiz* of the metal through the air. I wondered if they were imagining the blades slashing into human flesh, or if they were blocking the purpose of these deadly instruments out of their minds. They were like children playing war games back in the yards of their childhood villas. It was all fun until—

"She has escaped!" A shout from the courtyard cut through the silliness. I dropped the sword back on the pile and ran through the chapel to unbolt the side door. The two nuns who we had left guarding the abbess spilled into the chapel, flushed and wide-eyed.

"What happened?" I asked as the others swarmed behind me.

"She must have been gone for hours!"

"What do you mean?"

The older nun was huffing, trying to catch her breath, but the younger one spit out the story between gasps for air. "We went back and took our posts . . . and waited. But then . . . we wondered why it was so quiet inside the hut . . . We thought maybe they were napping."

The circle of nuns around us grew tighter, everyone leaning in to catch her words.

"Finally, we knocked on the door. No one answered, and we realized it was unlocked. No one was there. It was empty!"

"Do you know where they went?"

"We stood there for a minute. I did not believe my own eyes," the older nun said, having finally caught her breath. "I turned, and the bishop was standing behind us, grinning."

Needing not another word, we knew the rest; it was clear what had happened. But she continued. "He said that Basina had come to realize her sins and asked Lebover for forgiveness. She stood by Lebover's side when the army commander Flavian came and took them both to Maroveus's palace."

"This had to be hours ago," I figured aloud, "when you two were here with the bishop's warning."

They nodded.

"And yet, he let you come back here?"

"Well, we are much tougher than he," one of the nuns said, finally catching her breath, and smiling with pride. "Each of us alone. I do not think he could have taken anyone anywhere without Flavian doing his work for him."

I thanked them and sent them to our cots to rest.

I should have expected Basina's defection. Lebover had probably reminded her of the danger she faced outside of the convent.

Certainly, her stepmother Freda would waste no time ordering her kidnapping and, quite likely, her murder. My cousin's temperament had always concerned me, but I thought that keeping her out of the monastery as we planned our defense and keeping two strong nuns to watch her would defuse her changeableness. I thought she would not cause much trouble if she was in the hut, as much a prisoner as Lebover.

I had been wrong about this, as I had been about so much.

THIRTY-THREE

The sisters and I held our last Hour just as the sun dropped below the tall chestnut trees outside the monastery wall. They threw their hearts into prayer, their voices ringing out and echoing off the walls in the bare chapel. I, however, felt like my heart was sitting somewhere low in my body, leaden and despondent.

After a quick meal of bread and cheese, a dozen nuns stood and wished us a safe and honorable battle. They followed Desmona to the dormitory, and we listened for the heavy thump of the big bolt dropping into its slot behind the door.

"Let us get ready," I said. "Get your weapons and take your places."

I wondered if this is what the real leaders of the kingdom's armies would have said heading into battle. I felt like an imposter, imitating something I had no wish to be, as we gathered our weapons and scattered to our posts.

We expected that some of Macco's men would attempt to break down the front door, while others would breach the wall and attack the less fortified side door off the courtyard. Covina had demanded to be front and center—right inside the door that would likely be breached first. I could see what kind of a fearless commander she would have been if she had been born male and taken up the military career she seemed to crave. She gave a battle whoop that rattled the rafters and made me jump.

As I settled into my place near the broken altar, directly over the crypt, I recalled that Alboin had told me that this was where they found Lebover, covered with an altar cloth. Perhaps she had believed the relic would protect her from Alboin's kidnappers. It had not worked for her, and I did not think it would work for me either, but from there, I could see how the battle unfolded, and hoped I would have the sense and power to stop it before it became a massacre.

I anticipated that the men would arrive before dark, to eliminate the advantage we had of knowing our space. They would need light to make their way around; in the dark they would stumble.

The wait was short.

The drumming of horse hooves on the road outside announced their arrival, and my heart jumped from my stomach into my throat. Moments later, someone pounded on the front door.

"We are here under orders of the kings of Austrasia and Burgundy!" I recognized Macco's voice. "Let us in now or we will break down this door and take you by force!"

"The abbess is with the bishop!" I hollered back. "Go to the palace and you will find her. You have no reason to come here."

I could hear voices commiserating outside. It sounded like there were dozens of men. They probably only needed a few to subdue us, but it sounded like a whole century.

"We are here to bring you to justice, not to chat with the abbess," Macco finally answered. I heard the men laugh heartily behind him.

"We are armed and ready!" I shouted. "You do not want the

blood of nuns on your hands. Leave now, and we will surrender to the bishop." Of course, we had no plans to do that, but I still hoped to avoid bloody combat.

The ensuing quiet was more frightening than Macco's shouts. I waited, holding my breath for his next move.

Shattering the silence, something pounded at the wall outside the courtyard on the other side of the garden. Within moments, I heard the wall give way to the battering ram and the cries of the invaders. I knew it was only moments before they would reach Covina and two other brave sisters inside the side door.

"They are coming!" Covina yelled, and she crouched with two hands grasping the battle axe in front of her. "I get the first blow!"

It took only three strikes of the battering ram to break the wood bolt and knock the small door from its hinges. Covina raised the axe over her head as a dozen men in metal vests poured through. Before she could lower it on the first man's head, his sword slashed at her hands. The heavy weapon fell and skittered across the stone floor. Blood gushed from her wrists. Men grabbed her bloody arms, pulling them back behind her. The two sisters beside her backed away, waving their swords before them, but the soldiers were undeterred. They advanced, knocking the swords out of the sisters' hands with their own weapons, and quickly retrieving them from the floor.

Several men ran to the front entry, pushed Greta aside with little effort, and punched her axe out of her hands. They threw the bolt up and pulled open the door. A handful of nuns closed in behind the men, and two or three of them managed to slash the bottoms of the men's tunics, but most of their blows ricocheted off the men's metal vests, accomplishing nothing but a sharp din of metal on metal.

Through the door, Macco marched forward with a dozen

men. He headed straight toward me as I stood waiting at the altar. My sisters pushed forward, slashing with their swords, but drawing no blood before the men slashed back. I saw Greta fall, and her head bleed profusely on the stone floor. Merofled's sword caught in the folds of a soldier's tunic, and laughing, he swung his sword at her, catching her arm solidly at the shoulder and nearly splitting it from her body.

Horrified, I yelled. "Stop! Stop in the name of Radegund! Stop!"

The men marched through, as a few more nuns came out of their hiding places to swing axes and swords, doing little to stop the men's advance into the chapel. A couple of soldiers turned on them, and blood ran down the women's arms and faces as swords met their unguarded flesh.

I watched with horror as the men stepped over the writhing bodies of my sisters on the floor. As he approached, Macco laughed in my face. I raised my sword, and he stopped, an evil grin stretching from one side of his battle helmet to the other.

"So we meet again, Sister," he said. "This time, you will not force me out the door. I have come to remove you and your rebel cohorts to the jail. You can come with all of your limbs intact, or you can lose some"—he turned to wave at the carnage behind him—"as your sisters have." He laughed again.

Just then, Covina, who had dropped to her knees in shock, pulled herself to her feet along the wall and charged at Macco with a cry that froze my blood. He turned and calmly waited until she nearly reached him. Then he raised his sword and ran it through her stomach. She shuddered to a stop, hatred streaming from her eyes even as a deathly grimace gripped her face. Macco pulled his dripping sword back to his side, and Covina collapsed in a huddle at his feet, face down in her own pooling blood.

Macco turned back to me, his face calm as if he had just stuck his weapon into a melon rather than a human being. "Enough?" he asked.

"Frigga," I answered with a cry to the goddess in my mother's tongue. "Save my sisters from this evil horde!" I reached behind me for the metal container I had stashed in the altar's broken supports and held it before me. "Stop this murderous advance, now!" I screamed at Macco. "As I hold the holy relic of the cross of Jesus Christ, this powerful remnant of your savior's suffering, I beg you to let me and my sisters live! We are royal princesses and cousins. Our kings will exact their revenge!"

Macco stopped and stared at the object in my hand. He seemed puzzled. Did he not know what it was? Was he so immersed in his military world that he knew nothing of the monastery he had just invaded? Then, without a flicker of warning, he swung his sword against mine, and I was knocked to the ground.

In just a few minutes, the battle was over, and the casualties were all on our side. I lay with the tip of Macco's blade at my throat and met his laugh with another prayer, one that summed up our purpose and our folly. "Frigga, cleanse this home now bloodied with our sacrifice, so my sisters may return to it in peace and communion."

The irony flooded over me. I pretended to hold the relic, so precious to the Christians who had ordered this attack, while I prayed to the goddesses of my mother and grandmother, the wife of Woden.

I had been stalled at a crossroads of faith for some time, unsure of which path I would take. But now I was certain. The guardian of my ancestors would be the goddess of my future.

THIRTY-FOUR

That was not the way the battle was recalled by Macco and the bishop later on. Neither did they agree with my recollection of the words I had spoken as I stood with the relic's container high above my head, calling on Macco to respect its power.

The men who have assumed the right to tell our story insist that my sisters and I were bloodthirsty and bellicose. But the blood that soaked into the mortar between the stones on the floor that day was that of my sisters, not soldiers. Merofled died on that floor. Covina fell as a warrior, the same fate she likely would have suffered if she had been born with a penis instead of a womb. Others were dragged outside, tied to stakes, mutilated, and beaten. I was taken away in shackles, unharmed but broken-hearted.

Less than a month after our battle, Bishop Gregory finally did what we wanted him to do all along: he gathered a convocation of his peers. But the assembled had not come to listen to our concerns about life at the Holy Cross and Lebover's perfidy.

Rather, it was to weigh our sins and pass judgment. This convocation consisted of the same bishops who could not be bothered to hear us until the bloody battle had taken its toll.

Basina, who had allied herself with Lebover through the bloody battle, escaped injury, but after realizing the carnage inflicted by Macco's men, she realigned her sympathies with us, and so was put on trial with me to face the bishops. I was grateful that none of the other sisters were called before this jury. But their punishment was far worse: death for two of my best friends, the loss of a limb for some, and for others, having to live under Lebover's punishing leadership for as long as she lived (which, it turned out, was not long).

We could not have faced a trio of judges any more biased against us than we did: Gregory and Maroveus, whose direct orders we had disobeyed, and Godesigel, the bishop who had ridden his horse into the river after we chased him out of St. Hilary's. I knew I had little hope for justice and so I decided to go into the proceedings humbly admitting I had sinned.

Our trial was held in the long hall of the bishop's palace in Poitiers, the grandeur of which, like the bishopric in Tours, had been paid for by my father. Basina chose to sit out the hearing in our prison, which was not a prison at all but the same rustic hut where we had kept Lebover, without putting up a defense. She told me she expected her "true" status as a royal daughter was all the defense she needed, making it clear that she was comparing her legitimacy with my lack of it.

I sat in my appointed chair where I could be viewed easily by all, as the bishops took seats on the benches borrowed for the occasion. The voices of the three judges echoed off the high ceiling of the chamber while they chatted amiably, as if they were there for a good meal instead of a trial. They had arranged themselves at a long table facing the gallery of bishops.

As the seats began to fill up, four men carried Lebover in on a litter and helped her slide her huge body onto one of the front benches. Following closely behind the litter, Macco and some of his lieutenants took their seats. Then there were two I did not recognize. But after I studied their faces, I realized one was Reoval, the diocese's chief physician, and the other, the man I had seen in Lebover's chamber, still dressed in a woman's robe.

Finally, Gregory stood to quiet the crowd, and the low roar of the audience subsided. He started by enumerating the charges against Basina and me, and then launched into his argument with a bishop's verbosity. "The scandal, which by the help of the devil, arose in the monastery at Poitiers led by Clotild and Basina. They seceded from the monastery with a large following of nuns."

I could not take his bombast seriously. If the devil was helping me, I thought, he was ineffective, if not useless—certainly not an entity these august men needed to worry about.

"Clotild was anxious for strife," the bishop continued, "having gathered to herself murderers, sorcerers, adulterers, run-away slaves, and men guilty of all other crimes. She gave them orders to break into the monastery at night and drag the abbess from it. Poor Abbess Lebover heard the uproar and asked to be carried to the chest containing the relic of the Holy Cross, for as you can see, she is painfully troubled with gout, thinking that she would be kept safe by their power."

Gregory calling the abbess "poor" made me want to snicker, but I remained still. I had not been "anxious" to fight, but leading my sisters out of the monastery and asking Alboin for weapons made it look that way.

"When the ruffians entered Holy Cross, they found the abbess laying over the cache of the relic. Thereupon one who was fiercer than the rest was about to cleave the abbess in two with his sword when he was given a knife stab by another. Divine providence aiding in this, I suppose."

It had been Alboin, not divine providence, who had saved Lebover by killing one of his own men. I looked at Lebover and saw tears running down her round cheeks. Was she reliving this frightful experience, was there actual remorse in her expression?

"The would-be murderer fell to the ground without fulfilling the vow he had foolishly made," the bishop continued with more flourish than necessary. "Meantime Justina, the prioress, and the other sisters had taken the cloth of the altar and covered the abbess with it.

"But the men with drawn swords and spears tore the nuns' clothes and almost crushed their hands and seized the prioress instead of the abbess, since it was dark. They pulled her robes off and tore her hair down and dragged her out with the intent of placing her under Clotild's guard at St. Hilary's church. But, as the dawn was coming on, they perceived that Justina was not the abbess, and they told her to return to the monastery. They returned then and seized the abbess and dragged her away."

A few of the bishops looked at me, and I hung my head with as much humility as I could muster.

Gregory called for a brief recess, and the gallery erupted with conversation. My heart was pounding, and I breathed deeply to slow it down. We were probably only halfway through the bishop's accusations, and I needed to remain calm.

☨

After ten minutes or so, Gregory quieted the crowd and picked up where he had left off. "At the next twilight, Clotild's army of criminals entered the monastery and when they found no candles to light, they took a cask from the storehouse which had been pitched and left to dry and set fire to it. They plundered the monastery, leaving only what they were unable to carry off."

At this, I could no longer hold my tongue. "Including all the loot that Lebover had collected for herself from our treasury and hid in her chamber!"

Gregory's head snapped in my direction, and he pounded his fist on the table. "You will speak only when I allow it! Until then, you will not interrupt me."

I stared back at him without as much as a nod. Lebover was now looking at the floor, the corners of her mouth turned down, as though embarrassed at the revelation of her larceny. Suddenly I felt another twinge of pity for her. Would she finally admit some of her own culpability in our rebellion?

After his eruption at me, Gregory continued, "This happened seven days before Easter. And as Bishop Maroveus was distressed at all this and could not calm this strife of the devil, he sent to Clotild, saying, 'Let the abbess go. Otherwise I will not celebrate the Lord's Easter festival, nor shall any receive baptism in this city. And if you refuse to let her go, I will call the citizens together and rescue her.'

"When he said this, Clotild appointed assassins, saying that anyone who tried to carry the abbess away from her imprisonment would be thrust with the sword at once."

Assassins? Was he referring to the two nuns who had been set to guard the safe house? They certainly had no weapons.

"Meanwhile, murders were being committed at the holy

Radegund's tomb, and certain persons were hacked to death in a disturbance in front of the very chest that contained the relic of the Holy Cross."

"What?" The word burst from my mouth. If there had been murders at Radegund's tomb, I knew nothing of it, and they had nothing to do with our rebellion.

"Sister!" Bishop Godesigel now yelled. "You will wait until we allow you to speak. If you are not quiet, we will remove you to the jail, where you can stay until we render judgment on these crimes."

Maroveus smirked.

Gregory nodded and resumed. "And since this madness increased daily because of Clotild's pride and continual murders and other deeds of violence were being done by her faction, she had become so swollen up with boastfulness that she looked down with lofty contempt upon her own cousin. Basina then repented and said she had done nothing wrong in supporting the haughty Clotild."

The bishop was embellishing and mixing up what had happened, but part of his story was true: that cousin of mine had changed sides more often in twenty-four hours than I had changed clothes in the twelve years I lived at the abbey.

"Afterward, scarcely a day passed without a murder, or an hour without a quarrel, or a moment without tears."

I looked around the chamber at the sober faces of the other bishops. I would have a chance to refute this fantastical tale, but would anyone listen? Gregory's story was growing with exaggerated blood and mayhem, padded with events far more vicious and more deaths than had occurred. I imagined he was already composing this narrative for inclusion in the histories he was authoring. It was an epic tale of evil versus good, his favorite scold.

"King Childebert heard of this," the bishop continued, "and

sent an embassy to King Guntram to propose that bishops of both kingdoms should meet and punish these actions in accordance with the canons. And King Childebert ordered my humble self to sit on this case."

Humble? Again, I fought back a snicker.

"But I would not come to Poitiers unless the rebellion was forcibly put down. A command was sent to Count Macco, who is present at these proceedings and can tell his story." He pointed across the chamber at the count. I was surprised to see Macco staring straight back at me, his arms crossed over his chest, and his chin tilted up with pride.

"He was ordered to put the rebellion down by force if the nuns would resist. Clotild heard of this and ordered her assassins to stand armed before the door of the oratory, thinking they would fight against Macco and resist with equal force."

Is this what Macco had told him? That it was Alboin's men, not the nuns, who battled the count?

"So it was necessary for the count to go there with armed men and to beat some of the nuns with clubs, and when they resisted, he had to attack and overwhelm them with the sword." Then came his most damning embellishment: "When Clotild saw this, she took the Lord's cross, the power of which she had before denounced, and said, 'I am a queen, daughter of one king and cousin of another. Do not harm me, lest a time may come for me to take vengeance on you.'

"But the count ignored this and rushed upon those who were resisting. He bound them, dragged them from the monastery, tied them to stakes, beat them fiercely, and cut off the hair of some, the hands of others, and in a good many cases, the ears and nose. The rebellion was crushed, and there was peace."

Finally, Gregory's fiction came to a close. It was time for

me to refute his nonsense, but I sensed it was hopeless. I would undoubtedly be condemned for all the bishop had alleged, regardless of how false it was. The only hope I had was that my royal blood, however little I had, would save my head. And if it did not, perhaps the Valkyries would.

☩

After Gregory's long story, the men rose to relieve themselves in the sanitary house behind the palace while I was required to stay seated under guard. There was nothing I could do except hope that my fortitude was strong enough to resist my body's natural inclinations and that the rest of the proceedings would pass quickly.

Lebover remained seated as well, as the effort to move was too great for her. She had avoided my eyes throughout Gregory's tale, and even after the crowd thinned out, she refused to look at me.

When my trial resumed, I was given a chance to repeat my complaints about Lebover's abuse of power and the poor treatment we had received at the monastery, although I held little hope that my story would matter. Maroveus knew what I would say, and he was prepared with witnesses to rebut it all.

As I stood in front of them, I could sense the bishops' lack of interest in my story. Whatever transitory sadness Lebover may have felt at my tales of her gluttony had ceased. She had regained her composure and now wore an expression of victimhood rather than guilt.

After I finished my defense, Gregory nodded to Maroveus, who started questioning me. "Why, Sister, did you so boldly depart contrary to the *Regula*, breaking the doors of the monastery, and breaking the community of nuns in two?"

"Because we could no longer endure the starvation, the lack of adequate dress, the punishments, and the sadness that Lebover had brought to our monastery." As I started to list our grievances once again, I gained confidence, and my voice easily carried to the back of the room. "The *Regula*, which you bishops confirmed as binding on the Holy Cross, commands the abbess to 'think constantly of the need for bodily nourishment,'" I quoted from memory.

I described our hunger, the cold rooms starved of fuel, the men who bathed in the tank that was meant for nuns in the infirmary, the games the abbess played in her chambers, the number of visitors she entertained without supervision, the dress that she had made for her niece out of a silk altar cloth, and the gold leaves from the treasury she had hung around her niece's neck.

Finally, I spoke of the most shameful of Lebover's sins: "She kept a man in the monastery who wore woman's clothes, although we all knew he was surely a man. He was with the abbess in her chambers at all times. There he is, in fact," I said, pointing to where he sat next to the physician.

The three bishops at the table bent their heads together and whispered, and when they had settled whatever matter concerned them, they motioned for me to return to my chair. I sat down, certain that I had changed no minds.

"The abbess may remain seated," Gregory announced. Given her gout and her girth, which bore witness to her gluttony, she could do little else. "Godesigel will seek your response to these accusations," he said.

The Archbishop of Bordeaux's first question made a mockery of the detail of my testimony. "What say you to all of this?"

Lebover glanced quickly in my direction. "The sister complains of starvation," she said. She motioned toward me, still fleshy from months at my uncle's house. "Obviously, they never endured too great a privation.

"As to the clothing, I suggest that if the bishops had examined their belongings before this sister brought the criminals to our cloister, they would have found the nuns had more than what was necessary." She would not accuse Alboin's men of stealing our clothing, would she?

"As for the bath, it was built in the time of Lent and it emitted a disagreeable smell from the limestone. I was concerned that it might do harm to bathers. In any case, it had been in common use by the servants through Lent and until Pentecost."

Lebover turned back to Godesigel. "As to the games I played, I had played those same games with Radegund, and it was not regarded as a sin at that time. There is no *Regula* nor canon that prohibits them."

Maroveus and Gregory, hearing this testimony, appeared to relax. If Lebover had an answer to each of my complaints, their determined judgment would be incontrovertible. They looked pleased.

"Now, regarding my niece," she continued. "I had received money for the behalf of her betrothal in the presence of the bishop. If this is a sin, I will ask forgiveness. To the charge of taking an altar cloth for my orphan niece's robe, let me call forth a witness who can impeach that charge."

Didimia, one of the nuns who had stayed in the monastery with Lebover rather than join our protest, stood up unsteadily. A member of a noble family—but not a royal one—she testified that she had given a silk robe to Lebover for her niece's dress.

Lebover continued, "The leaves of gold that Clotild referred to were purchased by me openly. They were not the property of the monastery at any time. You may ask Macco, who sits here with us. He handed twenty gold pieces to me from the girl's betrothed."

"And what of this man who the sister charges kept you company in your chambers?" the bishop asked.

"I knew nothing of this matter," she lied.

As if on cue, Reoval, the chief physician, cleared his throat officiously and gestured for permission to speak. Granted such, he waved his arm at the man who had entered the chamber with him. "This man, when he was a child, was diseased in the thigh and was so ill that his life was despaired of," Reoval said. "His mother went to the holy Radegund to request that he should have some attention. Radegund called me and bade me give what assistance I could. I castrated him in the way I had once seen physicians do in Constantinople and restored the boy in good health to his sorrowing mother." He turned to Lebover. "I am sure the abbess knows nothing of this matter." Her nod, however, indicated they had discussed the matter quite thoroughly.

Godesigel called the eunuch forward. "Come and tell us what truth you can," the bishop demanded.

The man in women's clothes stood up and hung his head so that his chin touched his chest. "I am indeed impotent and therefore put these clothes on," the eunuch mumbled. "But I do not know the abbess except by name. I have never spoken with her. And as I live more than forty miles from Poitiers, it is unlikely I have ever met the pious sister."

This contrived scene was such a blatant cover for the truth that I could not hold my temper. I turned toward Lebover. "So this is not your man? No matter. But what holiness is there in making men eunuchs and ordering them to live with you as if you were an empress?"

"Do you accuse the abbess of adultery?" Gregory shouted, cutting in on Godesigel's questioning. "Will you now say she also committed a murder or a sorcery or a capital crime for which she should be punished?"

"I have nothing more to say to this," I spat back. "I only know that the abbess has consistently acted contrary to the *Regula* in the matters I described. And yet it means nothing that the abbess was not harmed? That I steadily and forcefully demanded her safe transport and fair treatment?"

Gregory ignored me. "We will discuss these charges and will render our verdict quickly," he announced to the gathered holy men. "The prisoner will wait for the verdict, and the abbess is allowed to return to the monastery, where her leadership is sorely needed."

This dismissal, if I had had any doubts before, told me my fate was sealed. I should have stayed with Basina in the hut and saved my breath. In just a few hours, my future would be decided, and I had little reason to expect anything but the worst.

THIRTY-FIVE

The four men with the litter had just enough time to load Lebover and carry her away before Gregory read his verdict in the monotone of a dispassionate judge. He had taken less than ten minutes to write his decision, which I believe was proof that he had composed it before the "trial" had even begun.

"We have discussed these charges brought against the Sisters Clotild and Basina of the Monastery of the Holy Cross, and in God's name, we issue our verdict," Gregory announced.

I sat with as stoic an expression as I could muster. I imagined the bishops would love to see me squirm and I did not want to reward them.

"We have found no wrongdoing for which to degrade the abbess but we have expressed our concern for her pardonable faults and urge her to not return to any of the questionable activities she has been accused of here in this chamber. She has promised to bow her head and do whatever penance we demand." The bishop then glanced up at me. Seeing my steady face, he reproached me without looking at his paper. "We asked ourselves in our deliberations who had committed greater crimes? That is to say, who had despised the warning of their bishop not to go forth and had left the monastery under the greatest contempt, involving other nuns in their sin?" He turned back to his written decision. "It is most just that until the sisters Clotild and Basina make a suitable repentance, they shall be excommunicated, and the abbess shall continue permanently in her place."

He looked up to gauge my response. I gave none. "As to the property of the monastery and the deeds given by the kings, your kinsmen, which have been stolen and which you possess but disregard our orders and fail to return—"

"I have taken nothing, and I have nothing!" I interrupted. "Not even a comb. I have no home, no property. I cannot hide the monastery's furniture or all the fine chalices and candlesticks that Lebover had hoarded in her room. I, the daughter of a king, the poor relative of another, have nothing to call my own but the shift on my body and my filthy undergarment."

His eyes threw daggers of anger. "You must surrender that relic of the most holy and sacred cross, which you secretly and wrongfully stole from its safekeeping!"

"Where do you think I have stashed it?" I held out my arms with a shrug as I feigned confusion. I patted down my torso and dropped my hands to my sides. "Ask Macco what happened to it when he and his men threw me to the ground and shackled me."

The bishop only returned to his declaration. "To the kings, your kinsmen, we say, 'Do not permit them to return or think of returning again to the place which they so impiously and sacrilegiously destroyed, lest worse may come.'"

✝

Two guards from the bishop's palace walked me back to the hut where Basina was staying, and as we watched, they pulled the blankets off our narrow cots and shook them out, looking for our stolen treasure.

"I told the bishops I have nothing," I said. "Neither does Basina. We have been living as nuns."

The men's faces were taciturn as they searched our cloaks, the only other possessions we had, and then left, locking the door from the outside with the bolt that had been installed just for us. Hearing the bolt drop into the slot, I secured the door from the inside as well and turned to Basina.

"We are excommunicated," I said. My news, as I expected, was no surprise to her either. "They are coming to get us tomorrow to take us to the palace of our cousin, King Childebert, in Paris. They told us to pack our belongings." I laughed half-heartedly and gestured at the empty room around us. "I guess they did not believe me."

Basina stood in the semidarkness, expressionless, as if she heard nothing. Her shoulders slumped forward, giving her gaunt frame a tormented aspect. Her arms hung listlessly at her sides. I pulled her into a hug like Alboin had done before Macco's attack, but I doubted she felt as much comfort in my embrace as I did in his.

"They are bringing us a little food," I said as we finally pulled apart. "And then, I guess we will say our prayers and try to sleep. It is likely to be a difficult journey." The Christian prayers would be for her sake. I no longer expected anyone to hear mine, and if someone did, that omniscient deity would know I had already come to reject Him.

Once we ate the biscuits and drank the beer a servant brought to our door, we lay down on our cots. I started reciting the Vespers prayers and Psalms, expecting Basina to join in. But she uttered no sound, and I quit after the first prayer. I curled up under my blanket and silently said my prayers to Frigga. Instead of asking for anything, I simply acknowledged her presence and the meaning her throne brought to all women—prostitutes, virgins, and mothers alike.

I awoke by habit at the hour of Matins, but instead of waking Basina, I lay still and considered our prospects. I felt optimistic, despite my meager circumstances. Hilda would probably be at Childebert's palace or would arrive soon after she knew we were there. But what would I do with my life? My only roles in this world had been as a bastard daughter of a king, and a nun. With my father dead, and his kingdom absorbed into my uncle's, I had no claim to any title. My only chance at a fulfilling life had been as a leader of the monastery, and that was now no chance at all.

I was nearly thirty years old, and motherhood seemed unlikely. Prostitution or servitude was not necessarily below my station, *bastardis* that I was, but I had no appetite for either. And I had none of the skills required. The only things I was good at were raising herbs and vegetables, reading, and copying manuscripts. The first was a skill nearly every woman without royal privilege in the kingdom had; the second was only a pastime, not a profession; and the third was available only to nuns in monasteries. Who knew how long any nun would be allowed to pursue that vocation?

I heard Basina snoring quietly and decided not to wake her. For a woman with as few prospects as mine—and with a murderous stepmother likely stalking her—she managed to sleep well.

The count's guards who were assigned to escort us to Paris banged on our door just as the dawn started to brighten the highest leaves on the chestnut trees above the basilica complex. We had nothing to pack. We folded our blankets into a tidy bundle, donned our cloaks, and stepped up into the bed of the wagon. We did our best to make ourselves comfortable, but I knew, after two long wagon trips across the kingdom, that the ride would be brutal.

We rode over the jarring ruts past the city gate and then turned north on the road we had followed on our walk to Tours. By the time we were out of sight of the city, the day was bright. Crisp fall air made for a perfect blue sky, and the trees and shrubbery along the side of the road were shedding their leaves in a flurry of color. Farmers in the fields slashed at golden stalks of grain, shouting insults as crows and sparrows darted down to steal whatever seeds fell to the ground.

I remembered the story of Radegund's escape from the soldiers who had come to tear her away from the religious life she had chosen and return her to Clothar. As the story went, she passed a farmer planting oats in his field, and as the soldiers approached, the oats miraculously burst to their mature height, providing her with cover that allowed her to elude them.

I had no faith in such miracles anymore. I did not believe any godly creatures intervened in the world where we lived. But I thought it was a lovely story, merging agrarian prowess with a woman's strong will to do with her life what she wished. I hoped such a fate awaited me.

As we bounced north over the rutted road in the chill of the morning, Basina began to shake herself out of her torpor. She mumbled at first about being cold and about the rough road, but as the day warmed, she stopped complaining and stared wide-eyed at the green of the landscape and the purple line on the horizon of the distant mountains.

Still, she did not speak. My efforts to engage her in "what

now" speculation were met with a stony stare. Either she did not care, or she did not think she had a future. Either seemed perfectly rational, given our situation.

We stopped after a few hours so that the driver and the guards could relieve themselves. The guards tied their horses to the wheels of the wagon, and the driver hopped down without a word to us. I was hoping for some assistance in getting down from the wagon, but the men seemed unaware that we also had bladders. They disappeared into the woods. I threw my legs over the side of the wagon and jumped down, relieved that I had not twisted or jarred a limb in the process. I reached a hand up to Basina and helped her to the ground.

As I turned to lead her into the shade of the trees, I thought I glimpsed something on the road ahead. I stopped and stepped back to look again but saw nothing. It was probably the quivering shadows of the trees, I told myself. But my heart beat fast and hard, and as we climbed back into the wagon and the driver shouted at the dray to pull us forward again, it continued to thump in my chest.

"Halt!" A minute later, my phantom materialized in human form. A man stood in front of us on the road, his arms stretched out as if to block the bulk of our party.

"Who says so?" the driver shouted back.

"The royal guard of Queen Fredegund!" And just then, four burly barbarians joined him on the road.

There was no announcement more frightening for my dear cousin. Hearing the name of her vindictive and murderous stepmother, she crouched in the wagon and exhaled a high-pitched, pitiful whine.

THIRTY-SIX

Our guards put up no resistance to the five men sent by Freda to kidnap us. Instead, they agreed that we should all retire for the night to a nearby villa, vacated by its owners some time before, and now used by military men of all allegiances when it was convenient. There, they would discuss our fate. Their quick camaraderie raised my suspicions; the count's guards were only too happy to go along, and, fortified with a cask of beer carried by Freda's men, they settled into a jolly evening of dice and drinking. Even our wagoner joined them.

Basina and I sat just inside the door, strapped to chairs with rough twine, a few feet from the filthy table where the men gathered. Someone had started a fire in the hearth, which at first filled the long room with so much smoke they had to open the door behind us, which sucked out any heat and froze our backsides. Finally, the chimney started to draw, and the smoke cleared. But across the long room from the fire, we felt none of its benefit.

Basina shook with cold and, I had to imagine, fear. Some of

these men could have been the ones who had raped her at Freda's command years ago, although she probably did not remember their faces. The mind has a way of blocking out such memories. I had no idea how to comfort her. I realized I could no longer comfort either of us with my thoughts and I wished I still believed in Christian prayer.

As tears came to my eyes, I listened to the men joke and jab at each other in the same dialect that my father and his brothers, including Freda's husband, Chilperic, had spoken. I expected they would discuss their plans for us, but they guzzled their beer, threw dice, gnawed on tough strips of dried meat, and seemed to have forgotten about us.

I leaned a little closer to Basina and whispered. "They seem oddly aligned. Does this make you wonder who our guards really are?"

"I have to get back to the monastery," Basina hissed at me in Latin, ignoring my question. "It is the only place I will ever be safe."

"You would have to confess to sins you have not committed," I said, also in the Roman tongue. "And the bishop may not allow it."

"If I am not there, Freda will kill me long before I am married. You know that."

I nodded. She was right. The Holy Cross was her only refuge. Still there was no certainty she could get back in, even if she did what the bishops asked. My heart sunk lower. "Lebover could eject you again," I said. "She has no reason to embrace you. And clearly, her tenure is secure. If she can remain abbess in spite of all that she has done, she can make you suffer until she dies."

"I have sinned!" Basina grimaced with anger. "And there is no other place where Freda will not get to me."

Raucous laughter interrupted us. "Which one will you

choose?" one of Freda's men asked the others loudly. He jerked his head in our direction. "If, perchance, you eventually win a game?"

I blanched. I wanted to believe they were joking. Surely, they would not be allowed to rape us right in front of the count's guards. I glanced at Basina; her face was drained of its color. She looked at me, her eyes wide open and full of tears. She blinked a stream down her face and a high-pitched cry escaped her throat.

"Aw, stop that! You frighten the poor girl!" said one of the count's guards. "She is probably afraid you will choose the tall one instead of her." He laughed and shook the dice in his hand and spilled them across the table.

"She should be scared," Freda's man said. "And I should win!"

I studied Freda's five men. One of them seemed to be drinking very little but was apparently just as drunk as the others. How could a man his size become inebriated so easily? He disgusted me even more than the others for his weakness.

I closed my eyes and prayed to the goddess Frigga. Basina wept quietly, now stifling her sobs. In spite of her wavering loyalties of the past few months, I cared for her more than anyone else. She was more a sister to me than my own half sisters were, and other than Covina—poor Covina!—closer than any of the other monastery sisters had been.

The memory of Covina's collapse at the stab of a sword, of her blood spurting from her body, flashed before me. Why did my treasonous mind fixate on that image when I was already as vulnerable, both physically and emotionally, as I had ever been? She was so much like me, in both her courage and foolishness. However wrong it was, I wished she were sitting next to me, rather than Basina. She would have ideas. She would be brave and obstinate. I would be stronger for being in her presence.

The party at the table continued. Despite my uncomfortable chair, the men's laughter, and my fear, I eventually nodded off. Occasionally, my head bobbed violently, waking me up, but I fell back into a dreamless, exhausted sleep.

Then, someone grabbed my breasts roughly, jerking me awake. I screamed with pain. I opened my eyes to a huge, bearded man blowing his alcohol-laden breath in my face.

He growled. "We are going to have a little fun, Sister," he said, his nearly toothless grin writhing with mirth. "I'm going to untie you, and you will be grateful and do as I say."

I looked over at Basina, who had fallen asleep beside me. My shriek had not woken her, and her chin rested on her chest. She snored sweetly.

The man slapped my chin back to face him. "Not her!" he laughed quietly. "I know she is not a virgin. I had her a long time ago. It is you I want. I want to make you bleed."

With his knife, the man cut through the twine around my waist in one quick flick of his wrist. He held me down on my chair with his free hand. I looked around him and saw the rest of the men slumped at the table, the rattles of their snores indicating the depth of their drunkenness. My protests would never wake them, and even if they could, they might only encourage them to join in the "fun" my attacker promised.

My heart thumping in my chest, I took in a deep breath, ready to scream again, thinking that Basina might awaken and work her way free from her ropes to help me. But if she did, she would witness something that would only bring back painful memories. Instead, I leaned forward and bit the hand that held the knife as forcefully as I could.

"Bitch!" the man yelled as the blade clattered to the floor.

He shook his arm wildly, and blood splattered onto my face. He slapped me with his wounded hand, and I fell sideways onto the floor, my face scraping the cold dirt. I spit out a broken tooth and tasted blood, but it was his knee pressed into my back that hurt the worst.

Then with his hand on the back of my head, the brute smashed my forehead against the ground, and the world went dark.

☩

The crash of splintering timbers and shattering plaster woke me.

I was lying on my stomach, the skirts of my shift and cloak shoved up to the middle of my back, the cold air rushing across my bottom. I struggled to turn over and sit, but my arms were too weak to support me.

I turned my head under my shoulder to see the wide wood door fall onto the dirt floor and chunks of the wall disintegrate to powder under the rushing feet of a dozen men, their faces obscured by a cloud of white dust. The men at the table woke with a start. They lifted their heads from their arms and looked around, bewilderment distorting their faces.

"Do not reach for your swords or you will be cut down where you sit!" I recognized Alboin's voice, and a cheer rose from my throat without my summons.

He was over me in an instant, pulling my clothes down over my legs and lifting me to my feet. I fell against him. I saw the man who had attacked me lying on the ground, his hand in his pants and his throat sliced. His blood had already stopped flowing, and a dark stain of it had soaked into the dirt.

Alboin covered my eyes and handed me to the man I had

thought a weak drinker, who picked me up like I was a piece of parchment and carried me out the door. He set me down on a large stone and went back inside.

Where was Basina? I tried to stand up to find her, but my legs failed me. How hard had I struggled against that brute? I fell back down as Alboin emerged with Basina over his shoulder. He set her down beside me and turned back to the house.

Basina cowered, shrinking away from the scene. I gathered her to me and held her as tightly as my weary limbs would allow. "Do not worry," I said. "We are safe now. It is our ally, Alboin."

The cries of battle were loud, but mercifully short-lived. Basina and I sat with our arms around each other. She sobbed, but I shed no tear. I had no idea what had happened to me after my world went dark, and that was all I could think about. Had I been raped? How would I know? How could I not know? Why had no one ever taught me these things?

In only a matter of minutes, the cacophony inside the house fell with a few, tortured cries of violent death, and Alboin stepped over the debris at the door and clapped his hand on the back of the man who had carried me out. His spy, I realized. Was he the one who had saved me? Had he thrust the sword through the brute's throat?

"There is a wagon coming for you," Alboin said to me. He nodded at Basina. "And I assume she will go with you?"

"Yes, for now," I said, standing with his help.

"Then get moving. This will likely get ugly before it is over," he said. I wondered how much uglier it could get? There must have been guards and kidnappers who were still alive. They would not be for long.

Two men hoisted Basina and me into the wagon as if we

were feather pillows. We had barely settled on the sacks of grain lining the bed of the cart before the wagoner cracked the reins and we shot forward. Basina steadied herself with both hands and looked to me, her eyes both wide with surprise and severe with anger. "What is this?" she shouted over the clack of the axles. We tumbled around helplessly as the wheels bounced over the rocks and ruts of the path leading out to the main road. The two men who had tossed us into the wagon caught up to us on horseback. They rode on either side without looking down. "Where are we going?" demanded Basina.

"To Childebert's palace," I said. "Where we were supposed to go." I assumed so, anyway. It was the safest place for us to be—right where the bishop had ordered us to go. I believed that Alboin would know that as well as I did.

"How . . . ?" She closed her mouth without finishing her question. Her face softened, as if she finally realized we had been rescued and not simply kidnapped anew. She did not ask about the scrape on my face or the cut in my lip that I kept working with my tongue.

✝

As we rumbled away, I put the question of my possible rape aside. Hilda would know about these things, and given that I was not bleeding and felt no pain in that place between my legs, I was hopeful that I had been spared what Basina, so long ago, had not.

On the way to Paris, we slept at another abandoned villa— this time, on bags of grain that the men carried in for our beds. They were as comfortable as the cots in the monastery, and far better than the chairs where we had spent the night before.

I realized that men like Alboin knew great swaths of the countryside well—where the empty farmsteads were, where there would be functioning wells to water the horses, and where to watch for ambushes. I envied their worldliness and once again regretted the long cloister of my life. How little I had seen of the world!

We rumbled through Orleans, our unexceptional little party turning no heads as we tumbled past people and carts on the roads. The one-time stronghold of the barbarian Alans, now capital of my Uncle Guntram's kingdom, the city looked more prosperous than Tours or Poitiers. I wondered if I would ever have a chance to visit its baths and basilicas, but I settled for the sight of its sturdy old Roman bridge as we rattled across its stone pavers over the Loire.

Our reception late in the evening at the palace in Paris was subdued. Only a couple of servants came out of the house to receive us, and we were rushed off to a chamber without seeing our cousin, King Childebert. A tray of bread, cheese, and cider sat on a small table under a tall arched window. Across the room, a bowl of water and sweet-smelling towels sat atop a table, and the bed was lined with soft linens and topped with a feather comforter. I opened a large chest, and as I expected, I found two white sleeping gowns and two simple dresses for daytime.

Basina had been sixteen when she had last lived in such luxury, and I watched her face to see her reaction. Fear and exhaustion, however, had overwhelmed her. She was as stoic as a monk before a feast. I helped her slip out of her filthy shift and undergarment and handed her a cloth to wash with. I turned away to give her some privacy and sated my hunger with the provisions under the window. Dressed in her sleeping gown, Basina slipped under the comforter without a word and began snoring softly not a minute later.

The next morning, the servant who had shown us to our

room the night before woke us with a discreet knock. She brought a plate of biscuits and a pitcher of water for our washing bowl. I expected my cousin to have recovered some of her vigor after a night in the most comfortable bed she had slept in for more than a decade. But she remained elusive and sullen, her face weary and aged beyond her years.

"King Childebert will see you in the hall as soon as you are dressed," the servant said. She gathered up our undergarments and nuns' shifts and slipped back out, pulling the door closed behind her.

Childebert sat at the end of a table long enough to seat all the sisters of the Holy Cross. Plates of fruit and glasses of cider sat on either side of him, and he gestured to those places as we entered. "I understand you had quite an adventure on your way from Poitiers," he said, his face indicating he found no humor in the matter. Childebert was several years younger than Basina and at least a decade younger than I was. At seventeen, he had ascended to the throne, releasing my Aunt Hilda from her regency. I had never met him before, but I recognized his father, Sigibert, in his features: heavy eyebrows and an exceptionally long nose. I looked at the smooth skin of his cheekbones. Not a single gray hair spoiled his thick, dark mane or beard. How long could a man stay young like this while shouldering the burdens of a kingdom, I wondered.

"Thank you for receiving us," I said, dipping into a small curtsy before taking one of the chairs. "I hope we will not be a burden to your household."

He ignored my words. "Hilda will be on her way to visit today," he said stiffly. "I expect she will help you get situated and help you determine what you will do now that you have violated your vows."

I had not expected such harsh words from the young man. Basina's haggard face reflected a similar surprise.

"And Basina will return to Chilperic's court where she will marry according to her stepmother's wishes."

Basina shook her head. "I will be leaving as soon as I can to return to the Holy Cross," she said, her voice low, her eyes pinned to the untouched food before her.

"You have been excommunicated, Basina," he said. "You cannot return to the monastery. Nor can you participate in the sacraments."

Basina stared at her plate. Her heavily hooded eyes were nearly closed, and I feared she would start crying again. So many tears had she shed over the past three days!

"Basina is not safe in a country where Freda and her thugs have freedom to travel," I said. "She will surely be murdered."

Childebert breathed a deep sigh. I read it as an acknowledgment that I was right, so I continued, "It is within your power to ask the church to relinquish her from her excommunication. She will ask for forgiveness and return to the monastery, where she can be protected from your murderous aunt."

"Why does she not speak for herself, Clotild?" he asked. "Do you believe you can discern what others think and want?"

I could have suggested that the eighteen-month battle for my sisters' happiness and security had given me that talent, but I did not want to alienate him until I knew Basina was safe. After that, he and I could argue and disagree as much as he liked, and I could accept the consequences.

Hearing no protest from me, he turned to Basina. "You do not want to marry?" he asked. "You would be satisfied to live out your life in the cloister? You will not foment another rebellion?"

"It was me—" I started to protest, but Childebert's cutting glance stilled my tongue.

"Yes," Basina answered for herself, barely above a whisper. A tear dropped onto the table in front of her.

I watched Childebert's face soften, touched by Basina's humility and sorrow. For several minutes, he returned to his breakfast and said nothing. Then, finally, "I will talk to Gregory and see what the possibilities are for your return."

EPILOGUE

ANNO DOMINI 613

I am now an old woman but I have yet to suffer worms in the head as many people do before their bodies succumb to disease or abuse. For fifty-one years I have taken sustenance from this earth and given little back. I owe it something, and all I have to offer is my skill as a scribe, my knowledge of herbs and medicines, and this truthful story. My story is different from Gregory's, and I hope it will attenuate his slander against me and my sisters.

The rebellion at Holy Cross ended shortly after our arrival in Paris. Childebert attended the next church convocation and pleaded on our behalf that Basina and I be released from our excommunication. The bishops agreed, providing that we confess our sins, ask for forgiveness, and return to the monastery. Basina, grasping at the chance to evade Freda's murderous hand, obliged gratefully, and the bishops let her reenter the cloister at Poitiers.

I no longer belonged in that place, however. I had stopped trying to conjure up some semblance of faith in the Christian God and reverence for its clergy. I declined to return.

Basina's parting was so unremarkable that I have forgotten its details. I thought at the time I would miss her, and I did. But I was also relieved that I no longer needed to worry about her or wonder when she would switch allegiances again. She was now Lebover's problem, and Lebover deserved no less of a challenge.

I stayed with Childebert and Hilda for a couple of months. From Alboin's spies, I got the names of men, friends of Freda, who were living with Lebover. Childebert examined them and eventually let them go—not because they had done no wrong, as Gregory has claimed in his history of the Franks, but as ransom for Freda's promise that she would leave Basina and me alone.

That may have been a waste of a ransom, as Freda died only a year later, within months of the death of Bishop Gregory. Her son Clothar now rules her kingdom.

I was angered, not at her death, but at its peaceful nature. She deserved to leave this world screaming for mercy. But then, as anyone knows if she lives as long as I have, people rarely get the denouement they deserve. The world is a random, violent place, and those who expect justice or expect the just to be rewarded are deluded.

I, for example, have been rewarded with a peaceful and comfortable life that I did not deserve, given the pain I caused and the deaths for which I am partly responsible. I was, at least, naive—perhaps foolish. The failure of our mission was abetted by my shifting motivations. At first, I wanted to lead the monastery as abbess, a foolhardy idea given my pagan heart. In the midst of our rebellion, I sought to ensure the independence of the abbey for my sisters, a situation the church was never going to allow. And in the end, all I wanted to do was escape, which was not only cowardly, but blocked at every step by powerful men.

I returned to the villa of my father after Hilda persuaded Childebert to let me live there. It had been abandoned, like many great villas of the late Roman Empire. Alboin stationed some of his men in the villa for my protection and used it as a base for his military operations.

Hilda sent her slaves to repair the small hut where my mother and I had lived, which was more home to me than the villa. I resuscitated my mother's garden, and through study and practice, recovered my knowledge of the uses of herbs and weeds for treating injuries and pains. The church's promotion of the power of prayer and clerical blessings had suppressed knowledge of nature's medicinal gifts to near extinction, but I pledged to keep it alive. I became a healer, but a different kind than the faith healers who traffic in superstition around the countryside. My potions are far more effective in relieving pain and healing wounds than the incantations of the Christian charlatans who profit from the diseased and injured by the laying on of hands and prayers muttered in ersatz tongues.

I believe I have lived out my grandmother's prediction. My life's work has been to pass along the ancient traditions and beliefs of my grandmother's tribes to others. In my garden on nights of the moon's greatest girth and out of sight or hearing of the church, which gains more power over all aspects of life every year, women gather with me, and we recreate the rituals and goddesses of our pagan ancestors. It is my hope that these clandestine observances will continue until a time when the church's pernicious subjugation of women will run out of favor, and our communities can reclaim joy.

Until his recent death, the circumstances of which I have chosen not to learn, Alboin visited me regularly, and I discovered the carnal pleasures of womanhood in his arms. He did not try to make me his wife, and I did not ask him what favors he sought from other women when he was away. Ours was a union of mind and heart, not of creed or religion, and our only daughter—Covina, I named her—grew up as I did, with the rituals of my grandmother, but with no tribe of half brothers to torture her.

Childebert died young, only a couple of years after Basina and I left his palace. Hilda was drawn back into the palace to stand as regent for her young grandsons, and the enemies against her multiplied. I worried for her safety, for good reason. She was eventually murdered brutally, drawn and quartered.

I am in no such danger; I believe no one thinks of me anymore. The nuns who returned to the Holy Cross after our failed rebellion did not live long. I am not sure if one can die of melancholy, but I believe some certainly did. Others died from the injuries inflicted by Macco and his mercenaries. Basina, Bertie, and Veranda have all passed. Only Greta remains, serving now as portress for the shrinking community. The reputation of the Holy Cross, once the most prestigious royal monastery in Gaul, plummeted after our rebellion. But now, I understand, the monastery is rebuilding under a new abbess and will continue as a safe haven for royal women who choose that life for some time.

A few days after I heard of Lebover's death, a large, hooded figure rapped on the heavy door at the Monastery of the Holy Cross and, through the small door by which the cloister received letters and parcels, he handed the portress a small parcel.

The relic of the Holy Cross had returned to Radegund's monastery, where I believe it still rests. I had not needed it for ransom, as I once had thought. It stayed safely in Alboin's possession until I knew that Lebover would not be able to celebrate its return.

Now that I have written my version of our rebellion, I return once again to Gregory's *Ten Books of History* and see how the blinders of religious doctrine had destroyed his ability to assess the sins of men. "Whatever evils there may be in the world, you will doubtless see the worthiest of men as guardians of all faith and religion," he wrote, forgiving all manner of kings and bishops for countless of acts of rape and murder. To him, regardless of what men did, as long as they carried God—the Christian God—in their hearts, they were just.

What kind of religion, I ask you, is this that forgives Clothar, my grandfather, for his atrocities, fratricide, genocide, and pillaging, but orders the death of my sisters and condemns me for trying to save a monastery's nuns from debasement and starvation?

I wonder if history will judge our rebellion to have been an unforgivable atrocity. If only Gregory's words survive to answer the question, I am certain it will. But perhaps, if this manuscript survives, someday a woman will read my story and gain courage from knowing that, even in the face of unspeakable brutality and impossible odds, we sisters of the Holy Cross stood up for ourselves and, united, fought for our independence. Maybe then it will not have been for naught.

ACKNOWLEDGMENTS

The genesis of *The Rebel Nun* was a Great Courses lecture by Dorsey Armstrong, titled "The Medieval World." The Purdue professor devoted just a few sentences to the rebellion at a monastery in the late sixth century, but that simple mention set me off in search of the true story of the Monastery of the Holy Cross and the rebel nun. I thank Professor Armstrong for giving me this story and for igniting a passion for the history of the Middle Ages.

Helping me get my history straight were Tom Lutgen, a friend and the most dedicated research librarian I've ever known; Veronique duPont Roc, a native of Poitiers, an alumnus of Ecole Sainte Radegonde, and a part-time neighbor in California; and Samantha Herrick, Associate Professor of History at Syracuse University. Thank you for your time and the use of your big brains.

Emmett "Gil" Schaller generously shared with me his recollections of his life in the monastery and the priesthood. His experience with a cloistered life and knowledge of the liturgy and the Hours were immeasurably valuable to imagining such a life.

Christine Meyer—my friend and my niece—read this manuscript early on and provided the kind of feedback and critique that only such a smart, passionate reader could give. I would think she was brilliant and priceless, even if she weren't related to me.

I thank to the heavens Blackstone Publishing's Addi Black for her commitment to this story, Josie Woodbridge and Megan Wahrenbrock for shepherding of the project, and Ciera Cox for her gentle and polished editing skills. Thanks also to Holly Rodino, my editor, for all her fine-tuning and her nose for inconsistencies and timelines. No one creates lovelier, more striking book covers than Kathryn English, and I'm so grateful she was assigned to *The Rebel Nun*. Thank you, Katy. And kudos to the marketing team for the diligence and prowess with which they approach the task of introducing new titles and debut authors to a very competitive market: Jeff Yamaguchi, Lauren Maturo, Greg Boguslawski, Mandy Earles, and Hannah Ohlmann. And thanks to compositor Amy Craig for the beautiful format—spoken from the heart of a person who has formatted dozens of books and knows how much tweaking goes into each page.

Thanks to my agent, Joelle Delbourgo, for finding this manuscript a home.

The literary community here in the desert of Southern California is small but loyal and supportive. Thanks to Rose Baldwin, Lynne Spreen, Judith Fabris, Laura Watt, LaDonna Harrison, and Peg Goldstein for being on my team and sharing your writing lives with me. A special thanks to Peter Bart for giving me confidence; someday, maybe, I'll be one-tenth as successful a writer as he is.

Thanks to my best friends, Diane Larson, Gina Wilson, and

Janet Day for being you. And thanks to everyone in the Next Chapter Book Club for your encouragement and for sharing your love of books with me.

Finally, and mostly, I thank my husband for his love, his faith in me, and his instincts for story.

AUTHOR'S NOTE

One dark night after the death of Agnes, the first abbess of the Monastery of the Holy Cross, forty nuns rebelled against their new abbess and the bishop who installed her and walked out of the cloister. That much is unanimously accepted by historians, but it is about all the consensus there is about the rebellion.

Mine is a work of fiction that starts with that one small piece of accepted fact. The rest is the product of my imagination, supported by my research into the event and that period in the dynasty known as Merovingian Gaul.

I started with Book X of Bishop Gregory of Tours's *Ten Books of History* (later published as *History of the Franks*), the only extant record of the event that was written near the time of the rebellion. I then read many scholarly recapitulations of the events at the Holy Cross, which relied on his manuscript as the primary source of information about the rebellion.

Gregory's account is garbled, repetitive, and written with poor syntax and grammar (the latter for which he humbly asks the reader's forgiveness). It is generally accepted by historians that he exaggerated[1], which may be the case when he described the extent of the violence at the monastery ("scarcely a day passed without a murder, an hour without a quarrel"), and his rendering of the incident for political purposes, as well as ecclesiastical ones. It appears he had forgiven kings and soldiers for all manner of evil—murder and plunder—as long as they retained their Christian faith. To be a Christian to Gregory, then, was to believe in Christ, His resurrection, and His purpose on earth, not necessarily to act in ways we believe represent "Christian" behavior today.

Of course, Gregory wasn't the only historian in late antiquity or the early Middle Ages to use his pen for argument as well as for recording fact. As the academic and prolific author Peter Heather puts it, "Establishing the credibility of an ancient historian operating in the classical tradition is never straightforward. Back then history was a branch of rhetoric, and although it aimed at truthfulness, truth did not have to be merely literal. A high degree of artistry was expected, partly for the audience's entertainment . . ."[2] Heather's statements were written in the context of his review of Ammianus Marcellinus's histories, written some two centuries earlier than Gregory's book. While Ammianus may actually have been striving to create an entertaining read, I do not believe this was Gregory's intent, and neither do I or others find his writing as clear and "modern" as Ammianus's. But the point is still salient: Gregory's histories were as much rhetoric as they were reportage.

In this novel, I have chosen to simplify his story of the count's attack on the monastery and the fighting between the nuns led by Clotild's women and the count's men. Compared with Gregory's account of the battle, which is not only likely exaggerated but also jumbled chronologically and thematically, mine is more compressed, as I am loath to imagine more bloodshed was inflicted by nuns—even pagan nuns. It's possible that the fighting took place over more than one day, and that the men Clotild recruited to help stave off the bishops and the count continued to wreak havoc elsewhere in Poitiers. A clear chronology is hard to recreate from Gregory's history. For the sake of a tellable tale, I have trimmed Gregory's rambling narrative to a few essential battles.

My main break with Gregory's account, and what inspired me to write this novel, is with his characterization of what motivated Clotild's rebellion. He repeatedly reported that she was full of pride and incited by the devil, describing her rebellion as "reckless."

I believe a woman would have viewed Clotild's circumstances very differently. With no options other than religious life, prostitution, or marriage with its attendant danger of childbirth, Clotild must have felt compelled to find meaning for her life within the confines of the convent. The church had already taken away other respectable clerical opportunities for women, including ordination as deaconesses and participation in the sacraments and liturgy alongside their priest husbands, and only appointment as abbess would have afforded her a leadership role in the church.

Not every Medieval scholar will agree with me, of course. In an exchange of emails, the eminent Dr. Georg Scheibelreiter, Medieval studies professor in Wein, Austria, rejected my theory of Clotild's motivations, suggesting that the concept of female independence and leadership is a twenty-first century phenomenon, and that no such ideas could have occurred to women in a sixth-century monastery. Certainly, Gregory of Tours harbored no such speculation.

However, I am unable to accept that female introspection and dissatisfaction have evolved only in the past 1500 years.

Rebelliousness is not a purely male trait, and probably never has been. Several women historians have also described Clotild's dissatisfaction as acute, most notably Lina Eckenstein, who wrote *Woman Under Monasticism* back in 1896. "The feeling of indignation in the women must have been strong," she wrote, "as nothing he (Gregory) could say would dissuade them from their purpose."[3] Other authors have reimagined the women of the Middle Ages in the novels of *Pope Joan, Confessions of a Pagan Nun, The Birth of Venus*, and others, demonstrating strength, perseverance, determination, leadership, and rebelling against rigid patriarchal limits. Whether these stories truly represent the minds of women in late antiquity, we will never know, as most histories throughout time have been written by men.

That said, I am grateful to Dr. Scheibelreiter for his willingness to engage in a conversation about this incident, and to all the historians who contributed to this narrative, whether knowingly or not, with their research and scholarship.

FACT VERSUS FICTION

Whenever I read historical novels, I always wonder what the author has discovered in her research, and what she made up to complete the narrative. I love an author's note that clears that up. To that end, the following details included in my narrative were reported as fact by Gregory and historians of the period:

- The existence of all the main characters except for those indicated as fictional below.
- Radegund's history, which is supported by hagiographies written by Fortunatus and others, in addition to Gregory's

report. The only fictional element is my characterization of her relationship with Clotild.

- The rulings of the various church councils in the fifth and sixth centuries that limited women's roles in the church and in marriage to priests.
- The *Rule for Nuns of St. Caesarius of Arles* (*Regula virginum*) and Radegund's implementation of the Rule.
- The Hours that would have been observed by the nuns.
- During Radegund's time, the escape of a nun named Agnes, who was captured and forced to reenter the cloister by the same rope with which she escaped.
- The unsatisfactory relationship Maroveus, Bishop of Poitiers, had with both Radegund and Bishop Gregory. Gregory and Radegund, however, were friends.
- Maroveus's refusal to install the relic of the Holy Cross, which Radegund acquired from Justinian in Constantinople. He also made himself conveniently absent when he would have been expected to preside over her vigil, funeral, and burial.
- Clotild as the daughter of King Charibert. She is not known to be the daughter of any of his wives.
- Clotild's entry into the monastery at her father's death.
- Fortunatus as a friend of Charibert and Radegund. It makes sense that he delivered Clotild to the monastery, but it is not recorded anywhere as having happened.
- Fredegund's many crimes. She was accused of the murders detailed in this narrative by her contemporaries, including those of her rival wives. She died peacefully, while Brunhilde (Hilda) was drawn and quartered by horses at the order of her political enemies.

- Brunhilde's marriage to Merovech and his subsequent suicide. I have, however, moved the marriage and death later in time so that if fits within Clotild's narrative.
- Clotild's expectation of being named abbess when Agnes died. Maroveus named Lebover instead, despite the usual practice by which monasteries elected their own leaders.
- Justina was named as prioress, and she was Gregory's niece.
- Lebover's gout.
- Lebover's alleged misdeeds. They were part of the testimony at the trial of Clotild and Basina. How many of them she was guilty of will never be known.
- The escape from the monastery. The nuns traveled to Tours by foot, although their means of the return is my speculation.
- Clotild's visit with Gregory in Tours, and Guntram in Chalôns-sur-Saône. Guntram did promise to convene the bishops, but the convocation did not take place.
- The break with cloister by some of the nuns who took sanctuary in Tours. Many married and became pregnant.
- The recruitment of local ruffians, although the means by which Clotild knew or hired them was not recorded by Gregory. The meeting I have imagined with Alboin is my fiction.
- The bishops' attempt to remove the nuns from the basilica in Poitiers. The bishops were driven away, although it is not clear how or by whom.
- The monastery raid by men recruited by Clotild. They captured the abbess, kidnapping Justina first by accident. They also set fire in the abbey to a cask that had been pitched. One of the men was killed by his own comrades as he appeared to try to kill Lebover with an axe.

- Maroveus's threat to cancel Easter services if Lebover wasn't set free.
- Basina's wavering loyalties.
- The count's raid of the monastery. At least one nun died. Clotild did brandish the relic, or at least pretended to, although what she said at the time is uncertain, as Gregory was not there when it happened.
- The trial of Clotild and Basina by Gregory and two other bishops. It is not certain that Maroveus was one of them. Much of the dialogue in the trial scene in this novel comes from Gregory's record of it.
- Clotild's and Basina's excommunication, Basina's return to the monastery, and Clotild's return to a villa thanks to Brunhilde's benevolence. Historians say Clotild vanished into history, although one historian surmised that she started a new monastery. I imagined a different future for her, based on her bastard status and likely pagan heritage.

☩

The following events and ideas are wholly imagined by me, and not reported in Gregory's history or any of the historians who have written about the rebellion since:

- Any information about Clotild's mother and grandmother is fiction, including their names, vocations, and backstories.
- Greta, Bertie, Vivian, Ingund, Veranda, Desmona, Marian, Covina, Merofled, and other minor characters in the monastery were invented by me. Alboin is an invention, as are the scenes in which he and Clotild meet.

- The suicide of Marian.
- The means of escape from the monastery. Gregory called it a "break," but I have characterized it simply as walking out the door in the middle of the night.
- Clotild's vocations as scribe, gardener, and cook.
- Visits to Clotild in the monastery by Fortunatus, Brunhilde, and Clotild's grandmother, and Clotild's receipt of the amulet.
- Details of Clotild's trip to Chalôns-sur-Saône and her visit with her uncle Guntram.
- Their kidnapping by Fredegund's men on the way to Childebert's palace, and rescue by Alboin.
- Clotild's polytheism and return to paganism, her relationship with Alboin, and the birth of her daughter.

A NOTE ON NAMES

Most of the historical characters in this novel are real, including our protagonist, kings, queens, their children, bishops, abbesses, priests, poets, philosophers, and founders of monasteries. In many cases, their names are difficult for modern readers to keep separate or to pronounce. In a short period of time, Gaul had two kings named Childebert, two named Clothar, plus at least one Charibert, Chilperic, and Guntram (and these are the simplified spellings). The queen's names were no less difficult, if more distinguishable: Fredegund, Brunhilde, Audovere, Ingoberga, and Galswinth, not to mention Radegund. Clotild is spelled in various histories in innumerable ways, including Chlotilde, Chlotield, Chrododield, Chrodield, and Chrodechilde.

I have included the family tree for the Merovingian royalty

in this book in hopes that it will help readers keep the characters straight. And to increase readability, I've chosen to use the simpler "Clotild," and shortened Fredegund to Freda, and Brunhilde to Hilda; and simplified some other names while trying to retain their Germanic, Medieval character.

1   Ian Wood, "The Individuality of Gregory of Tours," *The World of Gregory of Tours*, ed. by Kathleen Mitchell and Ian Wood (Leiden: Brill, 2002), pp. 29-46. See also: E.T. Dailey. *Queens, Consorts, Concubines: Gregory of Tours and Women of the Merovingian Elite* (Leiden, The Netherlands: Koninklijke Brill, 2015), p. 2.

2   Peter Heather. *Empires and Barbarians: The Fall of Rome and the Birth of Europe* (New York: Oxford University Press, 2009), p. 155.

3   Lina Eckenstein. *Woman Under Monasticism*, a reproduction (London: Forgotten Books, date unspecified), p. 66. The original book was published by Cambridge University Press in 1896.

BIBLIOGRAPHY

Bateson, Mary. "Origin and Early History of Double Monasteries," *Transactions of the Royal Historical Society,* New Series, Vol. 13, 1899, pp. 137-198 Published by: Cambridge University Press on behalf of the Royal Historical Society.

Brittain, M.A., F., ed. *The Lyfe of Saynt Radegunde* (Cambridge, UK: Cambridge University Press, 1926) English translation.

Eckenstein, Lina. *Woman Under Monastacism,* Chapters on Saint-lore and Convent Life between AD 500 and AD 1500 (Cambridge University Press, 1896) Transferred to Print on Demand, 2015, Forgotten Books.

Edwards, Jennifer. "Their Cross to Bear: Controversy and the Relic of the True Cross in Poitiers," *Essays in Medieval Studies 24,* 2007, pp. 65–77.

Ehrman, Bart D. *The Triumph of Christianity: How a Forbidden Religion Swept the World* (New York: Simon and Schuster, 2018).

Gregory of Tours, *History of the Franks*, Book X, 591

Guigot, M. Francois. *A Popular History of France*, republished on CreateSpace, translation by Robert Black, 2016.

Halsall, Guy. *Barbarian Migrations and the Roman West, 376–568* (Cambridge, UK: Cambridge University Press, 2007).

Hen, Yitzhak. *Culture and Religion in Merovingian Gaul AD 481-751* (E.J. Brill, Leiden, The Netherlands, 1995).

Hochstetler, Donald. "The Meaning of Monastic Cloister for Women According to Caesarius of Arles," *Religion, Culture and Society in the Early Middle Ages*, ed. Thomas F. X. Noble and John J. Contreni (Kalamazoo, MI: Medieval Institute Publications, 1987).

Lallemant, W. Marjolijn J. De Boer Ave. "Early Frankish Society as Reflected in Contemporary Sources, Sixth and Seventh Centuries" PhD Thesis, Rice University, 1982.

Lifshitz, Felice. *Religious Women in Early Carolingian Francia* (New York: Fordham University Press, 2014).

MacMullen, Ramsay. *Christianity and Paganism in the Fourth to Eighth Centuries* (New Haven, CT: Yale University Press, 1997).

McCarthy, Mother Maria Caritas. *The Rule for Nuns of St. Caesarius of Arles: A Translation with a Critical Introduction* (Washington, D.C.: The Catholic University of America Press, 1960).

McKitterick, Rosamond. "Knowledge of Canon Law in the Frankish Kingdoms before 789: The Manuscript Evidence," *The Journal of Theological Studies*, New Series, Vol. 36, No. 1 (April 1985), pp. 97–117 Published by: Oxford University Press.

Musset, Lucien, *The Germanic Invasions: The making of Europe 400–600 A.D.* (New York: Barnes and Noble Books, 1993) First American Edition.

Norris, Janice Racine. "Nuns and Other Religious: Women and Christianity in the Middle Ages," *Women in Medieval Western European Culture,* Ch. 16, ed. Linda E. Mitchell, (Garland Publishing, New York and London, 1999).

Wells, Peter S. *Barbarians to Angels: The Dark Ages Reconsidered* (New York: W.W. Norton and Company, 2008).

Wimple, Suzanne Foray. *Women in Frankish Society: Marriage and the Cloister, 500–900* (Philadelphia: University of Pennsylvania Press, 1981).

Wickham, Chris. *The Inheritance of Rome: Illuminating the Dark Ages, 400–1000* (New York: Penguin Group, 2009).

Whitney, Elspeth. "Witches, Saints, and Other "Others": Women and Deviance in Medieval Culture," *Women in Medieval Western European Culture*, Ch. 17, ed. Linda E. Mitchell, (Garland Publishing, New York and London, 1999).

Wood, Ian. *The Merovingian Kingdoms 450–751* (Routledge: London and New York, 2014).